By Andrew Grey

Published by DREAMSPINNER PRESS
www.dreamspinnerpress.com

By ANDREW GREY

Published by DREAMSPINNER PRESS
www.dreamspinnerpress.com

PAST HIS DEFENSES

ANDREW GREY

Published by
DREAMSPINNER PRESS

5032 Capital Circle SW, Suite 2, PMB# 279,
Tallahassee, FL 32305-7886 USA
www.dreamspinnerpress.com

This is a work of fiction. Names, characters, places, and incidents either
are the product of author imagination or are used fictitiously, and any
resemblance to actual persons, living or dead, business establishments,
events, or locales is entirely coincidental.

Past His Defenses
© 2022 Andrew Grey

Cover Art
© 2022 L.C. Chase
http://www.lcchase.com
Cover content is for illustrative purposes only and any person depicted
on the cover is a model.

Mass Market Paperback ISBN: 978-1-64108-255-6
Trade Paperback ISBN: 978-1-64405-945-6
Digital ISBN: 978-1-64405-944-9
Mass Market Paperback published July 2022
v. 1.0

Printed in the United States of America
∞
This paper meets the requirements of
ANSI/NISO Z39.48-1992 (Permanence of Paper).

Chapter 1

ROBERT STARED at the once nice home, which, after years of neglect, was now barely standing. He'd been called to the scene along with a number of other units. Robert remained calm as he watched the front of the house for a few seconds, then reached for the microphone built into the car. "I'm sure you can see us, so you know we have the house surrounded. It's over and no one needs to get hurt. Step out of the front door and give yourselves up." God, he sounded like he was reading a script from a cop show. He got no response and looked over at the captain, who motioned for him to keep talking. "If you come out quietly, no one is going to hurt you." His calm voice belied his rapidly beating heart and senses on overdrive. Every time his partner at the other side of the car shifted his weight, the sound of the leaves crunching under his boots made Robert's nerves jangle.

Robert tamped down the urge to rush into the place, gun drawn. A show of overt aggression wasn't going to defuse the situation. His job was to de-escalate and get the suspect to come out without hurting his hostage. Robert and his team had tracked the perp for days, following every lead, and finally got a break when the

man was seen heading in this direction. One of their units, now stationed in the woods, had followed him here. Robert knew the guy was inside, but the longer the suspect was quiet, the more he worried.

It was the quiet ones who did crazy things. The ones who yelled and bellowed at least had an outlet for some of the anger that drove them. It was the silence that made Robert nervous.

"I'm not going anywhere, and neither is she."

A high-pitched scream split the air, and Robert turned to the captain, who nodded. "Come out and let the girl go. Her parents are worried about her, and they're worried about you too. They just want their daughter back," Robert called out.

"I know what's going to happen. I'm not going to make it out of here alive," the suspect said. Robert detected a shakiness in his voice that hadn't been there before.

"Let the girl go. Just let her walk out the front door." Robert waited and hoped. Then the front door opened and a little girl, about six years old, appeared in it. She looked back and then took a step forward, followed by another. Robert allowed himself to release his breath slowly, motioning for her to continue walking. He heard her crying and saw the tears running down her dirty face. She wiped them away and continued walking, then jumped as a deer raced from the woods, probably scared up by one of the units. It bounded partway across the yard, saw the men, the girl, the house, then bolted in front of the police cars, probably panicked.

A shot rang out, echoing off the trees and through the clearing. The girl screamed as a second shot followed, and then she crumpled to the ground. Units

raced toward the house, and more shots were fired. But Robert couldn't take his eyes off the little girl.

"Shit, shit… God, let her be all right," he repeated in his head until the men yelled that the cabin was clear. He raced forward to where the little body lay on the ground. "Holly," he called, and it wasn't until the words were past his lips that he realized what he'd done. "Honey," he corrected quickly. "Grace." He checked for a pulse and found one.

"Get an ambulance here now," Robert bellowed, and the men around him jumped to make the call.

"Here's the med kit," Branch, his partner for the past five years, told him, and Robert immediately began first aid. She'd been shot in the back, and he hoped it wasn't too bad. The wound seemed to be near the shoulder, and she groaned and then began to cry. Thank God. He had never been so grateful for tears in his life.

"Just hold still. I'm a policeman and I'm here to help you. We have your mom and dad on the way, and so is an ambulance. I need you to lie still for me." He needed to stop the bleeding, so he applied pressure. Grace screamed and cried more, but he held the clean bandage over the wound. "I'm sorry it hurts, but you're going to be okay." He turned away. "Where is that ambulance?" he asked Branch. His partner patted his shoulder once and went off to find out.

At this point, Robert wasn't sure what had happened to their suspect, and he didn't care. He and the captain had already worked out that he would concentrate on the victim and the captain would take care of the rest. Robert had seen more than his share of battlefield wounds, and just because the victim was a six-year-old girl didn't mean that this wasn't a battle wound as far as

he was concerned. Heck, little Grace had seen about as much hell as some of his brothers in the corps.

"Five minutes," Branch reported.

"It's going to be okay," he told the child. "The ambulance is almost here. They're going to take you to the hospital and make you all better." A lump formed in his throat, and he swallowed it down. "I promise you everything is going to be okay." He gently took her hand and squeezed it as Branch put a blanket down that she could use as a pillow. "We're getting help. Okay?"

"Yes," Grace answered. "It hurts."

"I know it does, sweetheart, and as soon as…."

Sirens sounded in the distance and grew nearer. The pitch was different from the ones they used, so he knew it was the ambulances. The police vehicles were moved and an ambulance pulled into the clearing. EMTs jumped out and hurried over. Robert explained what had happened and the kind of wound she had. Then he let them take over, but sat on the ground near her head, not letting go of her hand. "It's gonna be okay," he repeated a number of times, struggling to keep his voice from cracking.

"Is that better?" one of the EMTs asked.

"Yes," Grace answered with less stress. Robert assumed that they had given her something for the pain.

"Gracey," a woman called frantically, and then she was right there next to him.

"Mommy," she said, then began to cry again. Robert released Grace's hand and backed away, letting the EMTs do their jobs and Grace's mama do hers.

Robert took a step toward the trees, turning away from the scene, wiped his eyes, and squared his shoulders. He had to get himself under control and had just seconds to do it. He couldn't let his thoughts of

his sister, Holly, take over now. Thankfully, his game face slid into place and he turned back and surveyed the scene. The EMTs were preparing Grace for transport, and her mother was with her. Grace was talking but looked very pale. Still, she was awake, and that was a good sign.

A second team of ambulance personnel walked toward the house and went inside.

"Is the suspect dead?" Robert asked Branch, who nodded once.

"Yeah."

Robert felt nothing at the news. All he could do was watch as Grace was lifted and loaded into the back of the ambulance.

"Are you there?" Branch asked, and Robert realized he'd zoned out. "Geez, where did you go?" He nudged Robert's shoulder, and Robert forced his attention back to the present and out of his memories, which threatened to spring to life right in front of him.

"I'm fine," he answered as Grace's mother climbed into the ambulance and the back door closed. He couldn't take his eyes off the ambulance, watching until it turned out of sight. Only then did he allow himself to breathe again. "She was a lucky little girl."

"Wendel," the captain called, and Robert hurried over. "Status on the girl?"

"She was awake and talking when the EMTs took over. Her mother is with her, and they're on their way to the hospital. I'll stop and check on her on my way back to the station and give you a report." He easily switched back to his full-on professional demeanor. Robert knew a lot of the men thought him a cold, calculating asshole, but staying professional and somewhat detached was

the only way he'd found to keep himself from going around the bend. "What about the suspect?"

"He'll be brought out as soon as the coroner is finished at the scene," Captain Willows told him. "What a fucking mess. We should have been able to get him out of there without ending up with a wounded little girl and a corpse. Who'd have ever guessed we'd have Bambi to blame."

"Yes, sir," Robert agreed automatically. "At least we can hope that Holly will be okay." He blinked as he realized the memories of what had happened to his sister were overlapping with the present. "I mean Grace."

The captain nodded but let the subject drop. "I've got men combing the area for evidence, and we have the car he arrived in." He scratched his head, a habit that Robert knew meant he was trying to puzzle something out. "Why in the hell did he do this? Why this little girl? We were fucking lucky they were spotted."

They had spent a lot of time trying to locate the suspect after the child had been snatched from outside the school. A few kids had seen the man and described him, but that was all they'd had. Harley Grant wasn't one of Grace's relatives, and once they knew the kidnapper's identity, they had found nothing to tie him to Grace or the family. The crime seemed to be random. And it looked like the answers they wanted had died along with Harley in that run-down house in the woods.

"Yes. Maybe there will be something inside the house, or in the car, that will give us some answers." More than anything, he wanted the family to have some peace, if it was at all possible. "The guy is dead and he's not going to rip apart anyone else's family. At least

that's something." He turned to the captain, who took a tiny step back. Robert knew what the captain was seeing. It was his all-out, "don't fuck with me or I'll take your head off" Marine look.

"You need to calm down. I'm not the enemy here." The captain's gaze hardened, and Robert forced his stance to relax. He'd been on full combat alert and needed to stand down.

"Yeah. He's dead." *Exactly what he deserved.* "Do you need anything more from me and Branch?"

"Just your statements and a weapons report." Thank God neither of them had fired a shot.

Branch had already put away the first aid kit and the other things he'd pulled out. He sat in the driver's seat, which irked Robert, even though it was probably for the best. With the way he was feeling, they'd either arrive at the station doing one-twenty or get wrapped around a tree.

Robert yanked his door closed and stared straight ahead as Branch pointed the vehicle back toward the station just off Thirty-Sixth Street. "What's wrong with you?" Branch asked.

"Nothing. I'm fine," Robert snapped.

"I'm calling bullshit. I've known you for years. You're the guy who plays in the backyard with my kids and the dog. Hell, last summer you got on all fours in the grass to give Brittany horsey rides. And Brandon thinks you walk on water. But if the kids saw you right now, you'd scare the shit out of them. So what the hell is with you? I know it wasn't perfect, but I called the hospital and spoke to Grace's mother. Grace is in surgery to remove the bullet and pin her cracked shoulder blade together, but the bullet didn't go any farther. She's going to be okay, and her mother thinks you are

the hero of heroes because you stayed with her and held Grace's hand until she got there." Branch pulled the car over to the side of the road.

Robert glared at his partner. He so didn't want to go into all that shit about his little sister and how she'd died in a situation so much like this one. If he talked about it, he was going to have to open the box that contained all the hurt and grief, and there was no way in hell he could do that—not here, not now. The entire situation had weakened his defenses. What he needed was the time to shore those defenses back up again— not have some kind of soul-searching, touchy-feely session. "I'm fine, Branch. She was just a little kid, and I wanted to go charging in there and rip that motherfucker's head off."

"So now you're about to take my head off instead. Why? Because you didn't get to take out the suspect, or because the kid got hurt?" Branch was one of a few guys who poked the bear and didn't get ripped to shreds.

"Look, I can't deal with this right now."

Branch was one of the coolest-headed people Robert had ever met, and he simply tried to stare him down. Robert stared back, refusing to let Branch get the better of him. Finally Branch turned away. "What you need is a vacation. You're wound as tight as a drum. And while you did a great job of trying to talk the kidnapper down, it just didn't happen. What happened today wasn't your fault."

"I know. But you can cut the vacation bullshit. I'm fine. Now pull back onto the road so we can finish the mountain of paperwork we have waiting for us. That way you can get home to Jeanine and the kids before

they finish high school." He flashed a smile, and Branch got them on the road again.

"YOU HAVE two choices. You can go on a fucking vacation and get the hell out of this station—and preferably the state—or you can sit with the department doctor and he can try to shrink that thick head of yours for a few weeks. It's your choice." The captain stood behind his desk, glaring hard at him. Robert knew there was no getting out of this. "You haven't taken any leave in two years, and…." He slowly sat down. "Don't think I don't know what's behind all this."

Robert cocked his eyebrows.

"I know who Holly is. I've known about that ever since you joined my team. And I know what happened to you today. I get it."

"Then I'll be fine."

"No, you won't. You have been working yourself to the bone for years. If one of the guys needs someone to take a shift, you do it. Holidays… you work. The rest of the team loves you for it, but it's wearing you down. I can see it." The captain leaned back in his chair. "You're a damned fine officer, and I want to promote you. You have great instincts and you know how to use them. Your integrity is above reproach, and I have never, ever, heard you complain about anything. But you need to give yourself a break. There's a lieutenant's position opening soon, and I want you to fill it. But you need to chill."

"After a year in a desert foxhole—"

"I get it. But it's my job to look out for my men. And right now, you're the one who needs my attention.

You have the back of every officer out there… without question."

It was what he had been trained for, had drilled into his head from the first day of Marine training years ago. It was who he was.

"So now I have yours," the captain continued. "And I say you need a vacation. Figure out where you want to go. Pack your stuff and get the hell out of Dodge. You're on the schedule for two more days, and in that time, you're to finish up all your paperwork. Then it's goodbye Robert—for at least three full weeks."

"Captain… I…," he stammered and then snapped his mouth shut.

"You have a ton of vacation time. Call some old friends, go visiting, see buddies you haven't spent time with in a while. I don't know, but get yourself some rest. You need it. And when you come back, we'll talk about that promotion."

Damn it all. He did have to dangle the fucking carrot like that. "All right. I'll see what I can do."

"Put in your vacation request before you leave tonight." While he didn't respond, the captain used his "it's an order" voice, so Robert nodded. Then he left the office and headed to his desk, where he sat and wondered what the hell he was going to do.

The idea of taking time off to sit in his apartment, letting the four walls close in on him, was kind of scary. He opened his top drawer and pulled out his old date book, held it for a few seconds, then turned to the page where he'd recorded email addresses. A few minutes later he'd sent off notes to some old friends and his "brothers" from his unit, explaining that he was going to have some time off and was thinking of coming to visit. He sent his last email and was about to close the

book, but paused at a name: Dixie, the guy he'd let go and the man—the friend, the lover—he'd never gotten over. He'd skipped Dixie earlier, not knowing if he could open that particular part of himself again. Maybe the past was best left in there. It had been years, and though he still thought about Dixie and regretted the way things had ended between them, it was long over.

Robert sighed. Even after all this time, he could still envision Dixie in his full gear, every bit the Marine, but with eyes that looked at him as if he was the center of Dixie's universe. Taking a deep breath, he looked up the email and sent the note. It had been years, and a lot had likely changed for both of them. Then, exhaling, not knowing if he'd get a response, he got started on the paperwork.

GRACE WAS apparently doing well when he checked on her on his way home. He'd stopped in the gift shop to get a stuffed rabbit and then gone up to her room, where Grace's mother sat next to the bed of her seemingly sleeping daughter.

"How is she?" Robert asked, his voice just above a whisper. He had kept his uniform on because he didn't want the hospital giving him a hard time. The badge assured he'd get to see her.

"I'm bored," Grace whispered, and her mother chuckled.

"She's sleeping a lot," Grace's mother clarified.

Robert came inside and handed her the rabbit. Grace tucked it under her arm with a smile and then closed her eyes, going to sleep for real this time.

"Thank you for everything you did for her." Grace's mother smiled even as she wiped her tears. "You have no idea what it felt like when she was taken."

Robert swallowed hard. "Actually, I do, ma'am, and I'm glad she's going to be okay. I know she needs her rest, but I wanted to make sure she's going to be okay." Someone from the department would need to speak with her eventually, but Robert didn't want to bring that up right now. He was going to be on vacation, so that little chore would fall to someone else. They shared a smile, and then Robert excused himself. He had what he really needed, which was to see that Grace was truly okay.

He strode out of the hospital and headed right home, then texted the captain that he had seen Grace and that she seemed to be on the mend. Sometimes their jobs were hard as hell, so good news was something to be shared.

At his apartment on the east end of Grand Rapids's Twenty-Eighth Street, he climbed two flights of stairs, unlocked the door, and entered the small one-bedroom place he called home. He set down his phone and went right to the bedroom, changed out of the uniform, and put his gun in the lockbox he kept near the bed. Now in civilian clothes, Robert felt like he could finally relax.

And the first thing on his list was to check his email. Hank had responded first to say that while he would love to have Robert come visit, his kids had the flu and Robert definitely wouldn't want to catch that. Cecil's response was next, saying that he and his wife were out of town for three months in Kuala Lumpur, but if Robert wanted to visit Chicago, they could arrange for him to stay at their place. A vacation alone

didn't particularly appeal to Robert, but he thanked both guys, wishing Hank and his family a speedy recovery and Cecil a good trip. He was about to close the app when another message arrived, and he couldn't hold back a smile.

Hey, buddy. It's so good to hear from you. It would be great to see you if you're traveling my way. Henri and I would love to have you as our guest. So if you're truly planning a trip to Paris for a few weeks, please come. We would love to show you around, and Henri will gladly explain to you all the wonders of everything French.

Robert smiled, even as a slight hint of jealousy crept in that he pushed away. He had no reason to be jealous. If Dixie was with someone, that would make things easier. He'd have no reason to worry about getting muddled up in his old feelings and regrets. His relationship with Denton—Dixie—Halewood was long and a little complicated. And though any romance between them was long over and he regretted how things had ended between them, basically nothing had changed. Even after all these years, he still considered Dixie to be his best friend and his brother in the corps. For about a month, they'd wondered if there could have been more between them, but it was not to be. Still, he was happy that interlude hadn't destroyed the bond between them.

Robert reached for his phone, but realized it would be well after midnight in Paris, so he typed a response instead, letting Dixie know that he would love to visit him in Paris if it was really okay. *I can get a hotel in the area if you point me to one that's close by. I don't want to crowd you, and I look forward to you and Henri showing me around.* The message was friendly and

in the same tone as Dixie's. Maybe it was best if they were indeed just friends now. Dixie had truly moved on, and Robert needed to stop thinking about what wasn't meant to be and figure out his future. It had been so long since he had done anything fun that he wondered if he could remember how. One thing he was going to need were some new clothes… maybe a few pairs of shorts and some shirts. A quick trip to the mall was probably in order. But first he had to finish up his message. *I have three weeks' vacation and need to get away. I plan to leave in a few days, provided I can get a flight that doesn't cost an arm and a leg. Talk to you soon.* He sent the email and turned on the television before rummaging in the refrigerator for whatever he had on hand. If he was going to be gone, he might as well eat stuff up.

With his dinner—a hodgepodge of a sandwich with some tomatoes and sliced cucumbers on the side—in front of him, Robert sat on the sofa and ate, wishing he had some ranch dressing for the veggies. The computer dinged, and he checked it, surprised to find a reply from Dixie.

Definitely come on over. It will be amazing to see you, and I've told Henri all about some of the things we did. Our place is in one of those quintessential Paris residential neighborhoods and is a little unique, but we have a tiny yard and a small spare room that you're welcome to. Henri and I are thrilled that you'll be visiting. He loves to have guests. Paris is an amazing city, so bring a list of sights you want to see, and your appetite, because the food here is incredible. Let us know when your flight arrives, and we can arrange to get you from the airport. Can't wait to see you!

Robert read the email a second time and then checked for flights as his excitement grew. He had a passport and some luggage, so there was no issue there. Suddenly he was ready to be away from work for a few weeks. Maybe a trip to Europe was exactly what he needed.

Robert went on the travel sites and nearly choked at the initial cost, but with some finagling and a last-minute deal on an empty seat, he was able to get a flight at a reasonable price from Detroit to Philadelphia and then from there to Paris.

Robert bought the tickets, sent Dixie the details, and then got out his bags and started to pack. He left in two days. He messaged his captain to explain when his flight was and that he needed to leave a little earlier than he'd anticipated.

Bon voyage and get the hell out of town, was the captain's almost immediate response.

And that was it. Robert was all set.

"Paris, here I come."

Chapter 2

ROBERT'S LEGS ached something fierce, and he shifted in the seat for the millionth time, trying to get comfortable. He had never been happier in his life than when the pilot had announced that they were making their final approach into Paris Charles de Gaulle Airport and that this flight would be over soon. But it could have been worse.

Fortunately the gate agent in Detroit had taken pity on him and gotten him an aisle seat rather than a center one for his connecting flight. But other than that, the eight-plus hours had made him feel as if he'd been squeezed into a can. After about an hour, he decided that he might as well go to sleep. Thank goodness for his Marine training, which had left him with the ability to sleep anywhere, any time.

The crew had served a little breakfast just after he woke up, which took the edge off his hunger, and now his ears popped as they descended. The wheels touched down and they slowed, then eventually pulled up to the gate. Robert texted Dixie to let him know that he had landed. As soon as they stopped at the gate, he stood up to stretch his legs and got his bag out of the overhead compartment.

"Pardon...." The woman who had sat next to him the entire flight tapped him on the shoulder. Then she pointed to a bag and said something that he didn't understand in French. Robert pantomimed getting down her bag, and when she smiled, he pulled it out of the overhead bin for her and set it on her seat. "Merci," she said with a smile.

Robert waited until the people ahead of them moved before letting her go before him.

Then he walked down the aisle and off the plane onto the Jetway that led to the terminal. Dixie had explained that they wouldn't be able to meet him until after he had cleared customs, so he followed the pictorial signs, waited in line, and had his passport stamped before getting his luggage and thankfully zipping through the "nothing to declare" line. He entered the busy terminal and looked for Dixie. Robert checked his phone, noticing that Dixie had sent him a picture of a sign. He searched overhead, found the sign, and made his way in that direction.

And then suddenly, there he was, as tall and broad-shouldered as Robert remembered, with a full head of blond hair topping off his six-foot-four frame. Robert strode over, smiling as he embraced his old friend. "Damn, it's good to see you."

"It's been way too long." Dixie grinned the perfect toothy smile that made him the center of every picture they'd ever taken together. He stepped back. "Robert, this is Henri." He motioned next to him, and Robert looked for a man but lowered his gaze and found a boy of maybe six grinning excitedly up at him. Holy hell, Henri wasn't Dixie's partner but his son. God, he could feel the first crack forming in his defenses. Had Dixie been in a relationship, it would definitely be hands-off.

But did it really matter? Sure, he'd thought of Dixie over the years. But their past was the past. This changed nothing. He and Dixie had had their chance and made their decisions years ago.

"Bonjour," Henri said before speaking rapidly in French.

Dixie smiled. "Remember, we need to speak English. Mr. Robert doesn't understand French." He was so gentle. "But he does speak Farsi and Arabic."

Henri gaped as though that was the coolest thing ever. "It's nice to meet you," Henri said, extending his hand. Robert shook it. "There's a lady in our neighborhood. She's nice and always smiles at me, but I can't understand her because she speaks Arabic. Maybe you can help me so I can talk to her." He barely paused to take a breath, motioning with his hands. The left one looked like it hadn't grown completely and was quite a bit smaller than the right, with tiny fingers. Not that it stopped Henri for a second. "I speak French and English, and I'm going to learn German next." The child was all energy and light.

"Let's get Robert to the car," Dixie suggested, motioning toward the exit. "Mr. Robert is going to be here for a while, so you don't need to tell him everything all at once." Dixie grabbed his carry-on bag, and Robert lifted his suitcase and followed them out of the airport toward the parking lot.

The dark blue car was small on the outside but surprisingly roomy. He stowed his luggage in back and sat in the passenger seat while Henri got in the back. "Papa, can we get crêpes?"

"When we get home," Dixie answered, starting the car, which made no sound at all. Apparently it was a hybrid. Dixie backed out, and before Robert knew it,

they'd left the airport and were on the highway, moving slowly with the heavy traffic. "I'm glad you could come to visit," Dixie said, turning, his eyes full of meaning that Robert couldn't quite figure out.

"Do you want to go up in the Eiffel Tower? I like it up there. We can see everything, and I know what it all is. Papa says I should be a tour guide, but I want to be a college professor or a pilot." That was quite a range. "Maybe even a museum director." Robert's head was already spinning. Just about the time he was getting used to thinking of Dixie as a parent, now it seemed he was the papa to a six-year-old going on twenty. "But I'm not sure."

"You don't have to decide just yet. You have lots of time," Robert said.

"That's what Papa says too," Henri told him.

"Just sit back and relax. It's going to take a little while for us to get home. Traffic is always bad in parts of Paris." They moved forward, and Robert didn't try to determine where they were. He usually had a good sense of direction, but none of the roads seemed to be straight, so he gave up.

"I'm just happy to be here," Robert said softly.

"How was the flight?" Dixie asked.

"Long, cramped. I slept a lot of the way and wished I had bought some food before I left the airport in Philadelphia. They only serve child-sized portions on the plane." He chuckled and shifted in his seat. He was among friends, and he needed to relax. It seemed like it had been a lifetime since he'd been able to just let go and not be on guard. He'd spent six years in the corps after high school, a lot of that time in combat or in potentially hostile territory. After deciding not to re-up, he'd gone to school and joined the police force. All of

his jobs had required him to be vigilant and to keep his senses on high alert. It was hard to turn off years of that behavior. And it didn't help that Dixie was right next to him. Robert could close his eyes, but Dixie's voice was the same, and he still smelled like warm earth mixed with a touch of spice with just a hint of sweetness. For a second, Robert was back there, alone with Dixie in a quiet hotel room with the sea just outside. Damn, he wished things had been different and that they had been able to make things work back then. But the decisions they'd made were the right ones for the men they'd been. It was too late for regret now.

"Papa says that you're a policeman," Henri said from the back. "Do you get to shoot people with a gun, like on television?" He giggled, and Robert thought the reaction strange. "Papa doesn't know I watch those shows. I'm not supposed to—he thinks I'm too young." Robert couldn't help rolling his eyes.

"I do carry a gun as part of my work, but I try not to use it. I never want to hurt people." He turned to Dixie, hoping that was the right answer, and was relieved when he nodded. "Hurting people is bad, and I don't like to watch those kinds of shows on TV. They give me nightmares." He hadn't meant to say that out loud.

"I get nightmares too, sometimes. Papa says it's just my brain going anywhere it wants, and sometimes it goes to not-so-nice places. But then he says if you go to those places at night, you don't have to visit them during the day." Henri was a smart kid, but Robert's opinion of his father rose a notch.

"And you know you aren't supposed to watch *CSI* and shows like that," Dixie said, scolding his son lightly.

"I know. It was only once." Henri sighed as though the world just wasn't fair. It was the most kid thing Robert had seen in him so far.

"How long are you here?" Dixie asked Robert. He pulled to a stop as traffic ground to a halt.

"I have three weeks. My captain basically ordered me to take the vacation. He thinks I need a break. That's the reason it was such short notice." It was his turn to sigh.

Dixie simply nodded. "Unless you've changed, I bet you took every shift you could get. You were always working yourself to the bone." He patted Robert's leg. "Well, you can relax now. You're on vacation, and you're in Paris, the greatest city in the world. There are delights here that you've only dreamed about. We'll show you all the best places—Henri will make sure of it. This is the most incredible place on earth."

"I see you've already fallen in love with the City of Lights," Robert commented. Dixie practically glowed with happiness, and if Robert were honest, he was a little jealous of that. He looked out the window, trying to catch a glimpse of some of the city's famous sights, but the clouds were too low, and buildings around the freeway obscured the view.

Dixie nodded. "Henri and I have lived in Paris for the past three years. Before that, I wandered around a lot."

Robert was a little ashamed that they hadn't kept in touch. A lot of it had been his fault. The past few years, he had turned in on himself and hadn't been particularly outgoing… and it seemed he had missed a lot. "Then Papa met me," Henri chimed in. "I was in a…." He paused. "Orphelinat."

"The English word is *orphanage*, and you were. But then I found you, and now you're my son and you always will be."

"I know, Papa," Henri said very seriously. "People didn't want me because of my hand and my leg. I look different, and the parents wanted children that were normal. But Papa wanted me." Robert could picture that moment instantly. Hell, who wouldn't want a child as amazing as this bright-eyed, outgoing little boy. He knew that Dixie's upbringing had been strict. Everything had to be just so, and anything—or anyone—who didn't conform to his parents' views was not accepted. So yeah, Dixie would immediately be drawn to someone who didn't necessarily fit the mold of perfection, because he certainly hadn't met his parents' expectations when he was growing up.

"I can see why," Robert said, turning around to smile at Henri, who grinned back. Henri was adorable and so smart, it blew Robert away. He sat back in his seat. "When you sent your notes, I didn't realize that Henri was your son. I thought…."

Dixie seemed confused for a second and then laughed. "Right. I guess I thought it was common knowledge. I posted on Facebook about Henri's adoption and everything I went through at the time. And he feels like he's been my family forever. But now that I think about it…." He chuckled. "Must have been a surprise."

Robert nodded. "The best one I've had in years." And he meant it.

They continued their trip into the city, and Robert found his gaze alternating between the view outside the window and the one in the driver's seat. Not that he had any right to let his eyes go wandering. Dixie

was a father, and getting involved with him was a no-go. They'd had their chance and mucked it up once. They didn't need to risk that again, not now that there was more at stake than just them. Besides, Robert was only here for three weeks—not long enough to even start something, really. Still, the temperature in the car notched up a few degrees whenever Dixie smiled that huge, no-guile grin of his.

"When we get home, do you want to rest?"

"Papa, crêpes, remember?" Henri chimed in from the back seat. "You promised." Robert got the impression that if Dixie ever forgot a promise, he'd be reminded for the next decade.

"I know."

"Actually, I could eat and then maybe sit a little. I slept on the plane, so I'm pretty good to go. Maybe Henri could show me around your neighborhood."

"Definitely," Dixie said as they got off the freeway and slowly made their way along relatively narrow older city streets lined with small cars. Eventually Dixie pulled into a really short driveway and came to a stop just off the sidewalk. "This is my spot. It comes with the apartment, which is a pretty rare thing in the city." He opened the door and got out. "We'll get you settled inside and then go eat."

Henri got out of the car and hurried toward the door, wobbling a little to the left, and Robert realized that his left leg was slightly shorter than the right. It didn't slow him down, though. He got his luggage out of the back and followed Henri and Dixie through a door that led to a small courtyard, a miniature private garden with vines, flowers, and a table and chairs.

"That's your room," Henri said, pointing, and Robert opened the door to a small bedroom. He set his

luggage aside and opened another door to a tiny bathroom with a corner shower. The room was impeccably
clean and, while small, wonderfully homey. "I picked
the flowers," Henri said from the doorway, and Robert
smiled at the small vase on the windowsill.

"They're very pretty," Robert said as he turned his
way. "No one has ever given me flowers before."

Henri's mouth hung open. "Really? Papa was dat-
ing Pierre a few months ago, and he always brought
Papa flowers." He scrunched his nose. "He was nice
to Papa but mean to me." He looked down at the floor.
"He said once that maybe they should cut off my hand
and give me a fake one. But Papa heard him and made
him leave."

"I see. Well, I think you're perfect just the way you
are. Pierre sounds like a real mean person."

"Papa called him a 'chercheur d'or.' Whatever that
means." Henri lifted his gaze, and Robert sat on the
edge of the bed, patting the mattress next to him. Henri sat as well, holding his hands together like he was
nervous.

"Some people are just mean, and that makes them
nasty. You can be anything you want to be." He smiled.
"You know, when I was little like you, I broke my
arm and they had to fix it." He pulled up his sleeve
and showed the old, faded scar. "See? I was small and
skinny, and I had to have a cast. But I grew up to be a
Marine like your papa."

"You're huge," Henri said.

"You've got a lot of growing to do. And when you
get bigger, you can be anything you want. Don't let
mean people like Pierre tell you any different."

"Henri," Dixie called.

"Ici," Henri called back, and Dixie stuck his head in the doorway.

"Are you keeping Mr. Robert from unpacking?" Dixie asked. "I thought you were hungry."

"Henri and I were just talking." Robert shared a wink with Henri and then stood. "I think I could eat a bunch of crêpes."

"Go get ready to go," Dixie told Henri, and he hurried off across the courtyard. "I'm sorry. He's so excited, and...."

"Nothing to be sorry for. Henri is amazing and apparently a very good judge of character. And he brought me flowers." That tickled Robert in a way he never expected. "He told me about Pierre."

Dixie nodded slowly. "That guy was incredibly two-faced. Apparently he couldn't deal with anyone who wasn't perfect. The doctors are hopeful that Henri's leg will grow and that the leg length difference will even out. Heck, even in the last year, the unevenness has lessened. He wears lifts in his shoes to help. His arm and hand, though, are another matter. Henri has symbrachydactyly, which he was born with. They are what they are, but he doesn't let anything stop him. To me he's perfect."

Robert couldn't agree more. "Without a doubt."

"YOU PROMISED crêpes, Papa," Henri said as they began to walk toward a busy intersection. "It's that way." He turned and pointed.

"I know. But the café we're going to also has crêpes, and Robert will be able to get something heartier. He's been on a plane and he hasn't eaten very much lately. Is that okay?"

Henri huffed and then nodded. "It's okay."

"Thank you," Dixie said. "The café is like a hundred other restaurants all over Paris. They're the French version of the American diner, except the food is so much better. I love the steak frites or the duck. I've also had the beef tartare, and it's wonderful too. There isn't anything on the menu that won't be good, because if it wasn't the best they could do, they wouldn't have it on the menu." Dixie held Henri's hand, and for a second Robert wished he could hold Dixie's hand as well.

Their fling, as Robert tended to think of it, had lasted a week. Granted, it had been hot and heavy, with both of them unable to keep their hands off the other. They'd been sharing a room while on leave and had gotten as far as a hotel on the eastern Italian coast. Their room had two beds, but they had used only one, and man, had they steamed up the windows. Even the old wallpaper was starting to give up the ghost by the time they'd checked out. But after that leave, Dixie had been called back to the States, and Robert had been sent to the other side of the world for two more years with a rifle, a foxhole, and a long taste of hell. Maybe he should have tried to keep in touch, but that kind of separation took a toll on any relationship. He and Dixie had their week in Italy, and Robert held those memories close to his heart. But he had to remember that was all they were—memories. Dixie had moved on, and Robert… well, he was supposed to have done the same.

"This is it," Henri said brightly, pulling Robert out of his thoughts. They stepped inside a bright restaurant that occupied a busy corner. There were many people seated, and the place buzzed with conversation he couldn't understand. Dixie spoke to the hostess in French, and they received a table. Robert was handed a

menu, and thankfully he was familiar enough with the food that he was able to figure out what things were. Besides, he was interested in the steak frites—something hearty and filling. Henri got his crêpes, placing his own order in French. Dixie did as well, then placed Robert's for him. It was easier and ensured that he got what he wanted.

"It's really nice," he said, looking around. The front of the café was open to the sidewalk, where people passed with bags, some just talking.

"There are places like this all over the city. The steak is going to be really good, and Henri here will probably help you eat your frites."

"You can have some," Robert told Henri, who grinned and kept looking toward the kitchen.

"What have you been up to these last few years?" Dixie asked.

"Mostly working."

"So why the sudden vacation?" Dixie asked. "I mean, the whole thing came about pretty fast."

Robert wondered what he could say in front of Henri. "I think I was getting wound too tight. Then I had a case hit a little too close to home and I nearly lost it."

Henri leaned closer. "What did you lose? Did you find it again?"

"It's just a saying. It means that I was having a hard time," Robert explained. "My captain thought I needed some time away, and he didn't exactly give me a choice." Though in hindsight, maybe a vacation was exactly what he'd needed. His shoulders didn't ache, and he didn't feel as if the world was closing in around him.

"I think I understand," Dixie said. "Did it have something to do with your sister?"

Robert nodded. Dixie was one of the few people who knew what had happened to Holly. He closed his eyes and drank from his glass of water. He needed something to take away the hurt that had lingered for too long. "It was a little girl this time too. She was hurt, but she'll be okay." He didn't want to discuss this anymore, especially since Henri seemed to be taking in every word they said.

"What do you want to do after lunch?" Dixie asked Henri, who shrugged.

"We could go to the tower, but that's cooler at night. Remember when we took Grandma there? She loved the lights, even if she was scared. I liked that she wanted me to hold her hand." Dixie's flash of frustration showed that he remembered the day with something other than delight.

Before he could offer another suggestion, the server brought their food and passed out the plates. Robert's mouth watered at the beautifully cooked steak and the frites with mayonnaise. The waiter spoke briefly with Dixie and then left them to their food.

Robert took a bite and groaned softly. It was delicious, with garlic and herbs, a little salt, and plenty of flavor. His stomach rumbled for more as his appetite kicked right in. Henri had his crêpe, and Robert shared his frites. Dixie got the duck, which looked wonderful, with green beans and onions. Robert dug in and had to remind himself that it wasn't a race. Still, he was hungry enough that he ate faster than the others.

"We can get you some more food, if you like," Dixie said. "It took me a while to get used to eating here. Meals aren't as big, but to make up for it, they

often have coffee in the afternoon, which comes with pastry of some sort."

"Can we get some on the way home?" Henri asked before shoving a bite of crêpe into his mouth.

"Yes, my dessert monster. We can get something, but you can't eat it until this afternoon. You don't get coffee, but you can have yummies when Mr. Robert and I have ours. Now finish your lunch." Dixie was so gentle. No one in the restaurant would know just by looking at his indulgent expression and gentle smile that Dixie could rip a person apart in about two seconds. Some of the things he had done—things they'd both done—would shock the other patrons in this almost genteel setting. Their tours had taught them constant vigilance—they had been on guard all the time. When attacked, they went full force. There was no halfway, no mercy. In life-or-death situations, they'd been taught to come out alive. The boys they were when they joined were soon replaced by hard, tough men, whether they wanted it to be that way or not.

Surprisingly, it was fantasy books—especially Tolkien, the only ones Robert read back then—that had initially brought him and Dixie together. When Dixie told him about his hard upbringing, the almost religiously oppressive way he had been raised and his obsessive need to hide who he was from his parents, that struck a chord with Robert, allowing him to open up about his own family situation, mired in loss. It was like he had found someone who finally understood. The situation had done the rest.

Robert ate the last of his steak and offered a few more of his frites to Henri. He could share, after all. Once they were all done, their waiter brought the bill,

and Robert had to grab it before Dixie did. "The service is included in the prices," Dixie told him softly.

"You mean you don't tip?" Robert asked.

"Not like we do at home. The service was good, so leave a Euro or two. That's all that's needed." He smiled, and Robert completed the slip before they got up and joined the others on the sidewalk.

"The patisserie is this way," Henri said, pointing. "They make good fruit tarts and strawberry cake." He licked his lips, obviously anticipating his afternoon treat.

Once they got to the bake shop, Henri looked at each of the items on display before making his selection. Robert let Dixie choose, and then they took their purchases back to the apartment, where Dixie put them away, then guided Robert to the living room. "Wow," Robert said as he stepped into the space. The room was nice-sized, with beautiful moldings and a chandelier in the center of the ceiling. This was a room designed to impress, and it certainly blew Robert away. He was used to living in his bland, small apartment in Grand Rapids—not a space like this. There were even paintings built into the plasterwork above the doors, and intricate parquet floors added to the warmth of the room.

"I loved it the moment I saw it. So I bought the place just after I got Henri. Before me, it was owned by a couple who'd lived their entire lives in these rooms. They didn't have any children, so it was being sold. I was very lucky. Usually places like this stay in the family for generations. There aren't a lot of homes that have the courtyard. The bedrooms for Henri and myself are upstairs, and I have an office up there as well. Then, of course, there's the little guest cottage that you're

staying in. We own this section of the building, but there's a small apartment above your room that doesn't belong to us, though I would like to buy it if it ever comes up for sale."

Clearly Dixie was doing very well in his business ventures. Robert knew only the barest details about what Dixie was doing now, other than that he was a consultant. But he wasn't going to pepper him with questions right now. After all, he'd just gotten here.

"It's so homey." Robert sat down with a sigh. Sure, the apartment was cozy, but it was more than that. Though the place was elegant, it was also warm and comfortable, making him feel like a fine blanket had been wrapped around him.

Now that he had eaten, the jet lag seemed to catch up with him. Although he was tempted to sleep, Robert knew it would be best to stay up until it was time to go to bed local time. That would allow him to acclimate more quickly. "How have things been? I mean…."

"Other than Henri?" Dixie supplied. "Sometimes good and sometimes not so good. There are nights I still wake up in a cold sweat because I'm back there. The incident in the market in Baghdad keeps replaying in my mind over and over again. I know that will be with me forever. That's part of the reason I chose to live here. Paris is so different from anything I've ever known. I hoped I'd be able to start over and maybe leave some of the nightmares behind." He chuckled. "I was wrong."

Robert nodded. "I remember the market." Of course he did. That incident had nearly gotten them both killed. They had been on the edge of the blast zone, blown off their feet by an improvised bomb meant to spread terror and upset life that had begun to come to some sort of normality again. They had both

jumped in to help survivors, and that was when the real terror had begun—the aftermath. It had been after that incident that they'd been given the leave they'd spent together.

"There are other things I remember as well," Dixie said softly, a glimmer in his gaze that lasted only a few seconds.

"Papa," Henri said as he hurried in.

"Mr. Robert and I were just talking." He patted a chair, and Henri set his bag on it. "Have you finished your homework? You don't want Madame Marie to be upset with you. Why don't you get it? Then we can look it over together to make sure." Henri sighed and got down, then hurried off and up the stairs.

"He's a smart one."

"Henri's brilliant, and that keeps all of us on our toes. He speaks English at home and French in school. I speak French as well, but not as well as Henri. I have to think about what I want to say, where for him, using both languages is as natural as breathing. The school wants to teach him German. He loves math, and he reads all the time at a level kids much older than him would struggle with. He's so advanced it scares me sometimes, and yet I have to remember that he's not quite seven, and has many of the other problems boys his age sometimes have. Like forgetting things. Homework is another thing. He hates it. Madame Marie tells me that Henri will work hard all day, head down, to get his work done so he doesn't have to bring it home."

"I get that. Home is his life with you, and he doesn't want school to interfere with it," Robert said. He understood that feeling very well. "Does he say much about the orphanage?"

"Not much. I think he's trying to forget—especially the loneliness and what it was like when others found homes." Dixie sighed, his eyes growing sad. "As long as I live, I will never forget the day I first went there."

"Papa?" Henri said as he brought his things to the table, and Dixie joined him. Robert let the two of them have their time together and rested in the chair, studying the fantasy painting of nymphs and satyrs frolicking through a vineyard with grapes and jugs of wine.

"That's pretty good. But what about your writing?" Dixie asked, and Henri made a face. He showed Dixie the paper, and Dixie sat down next to him. "I know you don't like it, but you need to finish it. So no moping. Get it done and then we'll have cake."

Henri sighed as though the world wasn't fair and sat at the table doing his writing. Dixie sat back down in his chair as Robert watched Henri work. He'd never seen someone so young concentrate so hard. Robert studied the boy for a while. His eyes drooped. But he managed to stay awake—barely.

"Coffee?" Dixie asked.

"Yes, please." He was going to relax himself to sleep pretty soon.

Dixie made coffee, the scent filling the room. Henri finished his work and showed it to Dixie, who gave him permission to go upstairs and spend an hour on his tablet.

Dixie brought Robert a mug and sat back down. "I was doing some logistical work for one of the parishes in the city, and I ended up walking by the local children's home every time I went to a meeting. I don't know why, but one day, on my way home, I stopped in to talk to them. There was this little boy, with his small

hand and something slightly off in his gait, who was sitting in a chair by the desk, head down, looking at a picture book. I said hi, and he looked up at me with those eyes...." Dixie inhaled deeply and released his breath slowly. "I thought I'd been punched in the gut. My reaction to him was so strong. The matron explained who he was, and I talked to him for a while. Within half an hour, Henri asked if I was going to adopt him. That's my Henri—he isn't afraid to ask for what he wants. I turned to the matron and asked her what I would need to do. Just like that."

Robert smiled at Dixie's impetuousness. That was so like the man he'd known. It was never in a bad way; he was just someone who always seemed to know what he wanted.

"There was a lot of paperwork—even more because I'm not a French citizen. But I'd lived here long enough at that point, and had all the required certifications." There was something Dixie wasn't telling him. Something nagged at Robert, but he couldn't put his finger on exactly what it was. "Anyway, eventually I was granted custody and took Henri home. From there, we finalized the adoption, and now he's my son." Dixie was a very proud parent, and Robert couldn't blame him.

"I think it's pretty amazing. You told me once that you wanted a family of your own." They had talked about everything during that week in Italy. "I'm sorry I missed it all."

"I posted a few updates on Facebook about the adoption, and I guess I expected that most people saw it. It was long enough ago that I never thought to explain who Henri was in my notes to you." Dixie snickered. "You should have seen your face at the airport. I

realize now you were expecting a husband." He seemed to get a real kick out of it.

"So has there been someone? Other than Pierre." Now it was his turn to tease.

"Henri told you about him?" Dixie asked.

"Henri said that Pierre used to bring you flowers, but that he was mean to him and that you caught him in the act." Robert hated the way Henri's voice had hitched while telling that story. It was pretty evident to him that deep down, Pierre's words had hurt pretty badly.

"I did. I grabbed the bastard by the neck and threw him out of the house. The things he was saying...." Dixie clenched his fists. "I wanted to beat him to a pulp, but settled for throwing him out, along with his damned flowers that always made me sneeze. He always brought daisies or some other cheap flowers. I would sneeze like hell after they had been in the house for a few hours." He put his finger to his nose, acting as if he were going to sneeze just thinking about it.

"How long ago was that?" Robert asked. He didn't want to pry, but he was more than a little curious. And if he was honest, he'd have to admit to the hint of jealousy that crept into his gut. He knew he had no right, but that didn't seem to matter.

"About three months." That explained why the hurtful words were still on Henri's mind. "I knew he wasn't for me, but I'd thought he was nice. Turned out my judgment was way off with him." Dixie drank some more of his coffee, his expression far away. "I'm glad you're here, Robert." He smiled and met Robert's gaze. They locked eyes for a few seconds, and Robert didn't want to look away. Robert had questioned his own instincts about other people many times, but the one

guy he knew, really *knew*, was Dixie. A wave of heat flowed through him, and once again Robert wondered what might have happened if things had been different all those years ago.

Chapter 3

WOW. DIXIE hadn't known what to expect once Robert arrived, but it hadn't been Henri telling Robert about his one other relationship, or the way his son had opened up to Robert right away. Henri was outgoing, there was no doubt about that, but he could be circumspect when it came to his feelings. And yet he'd told Robert about one of the most hurtful things ever said to him. At least as far as Dixie was aware.

Robert looked pretty much the same as he had the last time Dixie had seen him, though that had been a while ago now. Still, Dixie could already sense that Robert was the same man he'd fallen for in the corps. But he also knew that life could send someone on a lot of detours—he and Robert had experienced that firsthand. "What have you been doing since you mustered out?"

"I went to the academy and joined the police force in Grand Rapids, Michigan. It's a good fit, and my Marine training has come in handy. I really like it."

"Until last week?" Dixie asked, and Robert nodded. "It was that bad?"

"It really wasn't. I think I just wasn't prepared for it. You remember Westerhouse?"

Dixie definitely did. The guy was a rock. Nothing seemed to faze him. Roadside bombs, random gunfire, whatever—nothing got to him. He was calm and cool, almost a machine... until he wasn't. Then it had seemed as if he was broken and the pieces couldn't be put together again. "That bad?"

"I don't know. I think the whole situation brought everything—my little sister Holly's kidnapping and death—back." Robert leaned closer. "I actually called the girl Holly. She was about the same age Holly was. And once again, I felt helpless. Up until that moment, I thought I had everything under control, and then with a single word—my sister's name—it was gone." Robert seemed to pull in on himself. "At the scene, it was as if I was back there—once again consumed with worry, knowing that Holly had been taken. And then there was the nail-biting, waiting for some word, only to fall to pieces when we were told that she had been killed." He stood a little straighter, but it was an act, and Dixie knew it.

"Don't beat yourself up. There's nothing wrong with showing your feelings. Henri taught me that. Every time I bottle things up and get grumpy, he calls me on it. I think in part it's because some piece of him worries that if I get mad enough, I'll take him back. I would never, ever do that, no matter what, and I've told him that, but I know the notion is still in his head. He watches everything, and you can almost see him processing everything anyone does. So I have to be open and honest about how I feel and explain things. It's incredibly liberating."

Robert cleared his throat. "But it was drilled into us to not show any emotion. Bury it down deep and do your job. That's the Marine way."

Robert was right; that was what they'd been taught. When you're shot at, run toward the shooter and take him out. "But this isn't the corps. And Henri isn't a fellow soldier. He's my son and I love him, and I only want him to be happy. I don't need to hide what I'm feeling. I get to show him. And it's okay for you too. I already know you're a big, strong guy. I also know that inside, deep down, there's an ooey-gooey center that you keep buried." He leaned forward, holding Robert's gaze. "Henri knows it too. Kids have amazing instincts."

"And here I thought I had this reputation as a real tough guy." Robert smiled back. "Dang, it's good to be here."

"Nice segue," Dixie chuckled. Robert had always had a way of avoiding talking about his feelings if he could. Not that they weren't communicated, but as Dixie remembered, you had to look for them a little more closely.

"Papa, it stopped working," Henri said as he brought a tablet to Dixie. "Make it work again… please." He flashed his big eyes and pooched out his lower lip. Damn, the cuteness almost worked. Almost.

"I'm sorry. You had an hour of games today, and that's plenty. You get another hour tomorrow." Dixie had to be firm, even though he wanted to give in. Henri thrived on structure, and Dixie didn't want him disappearing into Minecraft for hours on end.

"Papa…," Henri whined. Seeing he wasn't going to get anywhere, he climbed onto the sofa near Robert and handed him the tablet. "Can you fix it?"

Damn, there went that look again, and Dixie could tell Robert had no defense against it. It had taken Dixie

months to develop the fortitude to consistently enforce his own rules with Henri.

"I can't, dude. It's the parental controls," Robert said, then turned to Dixie. "Do you have to get tickets for the Eiffel Tower?"

Henri seemed to forget about the tablet, at least for the moment. "Can we go when the lights are on? I love the lights. They're flashy and fun."

"We'll see. The tickets are timed, so I'll see if there are any available. The nighttime slots fill up first." Dixie pulled out his phone and checked the ticket site, though he wasn't particularly hopeful. He checked the date and was shocked to find slots open at eight. He immediately bought three tickets and, just for grins, checked again, and there were no more left. "Looks like we got lucky." Henri did a little happy dance, and Robert chuckled at him. "Okay, Baryshnikov, how about we have our cake?"

DIXIE GUIDED the three of them out of the Metro station and up to street level, holding Henri's hand. There were too many people and too much activity for him to let the boy walk on his own.

"There it is, Mr. Robert." Henri pointed as the lights on the tower flashed and danced. "We have to get in line, though."

"Yes. But it isn't going to be too long, and then afterwards we can get macarons. Okay?" Dixie said. Henri loved going up in the tower. They had done it three times so far. It was what he'd asked to do on his birthday.

"At the store on the tower?" Henri asked.

"If you want," Dixie told him. He thought those tasted plasticky and weren't very good. Tourists bought them by the dozen, but he didn't like them. "Or we can have chocolate cookies when we get home." Henri loved chocolate, so it was a no-brainer.

They got in line for their trip on the elevator with their timed tickets, and then they went in. As soon as the elevator door opened, Henri pulled Robert around the platform. "See, that's the Arc de Triomphe. Napoleon built it to celebrate his victories. It's very pretty up close." He continued walking around, showing Robert everything. Once they made it back to their starting point, they got in line to take the elevator to the top.

Dixie didn't particularly like this part of the trip, especially as the tower narrowed when they approached the uppermost stop. It always seemed to him that they were going to run out of steel before they got there. Once again, as soon as the doors opened, Henri played tour guide, showing Robert everything. It was funny because sometimes he slipped into French, but Robert didn't seem to mind. It was adorable. Robert's patience with Henri was incredible, especially since his son was wound as tight as a top, talking a mile a minute. Dixie trailed along behind Henri, with Robert holding his hand.

Maybe he'd made a mistake all those years ago. When the corps separated them, Dixie figured it had been for the best. Robert had been given the chance at a posting with Special Forces. It was what he'd always wanted, and Dixie hadn't been about to stand in his way. Just like Robert hadn't stood in his way when an opportunity opened up in Intelligence for him. When they'd gotten together, it had been like pouring gasoline on a fire—a huge rush of heat and flame. He'd

figured that once it was over, everything would burn out. He'd honestly thought they would end up like that. Their separate assignments only seemed to cement that vision, and after some attempts to stay in touch, they grew apart and both went on with their lives.

"There's the Statue de la Liberté on an island in the Seine. Papa says that when we visit America, he will take me to see the big one in New York." Henri's grin was infectious.

"Maybe I can see you then, and we can climb to the top," Robert told Henri, who nodded.

"Papa doesn't really like high place like this," Henri stage-whispered. "He thinks I don't know, but his hand gets jittery in the elevator."

Dixie rolled his eyes. It seemed he wasn't going to be allowed any secrets by his son, who seemed enthralled with Robert. Not that he seemed to be able to take his eyes off the boy either. Robert was all broad shoulders, big arms, and narrow waist, with a face carved out of stone. But then he smiled or turned to Dixie and his eyes danced, and Dixie's heart would flutter. It was ridiculous to think that after all these years there would be something left of what they'd had, but it was undeniable. Not that he had any intention of acting on it. Dixie was a father, and Henri came before everything else. It didn't matter what ridiculous notions his mind conjured up—Robert was only here on vacation, and Dixie wasn't up for another wild fling that ended with them going their separate ways. He could say what he wanted about the last time they'd parted, and he could rationalize about things being for the best. But it had hurt badly when they were forced apart, and he didn't want to go through that again. Still, it was hard not to fall for the guy just a little when he watched him

with Henri. Robert listened and even asked questions. "Henri," Dixie said gently.

"Papa, Mr. Robert had never been to the Louvre," he said as though it was a scandal. "I like the raft painting and the one of Napoleon." He stood straighter and put on his best impression of the emperor. Robert chuckled, and Dixie rolled his eyes.

"He's a little obsessed, as are many of the French."

Robert leaned close enough that Dixie inhaled Robert's heady scent. God, that brought back memories of the two of them naked after having very athletic sex, both breathing deeply and…. He pulled himself out of that line of thinking. He wasn't supposed to go there. "Does he realize that Napoleon lost?" Robert asked.

Dixie shrugged. "No one here really cares too much. Under him, the country was at some of its greatest power and influence. They controlled much of Europe, and that's what a lot of people want to remember. France endured two horrific world wars and had to struggle to get back to where they are today. A lot of people here like to remember the Napoleonic era as the good old days, ignoring the massive defeats and horrific loss of life."

"Everything is a matter of perspective," Robert said, and Dixie immediately knew he understood. "Maybe we can go to the Louvre and you can show me around."

"I'll have to work, but if you promise to watch over him, you and Henri can go. The Louvre is an all-day sort of thing, but he only lasts so long."

Robert smiled. "You know me and museums. After an hour or two I'm climbing the walls, so that will be fine. Then maybe we can walk through the Tuileries

gardens. Maybe get some ice cream. Or we could just go on a day that works for all of us."

Dixie immediately understood that Robert was saying that it would be more fun with the three of them. "Let me see what my schedule is like. We should take a boat ride on the Seine. Those are a lot of fun too. This city has interests almost crowding on top of each other. If you'd come before, I'd have suggested Notre Dame, but after the fire…. We can see it from the river anyway." Dixie guided them around the viewing platform and then back to the elevator. For him, the trip down was always the best part, and once they were on the ground, he breathed easier again. Dixie had determined that he wasn't going to impart his own fears onto Henri or let them influence what he did with him. Henri loved the tower, and if a little discomfort was needed so Henri could enjoy what he loved, so be it.

"Treats now?" Henri asked, taking Dixie's hand once they got off the elevator.

Robert crouched down, tickling Henri. "What is it with you. Do you have a hollow leg? You eat all the time." He tickled him again, and Henri laughed brightly. "Just like your Papa. When I knew him, he was always eating."

"Really?" Henri was almost wide-eyed. "He was like me?"

Robert glanced at him, grinning, and Dixie groaned inwardly. "Your papa and I used to be in the desert together, fighting beside one another. That was before he came here. And he always had food stashed somewhere. Granola bars, nuts, things that were small enough that he could carry with him. Our commanding officer could never figure out how he managed to get them." Robert winked, and Dixie sighed.

"How did you do it, Papa?" Henri asked. "Were you magic?" The delight in his voice and the shine in his eyes warmed Dixie's heart. But then again, Henri was the light of his life. He'd do anything for him.

Dixie took Henri's hand. "No. I was just good at hiding things. And the other guys in the unit didn't know they were hiding things for me." He'd always been good at sleight of hand, so slipping things in and out of other people's bags and pockets had been a breeze. Besides, while out on patrol, he and his teammates were gone for long periods of time, and he got hungry. So he made sure there was food around when he needed it. "Come on. We'll get you and Mr. Robert treats so he doesn't tell you any more stories about me." He flashed a look of mock annoyance at Robert. He hadn't told Henri much about who he was then.

Henri had already had enough loneliness and hardship in his short life. Dixie was told that Henri's mother had been alone and that once she saw that her child wasn't perfect, she didn't want him. The stupid…. He skipped over the expletive that rang through his head. After all, if she hadn't wanted Henri, then Dixie wouldn't have that bright light in his life. Still, the first few years of Henri's young life couldn't have been easy.

"But I want more stories. I like stories." Henri bounced as they walked back toward the Metro, but he was fading and his steps grew more labored. He never complained, but Dixie knew he was growing tired. The difference in his legs made it harder for him over longer distances. Doctors had told him that they weren't sure if the disparity would get worse or better as he grew, so it was a constant source of worry. For now, he was able to compensate for a lot of it with special shoes.

Dixie paused and lifted Henri into his arms. "You're almost getting too big for me to do this," Dixie told him as Henri put his arms around his neck and rested his head on his shoulder. It was moments like this that made part of him wish that Henri would always stay this age, so trusting and gentle.

"Such a good boy," Robert said softly and held out his hand. Henri took it for a second before releasing it and holding on to Dixie once again. Henri had been going all day, and it was past his bedtime. By the time they got home, Henri went right to bed with no fuss at all.

"YOU HAVE a nice life here," Robert said once Henri was asleep. Dixie brought Robert a beer, and they sat in the living room, talking quietly. "You've obviously done well for yourself."

Dixie nodded and sipped his beer. "After the corps, I started the system security business, and I've done very well. I really like Paris and the atmosphere here. Yes, there have been some issues over the past few years with some strikes and civil unrest." He sighed. He had his opinions on the real sources of that unrest. The world was shifting fast, and those changes were hard on people who wouldn't or couldn't change along with it. "They tend to come and go here."

"I've seen things on the news. So much division, and people making careers of furthering it. Just like home." Robert paused and drank the last of the beer. Dixie watched him far more closely than he probably should have.

There had been changes in Robert—lines that hadn't existed a few years ago—but he was pretty

nearly the same person. It was something Dixie was counting on. He really needed Robert's help. And tomorrow he told himself he'd have to explain what was going on with him and the reason Robert's note about needing a vacation had been a godsend.

Maybe it was just that Robert was familiar, but he doubted it. There was something about his brother-in-arms that drew him. Dixie wished he knew what it was so he could counter it, because he couldn't let himself get pulled in again. Not that he didn't want Robert in his life; he always had. But he knew it wasn't in the cards for them—not years ago, and not now. Dixie had grown up enough to know what was truly important. Still, he couldn't quit watching Robert—the way his shirt pulled tightly around the tops of his arms and how his chest filled out that shirt. The glimpse of chest at his open collar had Dixie wondering if the memories that still seemed so fresh were even accurate. Seven years was a long time, and Dixie knew that for him, there had been a lot of struggles.

"I should probably go to bed," Robert said as he stood. He took the empty bottle to the kitchen before heading to the back door. "I really appreciate you letting me stay with you."

Before Robert could react, Dixie pulled him into a hard hug. Robert patted him on the back just like they used to do in the corps. Then he backed away and left through the door to the courtyard.

Maybe all these notions about Robert that kept rushing through his head were just that—in his mind. Robert didn't seem to think of them as anything other than friends, and maybe that was how it should stay. All Dixie needed to do was relax and not let his imagination run away with him.

Dixie checked the doors to make sure they were locked and set the alarm system before going up to bed. At the top of the stairs, he veered to Henri's room and peered inside to where the boy was sleeping. Henri always kicked off all his covers and then curled up to try to get warm. Dixie straightened the bedding and pulled the covers back up over Henri, who settled immediately once he was warm again. This nightly ritual was something he'd done almost since Henri came to live with him. Soon enough, Henri was going to be too big for him to take care of like this.

He checked out his son's window to the sidewalk below, also something he did each and every night. The street was empty, and Dixie ensured that the alarm contacts were just as they should be. Then he quietly left the room, pulled the door partly closed, and went to the bathroom at the end of the hall to clean up before entering his bedroom across from Henri's. He closed the door only most of the way just in case Henri needed him.

Once he was all set, Dixie entered the secondary room off his bedroom, sat at his desk, and got to work. He was determined to spend as much time as he could with Henri, which meant he sometimes worked well into the night.

Fortunately he was at a slow point in his work, and a couple of hours brought him up to date. It wouldn't always be this way, but his work, like most, had peaks and valleys. He would enjoy this lull, because when the demands came in, he would end up spending a lot more time in this secure room.

Still, he was exhausted by the time he locked his systems and closed the door to the office, got ready for bed, and climbed between the fresh sheets. He should

have been able to go right to sleep—that was part of his training. But tonight his mind refused to turn off. Instead, it centered on Robert.

It was nice to have his buddy visit. He and Henri didn't get a lot of overnight guests. Dixie had a few close friends that he saw on a regular basis, and Henri had friends from school, but they often met for afternoons in the park or went out to dinner. Nobody stayed. Dixie considered their home to be their sanctuary, and he liked to keep it that way. And as far as he understood, that was the European way of doing things. He'd had a few close friends to dinner a few times, and he and Henri had been invited over as well, but mostly they met in cafés and coffee shops. It was just how things were done here, and it fit Dixie's life.

But having Robert in the house was a whole different thing. They knew each other, they had a past, and part of Dixie was really interested in making that past part of the near future. Although there couldn't be anything long-term between them. Robert was here for a few weeks and then he had a job to return to. Dixie's work was here, and going back to the States wasn't in the cards right now. No, he and Robert could be friends, but anything more wasn't going to happen. What he needed to do was figure out a way to get that part of his mind to shut down and go the hell to sleep.

"Papa," Henri said from right near his head, and Dixie ground his eyes open. He hadn't slept well at all. "There's beeping." He pointed toward Dixie's work room, and Dixie checked the time.

"Okay. Go on downstairs. You can watch TV until I get down there in a few minutes, and I'll make you

something to eat. I won't be too long." He gave Henri a hug and made his sluggish body move, but he waited until Henri was gone before entering his office.

"I'm here," he groaned and pulled up his messaging system. Some days with all this equipment, he felt a little like Batman, except he didn't have the car that did everything and a Batsuit or utility belt with all the gadgets. Damn it all. He brought up the message and reacted to it, provided the information requested, and waited for a response from Howard, his main contact and supervisor. Dixie had hoped that this would be fast, but it took longer than he expected to handle the issue—some of the data they had gathered contained extraneous information that kept obscuring the true picture. He finally got things cleared up and finalized, then pushed back his chair and left the office.

Dixie quickly cleaned up and dressed before heading downstairs to hear laughter coming from the kitchen area. Henri stood at the counter on a stool, with a lift under his shorter leg, helping Robert mix batter. "They're like crêpes?" Henri asked as he stirred.

"Yes. Pancakes are awesome. Your papa loved them when I made them for him, and I bet you will too." Robert leaned over to the check the texture. "That's perfect. You did a great job. Now that the pan is hot enough, I'm going to pour the batter, and then you and I can flip the pancakes together. Okay?"

Dixie leaned against the wall, just watching them, staying quiet as they worked. "It's bubbling!" Henri said.

"Yup. That's how you know they'll be light, fluffy, and really yummy. Now, I like mine with butter and a little cinnamon sugar. How about that?" Henri rubbed his hands together, and Robert helped him use the

spatula to turn the pancakes. "Great job. Okay, now they need to cook on this side, and then I'll put some on your plate and you can try them."

"Don't we have to wait?" Henri asked.

"Pancakes need to be eaten while they're hot and fresh. I'll make some for your papa when—" Robert turned and smiled at him. "He's right there," Robert whispered.

"Papa, I made pancakes. Robert says they're like crêpes only fluffier." He bounced, and Dixie helped him down, then handed him his plate.

"That's great. You are going to love them." He got Henri to the table and helped him get his pancakes buttered and ready. Henri dug in, making appreciative sounds as Robert continued pouring and flipping.

"I have some for you right here," Robert said as he handed Dixie a plate with bigger pancakes than the ones he'd made for Henri. "I bet it's been a long time."

"It has," he agreed softly. Dixie sat and prepped his pancakes, then ate slowly, savoring the simple flavor that brought back a ton of memories. They had just received their mail, and one of the guys had gotten a box from home that contained pancake mix. They'd used bottled water and managed to scrounge up some eggs from a local farmer, and Robert had made pancakes. The entire unit had feasted on the taste of home until the mix was gone and they were full. For an hour it had felt like they were back in the States instead of in the middle of Iraq. No one had been aware of it, and Dixie had never shared with anyone just how close to the edge he'd been back then. There had been thoughts of jumping on a plane and just getting the hell out, regardless of the consequences. Each and every day, multiple

incidents and too much death had worn his already frayed nerves down to a pulp.

Back then, Robert had set to cooking, probably to calm his own anxieties, and that taste of home had helped settle his nerves and he'd managed to get himself under control. Once he'd come to his senses, Dixie had been ashamed of himself.

"Papa?" Henri asked. "Why are you quiet?"

"That's when we all need to be afraid," Robert teased, making spooky noises that had Henri giggling.

Dixie smiled and ruffled Henri's hair. "It was nothing. The pancakes are good, aren't they?"

Henri nodded, putting another bite in his mouth as he smiled. Robert joined them at the table and set down a plate with more before taking the seat across from Dixie. "I hope it's okay. Henri was hungry, and you had the stuff to make them. He was a big help."

"They're really good. Thank you," Dixie said. He hadn't expected to take as long as he did, and he was grateful Robert had come to the rescue. "Did you sleep all right?"

"I did, but only to a point. It always takes some time to get on a new time schedule."

Dixie swallowed his bite. "What did you have in mind for today? I have some more work I need to do, and Henri has to get ready for school." He checked the time, then turned to his son. "You need to hurry and get dressed. Madame Brassard will be here very soon, and you don't want to be late." Henri raced off, and Dixie finished eating. Then he went up to check on Henri, who was almost ready. "We just have a few minutes. Put your shoes on and then get your bag from by the door."

Henri left the room, and Dixie followed him down, turning off the alarm. Henri hugged Robert goodbye, and Dixie saw him out just as Madame Brassard arrived with her daughter, Camille. Dixie thanked her for walking Henri to school before returning inside.

"If you want, go on up and get your work done. I'll clean up here and maybe take a walk around the neighborhood. I'm still trying to get my bearings, and some fresh air will do me good."

"You sure?" Dixie asked gratefully. He had things he needed to get a head start on, and the time to work would be helpful.

"No problem. I'll let you know before I leave." Robert flashed that smile of his that sent Dixie's heart beating a little faster. Dixie thanked him and hurried back upstairs. He had enough to do, and if he got it done now, he'd have more time with Henri and Robert later.

Dixie found it hard to think because of Robert, and he groaned at himself, drawing on his training to push those thoughts out of his mind and concentrate on his work.

Robert messaged him that he was going out, and Dixie told him to have a good time. Then he returned to the tasks ahead. In the short time since breakfast, a number of developments had unfolded, and he spent plenty of time on calls. He was just wrapping up when his phone vibrated on the counter.

You have a problem, Robert's message read. At a good stopping point, Dixie locked up his systems and left his work room, closing the door behind him. Robert wasn't someone to overreact, so he was curious as to what was going on.

"Robert?" Dixie asked when he found his friend standing next to the front window. He often kept the curtains drawn because of how close the house was to the sidewalk.

"I went out for a walk. You know all those years in a combat zone…. Well, you watch people, and I noticed a man getting out of a car as I left. He seemed to be looking for something as he went up the street, but seemed to center his attention on this part of the street. I went down to the corner, had a coffee, and wandered through the shops, just looking at the area. It's really beautiful here." He rubbed the back of his neck. "When I returned, I saw the same man still hanging around. I honestly wouldn't have thought anything about it, except that when I came from a different direction, the car was gone but the same guy was hanging around, wearing different clothes. Then he got into a different car, as if he'd left and returned, trying to look like a different person." He managed to look out the window without moving the curtains. "He's gone now."

"Did you take a picture?" Dixie asked.

"Yeah. I got one from inside, but it isn't very good. I'll text it to you." Robert pulled out his phone, and soon Dixie's dinged with the message. He reviewed the image and nodded.

"Would you please delete the picture on your phone," Dixie asked Robert. He knew that request was going to kickstart Robert's curiosity, but it couldn't be helped. "I have it here."

"Are you sure? I…." He thought Robert would protest further, but he deleted the image, and Dixie placed his phone in his pocket.

"He's no one to worry about." Dixie's racing heart settled, and he had a chance to think. It was time for

him to lay some of his cards out on the table. "While Henri's out, I think we need to talk." He had a fine line to walk here.

"I see," Robert said and sat in one of the living room chairs. "What's going on?"

Dixie sat across from him. "I can only say so much, but I need your help. It's part of the reason I asked you to come. I was really hoping it wouldn't come to this, but it has." It was probably best to tell Robert what he could. "I've been doing security work for various clients, and one of them is the government. *Our* government. They were smaller contracts, and I needed the work. No big deal… until recently, when I developed something important, by accident. And as it turns out, it's also potentially dangerous, because rival governments will want it."

"Come on. You were always brilliant with a computer. I know you may have joined the corps out of high school the way I did, but you kept everyone in the unit's technology working. Hell, you were a one-man tech team with a gun. You took college classes while the rest of us were playing on the game consoles you made sure remained functional. So I'm not surprised you created something important," Robert said, shaking his head. "What is it you developed?" He leaned a little closer, clearly engaged.

Dixie put up his hands. "I can't tell you what it is, but I'm pretty sure that it's made me a person of interest to several groups. I can deal with that, but there's Henri to worry about. I never dreamed my work would put him in danger." Damn it, he was so close to falling apart. Henri was his weakness, and he knew it.

"So you asked me here…." Robert's eyes darkened and his posture stiffened as if he was ready for combat.

Shit, he was messing this up. "Your email was a godsend. I figured you could have your vacation, and I had hoped that nothing would happen. I still do. But I realize it was wrong to not be up-front with you. There's a lot I can't say." He shook his head. "I hope to hell I'm wrong and that my secret is still just that. But if it's not and the kettle of fish I opened is what I fear… I could have put Henri in danger. I can deal with the consequences of my actions for myself. But Henri…." He paused; then the words tumbled out. "You were always someone I could trust, and damn it, regardless of what happened back then, I know I still can. You had my back when you told me that I should take the posting with Intelligence." He saw it now. They had both gotten the chance to have what they really wanted, and they had both encouraged the other to take it. He should have seen then what was happening, but he had been too young and stupid.

"Just like you did with me and Special Forces."

Dixie nodded. "You always had my back, the way no one else ever did. I'm hoping you will again." He clenched his hands into fists and then relaxed them.

"You lied to me to get me here?" Robert asked, his expression unreadable.

"I've never lied to you. Henri and I are both thrilled to have you here, and I would have invited you to come no matter what. I've missed you more than I realized." He stopped himself. This was not the time to confess that in all the intervening years, he'd never truly been able to get Robert out of his mind. Letting him go had been his one huge regret, and he'd be a fool if he didn't at least acknowledge to himself that Robert was the one he let get away. "But I also need you to have my back— and Henri's."

Robert sat in stony silence. Dixie wondered if maybe he had messed this up so badly that his friend would leave. "I see," Robert said, which told Dixie exactly nothing. "Okay. I understand, and of course I'll watch your back. I did then and I'll do it now. I just wish you had told me earlier, but it really doesn't change anything. If you and Henri need to be kept safe, then I'll do whatever I can to help."

"Thank you." He actually relaxed a little for the first time in weeks. His heart rate returned to normal, and he felt like he could finally breathe deeply. "Let's hope it isn't necessary."

"Amen to that." Robert held his gaze for a few heated seconds—at least they seemed that way for Dixie. Robert could still almost make him forget his name with just a look. It was excitingly frightening. He considered cracking a joke or something to break the tension, but thought better of it.

"Why don't we head on out? We can take the Metro to an area around the Seine where there are some wonderful little book stalls, and you can take a look around." Robert had always loved books, and he hoped the idea would give Robert something else to occupy his mind.

"Okay. What time do we have to be back to meet Henri?" Robert asked. "I need to get some things. I'll be right back." He strode out across the courtyard and returned in a few minutes with a light shell jacket. "I'm not sure if it's supposed to rain."

"It's hard to tell sometimes." Dixie grabbed a couple of umbrellas, and they were ready to go. He set the alarms and locked the door, then checked on his phone that everything was okay before guiding

Robert to the station. "The Metro is the easiest way to get around the city."

"I got a map when I was out so I can get where I need to go if you're working," Robert told him.

"And to answer your question—it's Monday, and Henri has a music class after school with Madame Brassard's daughter, so she'll take them right to the lesson and he won't get home until almost six. It makes for a long day for him, but Henri loves his violin class, and he's quite good already. But be prepared. When he gets home, he'll want to show us what he learned."

"Did you ever take anything musical?" Robert asked, and Dixie shook his head. "Neither did I."

"Henri asked to take lessons. I try to make opportunities available for him, but I don't force them onto him." They walked down the sidewalk side by side, and a few times, Robert's hand brushed his. Dixie reacted to each touch but tried not to make too much of it. "A year ago he came home very upset because all the other boys were going to be playing soccer—football over here…."

"Yes. I watched the last World Cup."

Dixie snickered because he knew Robert practically lived for the Packers. "He couldn't play and came home in tears. I've always told him that he could do anything he wanted, and that situation clearly made a liar out of me. He wanted to try to play, but physically, he isn't able to run that much. So I asked him what else he wanted to do. He told me he wanted to play violin." Dixie was so proud of him. "The amazing thing is that Henri is able to compensate for the more limited use of his hand. He has difficulty with certain movements but figures out ways around them." Damn, he actually sighed.

Robert bumped his shoulder as they reached the station. "I never pictured you as the proud papa type before. Though it suits you," he said as they descended the stairs.

"I spent a lot of time trying to find someone to share my life with, but no one measured up." He forced his mouth closed. The truth was that none of them could compare to Robert.

"Well, you have a great son and what seems like a good life." They bought their tickets before continuing down the tiled underground hallways to the platform. Robert's life was good, but maybe it wasn't complete, and the short time he'd spent here brought that into focus. "You know, I…." Robert turned as they waited on the platform. The display said they had five minutes before their train arrived.

"What were you going to say?" Dixie asked.

"I don't know. I lay in bed last night thinking about, well… you and me in a little town in Italy and…." He glanced at the display and then back at him. Seeing Robert acting nervous was something new. "I haven't been able to stop thinking about what happened between us." People joined them on the platform, moving around them, but Dixie barely noticed. His attention was riveted on Robert's full lips and intense eyes.

"I know." God, did he ever. "But that was seven years ago, and a lot has changed since then," Dixie said as carefully as he could. Part of him leapt when Robert brought up the subject, and hoped that he was interested in picking things up again. But Dixie had Henri, and Robert was only here for a few weeks. "We were young, and things got heated fast, but then life— and the corps—got in the way. We were young and

impulsive, and seven years ago, we let go." And he wasn't sure why.

"I know. We were definitely young and stupid. We should have tried to do more to keep in touch. Our time in the corps didn't last forever, and we were both discharged and free to go on with our lives."

That was very true. In fact, Dixie had thought at that time about looking Robert up and seeing if something was possible between them. But he never did.

"Maybe it's best to let sleeping dogs lie? You and I had something that I'll never forget, but we came out of it as friends, and maybe that's because it's how things were meant to be. You have a life of your own and a job you love because of it… and I have my work here and Henri. None of that would have been possible if we had taken a different path." He paused. "Do you regret it?" he asked.

Unfortunately, just then, the train pulled into the station, swallowing up Robert's answer. But there was no mistaking the way Robert lowered his gaze… or the disappointment Dixie saw in his eyes before he did.

Chapter 4

ROBERT BOARDED the train and took a seat, with Dixie sitting across from him, their knees nearly touching. He should have expected Dixie's response. It had been a long time, and Dixie had obviously moved on. Not that Robert could blame him. Dixie had a son and a life that he'd built for himself, and Robert was stupid to have gotten his hopes up, even in the smallest way. He wasn't sure what he should say and tried to keep from blushing like a jilted teenager.

"Robert…."

"It's okay, Dixie. Really." He needed to cover how he felt. Robert didn't want things to be uncomfortable for the rest of his stay.

"No, I don't think it is. I remember how things were and how we felt back then." Dixie leaned closer as the train barreled down the tunnel. "And I think I know how you feel now, because there's some part of what we had that didn't go away." He sighed, and Robert listened intently, his gaze locking on to Dixie's, looking for some sort of hope in those bright eyes. "But we have separate lives now. Do you really think it would be smart to just pick up where we left off seven years ago? Even if we could?"

Robert rolled his eyes. "Of course not. We're different people." He closed the gap between them. This might be Paris, but he wasn't comfortable talking about things like this in public. "But I haven't had a decent relationship since then, and from what your little reporter told me, you haven't either. I'm not saying that you and I should jump into bed together, but I'm here, and so are you. Maybe we could explore things and see what happens." It was the best argument he had, but Robert had already determined that he wasn't going to press Dixie any further. If he truly wasn't interested, then that was it.

"You're only here for a few weeks. What happens then if we go down this path and history repeats itself?" Dixie swallowed, the muscles flowing beautifully. "Leaving you broke my heart. I worried about you for months until you were discharged. I followed your career just to make sure you weren't hurt or killed. Then we got out and I hoped you might get back in touch, but…."

Robert sat back. "You could have called too." Okay, maybe that was a childish remark, but it was true.

"I know. But you were building a life of your own, and I was doing the same thing. It seemed best to let the past be a happy memory."

Robert snorted. "That's the biggest line of bullshit I've ever heard in my life. You were never someone who sat on his hands when you wanted something. Why start now?"

"Because…." Dixie began to explain and then faltered. "There are things I can't tell you." He rubbed his forehead.

"Like what that man was doing outside your apartment this morning, and why you don't seem particularly

worried about it? Or maybe why you have all those alarms in your apartment and the room off your bedroom that you work in?" He raised his eyebrow. "Henri told me it's your special workroom and that he doesn't go in there."

"We should—" Dixie stammered.

"No. I don't know what work you're doing, but from what I've seen, I know enough. And I'm confident that it's work for the greater good, because I know you. So I'm not going to bring it up again. Your secrets are your own—that's how it has to be for now. But don't use that as an excuse."

Dixie tensed and finally relaxed back in his seat. Robert had no idea what the hell that reaction meant, but he did the same. He'd said what he had to say, and whatever Dixie decided, it was up to him. Robert could do nothing about it. "I...." Dixie seemed to have been taken by surprise.

"I'm in your house, and I see things. I've gotten to know Henri a little, and he sees things. I'd never repeat anything that happened at your home to anyone." He glanced around at the others in the train car, thankful that they were many feet away and that there was plenty of background noise. "You were never the kind of person who made excuses." The train slowed down, and Robert cut himself off as the door opened and riders got on and off. It didn't take many stops for their car to fill, and Robert stayed silent until Dixie indicated their stop.

Once they were out of the Metro and up on the sidewalk, Dixie took him aside. "Look, it's—"

"Sometimes you have to go for what you want. I haven't done that, outside of my job, in a long time. You know what happened to Holly and what that loss

did to my family. My mother was never the same again, and my father managed to hold himself together for a few years before he took his own life. Mom didn't do that, but she faded away slowly, climbing into a bottle and never getting out again. I had a shitty adolescence and went into the corps to get away from all of it. I found a life there, then I found you, but one part of my life took another part away. Now I have the chance to put Humpy Dumpty together again… or at least see if the pieces might fit." He simply stared into Dixie's eyes. "If that's what you want too, then all you have to do is say so. If not, then we'll be friends and that'll be it. But one way or another, after seeing you again, I had to take a shot. I had to see if we can at least try. So now it's up to you." He turned, basking as the sun peeked through the clouds. "So, where are we going first?"

"How was your lesson?" Robert asked when Henri returned home, all smiles and excitement.

"I learned something new." Henri set his bag on one of the chairs and his violin case on the table. He opened it carefully, then withdrew the instrument. When he put it at his shoulder, it seemed too big for him, but he picked up his bow and began to play. Henri's tongue stuck out from between his lips as he worked his good hand hard to get the strings to do what he wanted, the determination in his expression unmistakable. It was a simple song, but pretty, with none of the screechiness Robert had expected.

"That's very good," Robert told him as Dixie smiled.

"You are getting to play so well," Dixie said. "Now put your instrument away and remember that you have to practice."

"I know. I got a new piece that I have to learn." He set the instrument in the case. "It's for the recital." He rolled his eyes. "I have to stand up in front of everyone and play." Henri pooched out his lower lip. "I don't wanna play like that. What if people are mean like Pierre?" He sniffled slightly, and damn it all, Robert was tempted to go out and find Dixie's ex just so he could pound him into the middle of next week.

"No one is going to be mean, and I'll be right in the front row to watch you play," Dixie promised.

"Will you beat them up if they're mean?" Henri asked, wiping his eyes.

Dixie shook his head. "No. But I will give them my best Papa glare."

Robert turned away when Dixie demonstrated. It was funny, but he didn't want Henri to see him laugh. He took this so seriously, and Dixie was determined to stand up for him.

"I'd really like to watch you play too. So, will you go?"

Henri nodded, and Dixie lifted him into his arms, twirling him around as Henri giggled happily. "Papa, I'm gonna woof." He giggled some more.

"Where did you hear that?" Dixie asked.

"Louis at school," Henri answered. "He isn't very nice and talks about stuff like that all the time. Though when he does, it's in French… mostly." Henri scrunched up his nose.

"I see." Dixie tickled Henri until laughter filled the house. "Go on and put your things away. Do you have homework today?"

Henri shook his head. "I did it already." He handed Dixie some papers before carrying his things out of the room.

Robert sat down, trying to stay out of the way. He and Dixie hadn't continued their earlier conversation, and Robert was determined that the next move would be Dixie's. Patience had been one of the most difficult things for him to master, but after years of the military's hurry-up-and-wait, he could wait until Dixie made up his mind.

"I really enjoyed today. Thank you," Robert said. They'd spent some time wandering by the Seine, checking out the book stalls. They also stopped in at Sainte-Chapelle, where Robert had been blown away by the medieval stained-glass windows. It was like being bathed in colored light from every direction. Robert had been mesmerized by how the colors changed as the light shifted, even just in the half hour they were inside.

"Did you go to the museum?" Henri asked.

"No. You get to take him there. We went along the river and into the chapel with the windows—all things you've done a ton of times." Dixie sat down, tugging Henri onto his lap. "You don't need to worry about taking Robert to see things. He's going to be here for a while, and you'll have plenty of time to spend with him. It's more important that you go to school. Maybe this weekend we can do something really special, okay?"

"Disney special?" Henri asked, and Robert groaned as Dixie rolled his eyes.

"You've already been there this year. We'll find something else that's fun to do. But first you need to clean up and get ready for dinner." He hugged Henri, who slipped off his lap and left the room.

"Is there anything I can do to help with dinner?" Robert followed Dixie into the small kitchen.

"I don't know what I'm going to make. Henri likes just about everything, thank goodness. But he won't eat certain vegetables." He began pulling things out of the cupboards. "He's partial to French food, but I've also introduced him to some American things." He brought out a package of ground beef from the small refrigerator. "How do you feel about hamburgers? They'll be on brioche instead of regular buns, though."

"Sounds good. Is there any onion? I could fry some to go with it." He chuckled. "Remember when Gunderson decided he wanted liver and onions and practically fumigated the entire camp making it? I'm still surprised the enemy didn't bomb us just to get rid of the stench."

Dixie chuckled. "And he made so many onions the entire unit cried for three days." He got an onion from the pantry, and Robert got to work cutting it while Dixie formed the patties.

"Can I help?" Henri asked as he slid into the room on sock feet, his left leg nearly slipping out from under him. "Ewww, onions." He held his nose and clamped his eyes closed.

"I'm gonna cook them. You can help if you want, but you should put your shoes on, and I'll get the stool. They'll be delicious when they're cooked."

Robert pulled over a chair and got a pan. He put in the onions to sweat with a little butter. When Henri returned, Robert got him in place and handed him a spatula. "Don't touch the pan, but keep moving the onions around. That's it. See how they smell better already?" He smiled, and Henri nodded, concentrating on his task. He made sure the heat was moderate so the

butter didn't spatter and glanced at Dixie, who winked back at him. "Do you usually help your papa cook?"

Henri shook his head. "I don't want to be burned."

"Of course not. That's why we have long spoons like this one and why you don't touch the pan. I remember cooking with my mama when I was about your age. She used to bake cakes, and I got to lick the spoon when she was done."

"Can we make cake?" Henri asked. "Like from the patisserie?"

Robert chuckled. "I can't make ones as pretty as that, but I think if your papa will help me get the ingredients, I can make a pretty good chocolate cake."

Henri's eyes narrowed and he scrunched up his nose a little.

Robert looked at Dixie, puzzled at Henri's reaction.

"Chocolate cake where Mr. Robert comes from is different than it is here. Not as fancy and lots more kid-friendly. I really think you'll like it a lot. And yes, I can help Mr. Robert get the ingredients. Though when my mom used to make cake, she used a box mix."

"So did mine. But somehow I doubt I'll be able to find one of those here." Robert grinned. He wasn't using one even if he found them. He could look up a good recipe on the internet and make it from scratch. "Still, if Henri wants cake, then maybe tomorrow when he gets home from school, we can make one together."

Henri tossed his arms in the air, scattering a few onions in his excitement. "I can make cake."

"Put the spoon back in the onions and watch what you're doing, okay?" Dixie said gently, cleaning up the floor as Robert moved closer to Henri.

"You're doing good. Now I'm going to turn these down a little."

"They're turning brown," Henri said, slightly aghast. "They're burning."

"No. They're browning, which is good. It makes them taste sweeter." Robert turned off the heat. "You did a great job. Now I need to put them in a bowl, and we can have them on the burgers your papa is going to make." Robert loved caramelized onions on a burger. "Will you try some?"

Henri put a finger to his lips as though he was thinking. "A few."

"That's my boy," Dixie said as he got started on the burgers now that they were done at the stove. "You did a great job."

"I helped Mr. Robert." Even though they weren't related by blood, Robert could see pieces of Dixie in Henri. Of the two of them, Dixie had always been the brains, and Robert knew he'd never be able to keep up with him that way. But then he'd help Dixie along, making sure he didn't fall behind physically. Together, they had complemented each other in a way that Robert hadn't experienced again since he'd mistakenly let Dixie out of his life.

"And you're the best helper I've had in a long time." Robert smiled at Henri. The boy grinned, then hurried out of the kitchen. Soon enough, the sound effects from his game drifted in from the other room. "Your son is pretty amazing."

Dixie nodded and held Robert's gaze. "He really seems to like you, and…." Dixie's voice trailed off as the meat began to sizzle, but he didn't seem to notice. "Maybe after Henri goes to bed, you and I can talk and see how this… whatever it is between us…

might work." Robert grinned, and Dixie scowled for about two seconds. "Don't look like you've won or something."

"Of course I did." He pressed next to him. "You can't take your eyes off me. I see you watching all the time."

"Yeah, because you keep watching me. I'm not blind either." Dixie sighed. "Look, don't get your hopes up or anything. You're here for a few weeks and then you'll go home. I have no idea what you think is going to happen or how you and I can make things work with an ocean between us. Also, I have Henri to consider, so you can't tell him anything about this." Dixie's expression grew stern. "He's already getting too attached to you as it is. After just two days, it's 'Mr. Robert this' and 'Mr. Robert that.' You do realize that now he's going to want to have onions with everything because he cooked them."

As if to emphasize the point, Henri came into the kitchen with his tablet. "Look what I did, Mr. Robert. I found the treasure chest." He showed the blinking and flashing screen to him. "See? I really did it." He bounded from one foot to another in excitement. "It's awesome."

Dixie threw him a cautionary glance. "That's so cool, buddy. But remember that you only have an hour to play."

Henri nodded. "I know." He hurried back to the living room and the sound effects began once again.

"I get it," Robert said, nodding. "And you have to know that I'd never do anything to hurt you or him." The kid was awesomeness personified. He was so smart and so… there. He understood things around him and was so eager to learn.

"I know you wouldn't. If I thought that, we wouldn't even be talking. But there's the possibility of leaving hurt in your wake, no matter what happens or what either of us intends. That's what I'm worried about."

Robert ran his fingers through Dixie's hair. It was just as soft as he remembered. "I know all that. And I also know that as soon as I saw you again, this wave of memories washed over me. I thought you had a husband and that it wouldn't matter. But as soon as I learned who Henri was, everything changed for me. You changed. And I can't seem to turn the feelings off." He spoke softly because he didn't want Henri to hear.

"Let's see how things work out, okay? I can't rush into anything, but… yeah… let's give things a little time." At least it wasn't a no. That was a step forward.

"Papa…."

"You know what happens when the time runs out," Dixie answered. "If the game has shut down, why don't you read a book? Dinner will be about ten minutes, and you need to wash your hands before you come to eat."

"Okay," Henri agreed, but there was no further activity or sound. Robert could just imagine Henri trying to figure out the key to get around the parental controls. A stream of steady French followed, and Robert grinned.

"He keeps trying," Dixie said. "But I don't work in cyber security for nothing."

"That isn't fair," Robert told him, but his mind flashed to the men outside the apartment and how Dixie couldn't talk about his work. Another piece fell into place, and Robert wondered just what kind of trouble Dixie had gotten himself into. He had always been

smart, but what the hell had he developed that required men outside his home?

"Actually, I set the code up so that he can break it if he works through the problem. He *can* figure it out. But I'm not going to give him any clues, and I don't stop him from trying. Henri is smart and advanced beyond kids his age. He's in an advanced class at school, but I don't want to take him too far, too fast. I want him to have a childhood. Still, I know there have to be challenges in his life, so I make sure he has them."

Robert nodded slowly. That made a lot of sense. "So you put the controls on his iPad so he would have to challenge them?"

Dixie nodded. "A couple hours a day playing his game isn't going to hurt him, especially since he plays mostly when I'm busy with other things. I know it frustrates him, so I let him try to get by it. Then I'll give him more time and change the code, let him try to figure that one out." Man, Dixie was devious. Robert hadn't realized that about him. He also hadn't known he was involved with developing cryptology. Maybe that was the kind of work he was doing up in his secure room? That was interesting and might shed a little light on things. Not that it was any of Robert's business. What Dixie did for a living was none of his concern.

"The burgers are almost ready," Dixie called, pulling him out of his thoughts. "Henri, come to the table."

"Oui, Papa," he answered. Robert loved how sometimes Henri morphed into French.

"The language thing must be hard for him sometimes," Robert said as he cut the last of the rolls before warming the onions slightly and putting them in a dish.

Dixie pulled condiments out of the refrigerator, and with the addition of the salad, they were ready to go.

Henri hadn't come in, and Dixie turned to the living room as Henri whooped and the sound effects of the game started to run. Dixie rolled his eyes and swore under his breath. Apparently he had expected it would take longer for Henri to figure out his code. "Henri."

He came in with the iPad, grinning. "I can play now." He sat down in his chair and set the tablet on the table.

"You can't play that at the table." Dixie didn't scold Henri, but he did reach for the tablet. Henri tugged it closer and then put it on his lap like a napkin. "You can play after dinner." Dixie took the tablet and set it aside.

Robert watched the two of them, how close they were, and an ache from deep inside rose up in him. Had he made different decisions and not let Dixie get away, this could have been his life. But instead, he was on the outside, looking in. And he'd only be able to do that for a brief period of time.

DINNER WAS good—a little taste of home, and even Henri liked the onions. As soon as he was done, Henri got his tablet and happily hurried away to play his game.

"Tonight I'll change the code. But for now, I'll give him an hour and a half before it turns off the application." He smiled.

"Papa, that's not fair," Henri whined from the other room. "I got the code fair and square." He came in, holding his tablet to his chest as if it was precious. "I

figured it out." He pooched that lower lip, and Robert could see Dixie's will begin to falter.

"I can't have you playing those games all the time. We made a deal when you got the tablet. I'm going to change the code tomorrow. Since your homework is done, you can play all you want tonight."

Henri huffed, and for a second he looked just like Dixie. He had definitely picked up some Dixie-isms. "Oo-kay." He sounded deprived as only a kid could. "Sometimes you're mean, Papa." He turned away, and Dixie lunged after him, lifted Henri into his arms, and set the tablet on the table before tickling Henri until peals of giggles filled the room.

"Is this mean?"

"Papa." More giggles followed, and Robert grinned and sighed. His own experiences with family were depressing, to say the least, and to see the two of them laughing and happy together, even after a fit of temper, was tender as all hell. After his sister's death, everything had changed for him in an instant. His happy family life had a pall over it that never seemed to go away. His mother rarely smiled. It was like someone had stolen her heart, and no matter what Robert did or how hard he tried, he had never been able to fill the void. It wasn't that his parents were bad people—they just seemed to have become lost in their grief and never found their way out. Life functioned on the surface, but underneath, there was little other than loss.

He turned away. Watching what he could never have hurt, so he finished cleaning up, letting Dixie spend time with his son.

"You didn't need to do that," Dixie said when he returned. Robert wiped down the counter and turned off the lights. "I'll put the dishes away later."

"I'm going to help if I'm staying here," Robert said, following Dixie into the other room.

The day had been full of activity, and Robert was glad to have a little while to sit and relax. He found it difficult not to watch Dixie as he turned on the television. The programming was in French, so Robert pretty much ignored it. Dixie and Henri watched for a while until Henri got engrossed in his game once more.

"I still find it hard to believe I'm in Paris," Robert explained. "I always wanted to come here and thought that at some point I'd get leave and be able to visit. But it never happened. Italy was as close as I got."

"Once I was reassigned, I got sent to the States and then transferred over here as a liaison for the Intelligence Services. From there, I found a talent for cyber security and encryption that I didn't know I had, and when I mustered out, I was already here and loved it— my life could be my own—so I worked for myself and stayed."

Robert shrugged, figuring there was a lot more to the story. But he wasn't going to pry, though the details Dixie shared helped him fill in a few tiny pieces of the picture.

"A few years ago, after I ran into a few difficulties, I thought of going back to the States. But once I met Henri, I decided to make Paris my permanent home. I like that we speak English at home, but at school, he speaks mostly French. The more languages he has, the better."

"I can't wait to start learning German," Henri piped up and then returned to his game.

"It's almost time for you to go to bed. You should wrap up your game and go upstairs for your bath. Then

when you're in your pajamas, I'll come in and read you
a story. Okay?"

Robert sat back while Dixie got Henri moving. He
got a hug good night, and then Henri left the room with
Dixie following.

IT TOOK almost an hour before Dixie rejoined him.
"Henri's asleep, thank goodness. He keeps going over
the list of things he wants to show you and makes me
promise that I won't take you while he's at school."
Dixie sat next to him on the small sofa. It was only
a little bigger than a love seat, but European furniture
was smaller in general than its American counterparts.
Europeans usually lived in smaller homes and had to be
much more economical with their use of space.

"What do you want to talk about?" Dixie asked.

Robert groaned. "God, I don't know. Henri is in
bed and the two of us are alone. We could talk about
anything, and yet I have no idea what the hell to say. I
mean, I've thought about you a lot, and you and I talked
earlier. But if I'm honest, I have no idea what going
slow means. Does that mean we hold hands?" He put
his over Dixie's, who threaded their fingers together. "I
feel like I'm in high school again."

Dixie chuckled. "Sometimes the simplest things
mean the most."

"I remember that." Robert closed his eyes, Dixie's
warm hand in his, letting his mind drift back to that
small hotel room on the Adriatic, above the coast. The
water was visible from their room, even if they were far
enough away that the sound of the waves was obscured.
"We'd spent the day in bed, and you decided we were
going out to get food. You took my hand as we walked

down the street. It wasn't for very long because neither of us wanted to draw attention to ourselves, but you did it."

Dixie squeezed his fingers. "Didn't seem so high school then."

"Nope. It was the first time anyone had ever done that." Robert grinned and shifted slightly. "There were a lot of firsts for me that trip, as I remember."

"I think that was true for both of us. I'd had a few fumbling encounters, but no one had ever engaged my heart before." He huffed. "You know I never talk like this with anyone. Henri and I talk about feelings, but not this kind of stuff." Robert snickered softly. "You know what I mean. We're men of action. We do shit, not talk about stuff. You remember in Italy, we were active for a week, but we didn't do a lot of talking."

"Maybe that was our problem," Robert countered. "Sure, we were great in bed together, but when they separated us, we didn't have anything to fall back on. I know a lot about you and you know a lot about me because we were in the same unit. But we never sat down and really talked to one another. We liked each other. We were both gay and had each other's backs when someone gave either of us shit. Thank God that wasn't all that often once the small minds learned they'd have to take us both on. I think we just assumed we knew all there was to know." Robert had spent quite a bit of time, particularly last night, thinking about what had gone wrong, and up until this moment he had no idea. "Hey, you know that my parents were gone, but I never shared with anyone that my father ended his own life from grief." Dixie gasped and his eyes filled with gentleness but thankfully no pity. That was the last thing Robert wanted.

"I guess what I'm saying is that we both could have done better," Robert continued.

Dixie nodded. "So what do you want to talk about?" Damn, the hint of obstinance in his purple-flecked blue eyes was hot. Who knew that blue could be that fiery?

"I don't know. What do you hope for?" He shifted on the cushion to get more comfortable. "What do you want for yourself and Henri?"

"I want Henri to be safe and to have the chance to grow up as normally as possible. Because he's gifted, there is a lot of pressure on him at school to advance and to move forward. I want him to have a childhood." Dixie bit his lower lip.

"And you're giving him that. He's something else."

Dixie shrugged. "Look, I can't talk a lot about my work, but...."

"Yeah... I get that. And I also get that with someone outside the apartment, there are folks who want to get at you. Maybe that guy was to check that you were safe and that there weren't any threats... or maybe he *was* the threat. I don't know. But things like that will affect Henri." He scooted closer. "Let me guess. You spend a lot of your days worried about him. He's in school and out of your sight and protection."

Dixie put his hand to his head as though he were fighting a headache. "I worry about so many things with him... and yes, his safety is one of them." The way he met Robert's gaze held a warning, and Robert figured he better back off. He was about to hit a brick wall of secrecy that would be impenetrable.

"But what do you want?" Robert asked. Dixie shrugged again, holding his breath. Robert was probably going to have to go first. If he wanted Dixie to

share, then he was going to have to be willing to as well. "After all the adrenaline of being in the service, I got out and didn't know what to do with myself. Everything seemed so tame, and yet I also craved quiet."

"You have to be kidding me."

"I know, weird combination. But I've always been a complex kind of guy." He cocked his eyebrow, and Dixie bumped his shoulder as he snorted in derision.

"Come on. You're a typical guy. You want three things: food, football, and sex. I swear if you could have sex in front of the television while watching the Packers and eating nachos, you'd think you'd died and gone to heaven. Remember, I spent a whole week alone with you." His laugh was infectious, but Dixie knew a lot less than he thought he did.

Chapter 5

"WHY DID you become a police officer?" Dixie asked as he realized that Robert was right. They didn't know all that much about each other, though they had great chemistry—or at least they had years ago.

"Well, ultimately I have skills that apply to the job. But really, I went into law enforcement because I wanted to help people. And I'm good enough at my job that the captain is looking at promoting me to lieutenant." Robert's breathing became rapid, and he turned away. "You know about Holly. But my last case involved the kidnapping of a little girl. Before we could get her back, she was hurt."

"Is that why you're here?" Dixie asked.

"Yeah. I almost lost it completely. I even called the little girl Holly at one point." He swallowed hard. "After Holly's kidnapping and death, my dad never recovered, and I was the other child. Mom and Dad were there, but not really. They sort of went through the motions until Dad took his own life, and then Mom stopped caring about anything. So I don't have the best memories of my family. But you already knew a lot of this."

Dixie nodded. "Why did this one get to you so badly?"

Robert lowered his gaze, unable to meet Dixie's gaze. "Because it was my responsibility to get her out safely… and I couldn't do it. I stopped by the hospital afterward, and the girl's mother was glad to see me. She was just so relieved to have her daughter back. But I felt like crap because nothing should have happened to her in the first place."

"You know it isn't your fault. You weren't the one who hurt her. The only one responsible for hurting that little girl is the man with the gun. Remember what we were always told—know who the enemy is. And the man who shot her is the enemy, just like the combatant who took out Wasinski two days before he was sched-uled to go home. Remember? He'd been on patrol in the market, and the enemy just took him out in a freak shot, right in front of us." Dixie's own guilt twisted in his gut. He and Robert been there to watch Wasinski's back and they'd failed. All they'd had to do was keep the guy safe for two fucking days. If they'd done it, Wasinski would be home with his family today. But he wasn't. And looking at Robert, at the sheer pain in his eyes, Dixie knew he had to be strong. He'd had his own brush with that same kind of loss. Just not as much as what Robert seemed to carry.

"Is that your version of 'shit happens'?" Robert asked.

"No. Bad people make shit happen, letting it rain down on innocent people. Those of us who try to help are not to blame when things go wrong. You didn't create that situation. But you had to deal with it." Dixie swal-lowed. "You know that sometimes all we can do is our best to protect and keep the innocents from harm."

Robert nodded. "I know. But this situation seemed different. The way I felt about this child and the situation with Holly got all mixed up in my head. They were both children who were taken and ultimately shot. And all I kept thinking at the scene was that I couldn't let her end up like Holly. Another family shouldn't have to go through that pain, not if I could help it."

"Losing Holly was a tragedy for your family. But this little girl's mother still has her, and that's partly because of you." Dixie put an arm around his shoulder. He wished he could make this go away for Robert, but the hurt he was sharing was bone-deep.

"Reality doesn't matter," Robert said.

Dixie paused. "Huh?"

"What's real or how I should feel doesn't matter. Holly's death cost me not only my little sister, but both my parents. And when that little girl got hurt, it brought it all back." Dixie tried to understand how powerful that experience could be. "The grief and loss are a part of me, just as much as the color of my hair or…."

Dixie sighed. "That's just it. It's something that you can let go of. And as for your hair, you can dye it, you know, even change the color of your eyes." He tried to be funny and was grateful when Robert gave him a smile, even if it was a little fake.

"Yeah. But your real hair always grows out, and the color is just contacts. Under them, you still have the same eyes you were born with. You can cover up who you are, but it doesn't really change anything." Robert crossed his arms over his chest, daring Dixie to contradict him.

"Yeah. Except you have things turned around. The grief you feel, the old hurt that you've taken down deep, doesn't have to define everything in your life.

You weren't born with that grief. In fact, I bet you were a happy, maybe overactive, towheaded kid."

Robert blinked at him. "I…."

"The grief may seem like part of you, but it isn't. You know my family life was all Jesus, prayers, and church. If I did anything wrong, real or not, my punishment was memorizing Bible verses, and then I was made to spend an hour praying for forgiveness. I came to resent my folks for never seeing beyond their own narrow beliefs. But I don't let all that determine how I run my life. I took a page from my parents' book and forgave them so I could move on and be happy. And while you can't just let go of what happened to Holly, you can let it be part of your past, not your future. But that's up to you, not anyone else. I can't take it away; only you can do that." Dixie snickered. "Sorry if I seem preachy." He hoped he didn't sound like the minister in the church he'd attended when he was growing up.

Robert nodded slowly, their gazes locking, neither of them moving. Robert licked his lips, pink tongue darting, and the temperature in the room shot upward. This wasn't the time for sexiness, but Dixie's body didn't seem to care. He didn't dare move as Robert drew closer and pulled him into a hug. Robert said nothing more, but held him in a vise grip. Dixie returned the hold, saying nothing, hoping Robert got what he needed.

Dixie hadn't meant for their conversation to become so serious so quickly. But maybe this was what they needed—to share some of the deepest parts of themselves. Before, they'd had sex and the time in the same unit. This felt a lot different, deeper, even if it was difficult for him to hear.

"I'm sorry," Robert said softly as he pulled away. "I don't know what happened to me." He straightened his shoulders, the Marine deportment sliding into place. Dixie sat back, glaring at Robert. "What?"

"We aren't in the corps now, and we don't have to put on that façade all the time. It's okay to be yourself. It took me a while to figure out that letting my feelings show wasn't a sign of weakness." He half smiled and leaned forward. "When I heard the stuff Pierre said to Henri, I was angry as hell and threw him out. But it hurt like crazy. I'd thought Pierre was someone special, someone I could care for."

"Henri said he brought you flowers." Robert scowled.

"He did, and he made dinner and took both of us out. Pierre took us to Disney. I thought he liked Henri, but instead…." He swallowed hard. "Look, the thing is, that was hard, and at the time, I tried to revert to being a Marine, just like you just did."

"What happened?" Robert leaned closer as well.

"Henri. He was terrified that someone would actually cut off his hand. So help me, I wanted to slice off Pierre's balls for saying that." Dixie felt the tears run down his cheek. "I had a little boy to comfort, and as soon as I did, I realized I was comforting myself too. I could feel shit and let it go. Henri cried, and I did too. Then, afterwards, we went on with our lives." He took Robert's calloused hand. "See, it took my son's distress to help me realize that by grieving for what I lost, I was helping Henri deal with his own fears." Dixie sighed and stood. "I know that Henri is always afraid that he's going to do something so wrong that I'll send him back."

"Really?" Robert asked.

"Last month I found him standing on the counter in the kitchen. He had climbed up there because he wanted one of the cookies on the top shelf. He got the cupboard open and knocked a few glasses out. They shattered on the floor, and I raced in to find him standing there, shaking and crying. As soon as he saw me, he burst into more tears and asked me not to send him back to the orphanage." Dixie kept himself together. "I know that part of it is him testing me to see what will happen. I'm well aware of that. But that fear is still there. Henri is largely a happy, incredible child, and I'm thankful every day that he's in my life. But he's taught me so much about what's really important, and being afraid to show who we are just isn't one of those things." He patted Robert on the knee. "I don't know about you, but I think that's about enough drama for today." Dixie leaned down and lightly kissed Robert on the lips. Damn, the taste drew him in, and he wanted to do that again, deeper, longer, but he straightened up instead. "I'm going to go up to bed, and I'll see you in the morning." He was determined to take things slowly, even if every fiber of his being wanted to press Robert back onto the sofa cushions and taste every inch of him. And if he stayed here much longer, he knew he'd do just that.

DIXIE WORKED and worked, staying up well past midnight to clear away everything he had on his plate. And even then, he began looking for more to do. He wasn't tired in the least. His entire body thrummed with excitement, and he had to do something to keep his mind off Robert.

The trouble was, keeping busy wasn't working. If he allowed himself to stop concentrating for even a few seconds, the taste of Robert's lips came roaring back, along with the desire for more. Then there was his worry that his work had suddenly brought potential danger to his and Henri's life. The encryption method he had almost accidentally stumbled on had the potential to add essentially uncrackable layers of security to sensitive government computer systems. However, if word of this got out, rivals would be desperate to get their hands on it, if only to get around it. The stakes were enormous, and now people had suddenly been parked just outside his door. He needed help, and Robert was the one person he knew he could trust to do so. That was the main reason Dixie had asked Robert to stay with them. He just wished he could tell Robert everything.

This wasn't working. Dixie pushed back his chair and locked his systems. He stretched his scrunched muscles and left the room, closed the door, and went downstairs to the kitchen. Coffee was not a good idea, though he desperately wanted a mug. He thought of tea, something to relax him, and began heating water.

Movement in the house made him pause. He felt it more than heard it. Someone was here.

Dixie turned slowly, reaching for a knife out of the block as some sort of weapon.

"You couldn't sleep either?' Robert asked, and Dixie began breathing again as he slid the knife back into the block.

"Yeah." He took a deep breath. "You startled me."

"I didn't know you were up, and I didn't want to disturb Henri or you if you guys were asleep. Sorry if I got your blood racing." Interesting choice of words,

and that fact had nothing to do with Robert putting him on alert. Dixie's blood had been racing for hours now, and he wished he could make it stop, at least enough to let him go to sleep.

"You have no idea," Dixie sighed.

Robert slid closer. "Oh, I think I do." Robert's gaze lowered, and Dixie followed it, remembering that he was wearing sleep pants that were loose and did next to nothing to hide this particular issue. "I think your feelings are very much on display."

Dixie snorted. "Come on. You have one of those too, and you know the damned things have a mind of their own." He rolled his eyes.

"Yeah, and sometimes it overrides what the big head says we should be doing." Robert closed the distance between them, tugging Dixie to him, sliding his arms around the back of his neck, rough hands teasing his skin. Dixie met Robert's gaze and let Robert draw him in. He wanted this badly, and as soon as their lips met, Dixie's arms engulfed Robert, holding him tightly. He finally let go of what had held him back and feasted on Robert's intense lips.

Robert pressed him down until the counter touched his lower back. Dixie held on, nearly surrendering under the onslaught. Damn, Robert was forceful… and sexy. The energy between them crackled through the room, and Dixie gave himself over to it, letting the tornado that surrounded them carry him away. It had been years since someone had given him what he needed and taken him on a trip to complete passion.

"Papa."

That one word brought Dixie crashing back to earth. He pulled away, wiping his lips as he turned to his son. Fortunately Henri was just in the doorway, and

Dixie could use the counter to give himself a few seconds to calm down a little.

"What is it?"

"I'm thirsty, and there are noises outside. And I wanna kiss too." Henri held a stuffed rabbit to his chest, scrunching it up against him. That told Dixie how stressed Henri was. He hadn't slept with an animal in some time.

"Okay. Let me get you some water, and I'll take you back to your room. It's probably just the wind."

Robert got the water for him and let Henri drink before taking the glass and giving Henri a loud kiss on the cheek.

"Come on. Let's go back to bed," Dixie said, glancing over his shoulder at Robert, in his tight T-shirt and little clingy shorts, and wishing he could stay. But he took Henri's hand and went up the stairs, put him back to bed, and made a show of looking outside.

He saw nothing, but spent a few seconds scanning both ways. The street was quiet, with no moving cars or people, only the trees swaying in the wind, a few branches coming close to the house that he probably needed to trim. Letting the curtains fall back into place, he sat on the edge of Henri's bed. "It's all good, just some branches that I'll trim in the morning," he said gently. Henri's eyes were already drifting closed, and Dixie stayed with him for a few minutes, then slowly got up and left the room, closing the door most of the way.

He went back down, and Robert handed him a mug of the herbal tea he had been making before he and Robert had gotten sidetracked. "Is he okay?"

"Yeah. Henri is asleep. There was nothing outside. I think he sometimes gets his dreams a little confused

when he wakes up. It happens." He sipped from his mug, letting the warmth of the tea slide down his throat, soothing away some of his jumpiness.

"I'm going to check outside, just in case. Then I'll return to my room." Robert turned to leave, taking his mug with him. "Not that I don't intend to pick things up where we left off, but somehow this late at night isn't the time." He smiled. "Go check on Henri again and then get some sleep. You have a little boy who's going to have you up pretty early in the morning." He paused in his retreat and returned to where Dixie stood. Robert tugged him close and kissed him hard enough to get Dixie's engine revving before pulling away once more. "I'll see you in the morning."

Robert left and went back through to the front door. Dixie finished his tea and waited until Robert returned before he checked the alarms and went upstairs to bed, knowing he had a restless night ahead of him.

DIXIE WAS up with the first stirrings in the morning. He turned off the alarm and forced his still-reluctant body out of bed. Downstairs, he found Henri and Robert making eggs for breakfast and joined the others at the table. "I made the toast," Henri said, passing over the almost burned toast with a wide grin. Robert shrugged and added eggs to the plate for him.

"Henri says he likes his toast dark," Robert said with a wink.

"I put the butter on too," Henri added, and there was no way Dixie was going to disappoint Henri, so he ate the nearly burned toast and his eggs with a smile. After all, he'd had worse while he was in the corps. Robert got him some coffee, which was a blessing,

and they all sat down to eat, Henri watching each bite they took.

"Finish your eggs," Dixie told him as he quickly finished up his breakfast. "Then you need to get dressed and ready for school. You don't want to be late for Madame Brassard."

Henri shook his head seriously. Madame Brassard was a good lady but tended to be firm, and she liked to be on time. The last time Henri was late, she talked to him about it the entire walk to school, and Henri had told Dixie all about it when he got home. It was an experience neither of them wanted to repeat. Especially since Madame Brassard had talked to him about it as well.

"I'm all done," Henri pronounced and slipped out of the chair to head upstairs. "I'll go get dressed." He walked out of the room, and Dixie took the few quiet minutes to finish his coffee.

"He likes the toast dark," Dixie said.

"Henri insisted that you did too." Robert ate his light toast. "I managed to convince him that I liked mine light. We had quite a discussion on the doneness of toast."

Dixie could just imagine. "I'm going to check on him. Since you cooked, I'll clean up when I get back." Now that he was alone with Robert, some of the agitation from last night had returned. The two of them were going to have much of the day alone together, and he was more than a little jittery, wondering just what kind of possibilities the day would offer. Maybe, if they were lucky, the two of them could pick up where they left off before Henri had found them last night.

Dixie pulled his thoughts back to Henri and went to find him in his room. "Dude, you can't go to school

like that." He had on yellow shorts and a wild purple shirt. "Come on. You can wear the shirt, but you have to wear regular pants." Dixie picked some out and helped a now-grouchy Henri get them on and then find his shoes.

"But why?"

"Because the colors will make your teacher's eyes bleed," he teased, lifting Henri and tickling him. "No one wants bloody eyes. Now let's finish getting ready." He continued tickling Henri for a few seconds before letting him up. Dixie loved the sound of his son's laughter. As far as he was concerned, there was no more joyful sound anywhere. "Okay, first the shoes, and then let's get your school stuff."

Henri put on his shoes, and Dixie checked him over, then took Henri downstairs. By the time they had his backpack ready, Madame Brassard had arrived with her daughter. Henri waved as he left with them. Dixie wished them all a good day before closing the door. Only then did he realize that Robert wasn't around. He figured he'd gone to his room, and Dixie got ready to go to work as Robert came back inside.

"There's something you need to see," he said very seriously. "Where's your computer?"

"In my office. Why?"

"I have something that you need to look at. I'd take you outside, but I don't want to draw attention right now. You need to see this, and then we can figure out what to do."

Dixie motioned toward the stairs. "What are you talking about?"

Robert paused at the top of the stairs. "Remember last night when Henri said he heard noises? I think he really did." He held up a small camera, and Dixie

sighed before leading Robert to his bedroom and then into his office. He turned on a small computer that wasn't attached to any of his networks and motioned to the chair. Robert sat down and connected the camera.

"I took this from across the street, playing tourist as a cover. I took pictures up and down the street, but those aren't important." Robert brought up the picture of the front of the building. "This is the outside wall, and if you look closely, you can see where there are chinks in the stone." Robert zeroed in on them. "Each one is a small cleat. I doubt anyone would even notice them if they weren't looking, but they're there." He blew up those areas.

"What the hell?" Dixie leaned closer. "What are you saying?"

"Someone was outside your home last night and at least partially scaled the front wall. The cleats end a few feet below Henri's window and just off to the left of it. I don't know what the intention is or why some-one would do that, but I believe Henri really did hear something."

Dixie went cold, slowly rubbing his arms. "We need to get those damned things removed, and I need to install sound sensors of some kind around the house. I can't have someone climbing the building trying to get in." Why in the hell would anyone even try that? It was the front of the house and highly visible. Though people rarely looked up, and if it was at night and dark, it was possible that someone could reach Henri's win-dow. Shit, there was no way he was letting anyone get near his son. The very idea of a kidnapping to get at Henri was frightening as all hell.

"Yeah. And I have an idea. I noticed that the paint around a few of the windows needs to be touched up.

Get me a ladder and I'll do that today. While I'm up there, I can render the cleats unusable while I paint the window frames."

"You have to be kidding. I can take care of it myself. You're supposed to be on vacation," Dixie said, even as he wondered how he was going to take care of this problem without drawing attention.

"A bigger question, instead of whether I'm going to be spending a little time on a ladder, is why someone would do this." Robert swiveled around in the chair. "I know you are working on sensitive projects and you said you might need help." His gaze scanned the room. Dixie already knew there was nothing incriminating and not a hint to give away anything that he'd been doing. "It looks like that maybe has been turned into a definite."

"I can't really talk about the details," Dixie explained. It was the most honest answer he could give, even though he wanted to tell Robert everything and wished to hell he had never gone down this road with his work in the first place. The thought of putting Henri in harm's way scared the hell out of him. "I have alarms on the house, and they'll screech if someone so much as opens any of the front windows."

"Maybe these people don't need to get inside. Maybe they're trying to tap into your data feed or wire the house for sound."

Dixie shook his head. "My data feed is secure eight ways from Sunday. All they're going to hear if they wire the house for sound is me and Henri talking. This room is already soundproofed and secured. The only way in is the way we got here."

Robert looked up. "What's above it?"

"The attic space and roof."

"Then we need to check those out. You do that while I take care of the painting. There has to be a reason why they're so focused on your place. And if you're going to be safe, we need to figure out what they want." Then Robert gasped. "What about Henri while he's at school?"

Dixie snickered without a hint of mirth. "Henri is perfectly safe. He's being watched over while he's out of the house. The people I work for are as committed to keeping him safe as I am." Still, he didn't like this. "Okay. Paint the windows and take care of the cleats. I'm going to check out the attic."

"Look for honey hooks of any kind. If the network is wireless, then they might try to install their own repeater that would send your signal to them."

"I know what I'm looking for," Dixie said. "There's a small shed off the courtyard. Inside, you'll find a ladder and brushes, along with some of the paint that was used the last time the building was fixed up. Just touch it up and get done as quickly as you can." Dixie wanted to make sure they were all safe, and then he was going to have to report this to his superiors. What was going on was concerning, but even more so was the fact that someone had figured out what he was doing. There was a leak somewhere, and his NSA bosses were going to need to plug it. But first he needed to figure out if any of his systems had been compromised.

"I'll get started," Robert said, leaving the room. Once Dixie was sure that Robert was gone, he started a special tracing program that would follow all of his data connections. If someone had managed to tap into them, this would find it and alert him. While the program ran, he went into Henri's room and into his closet,

opened the small door in the back, and stepped into the attic space.

DIXIE SNEEZED for the eighth time in three minutes before climbing out of the attic and closing the door. There had been nothing up there, and in his office, the program showed no threats to his network. At least that was good. Dixie called Howard to inform him what was happening and what he suspected. Howard agreed to add some more exterior security to the building, including sensors for vibration on the building itself. Dixie had told him that the cleats had been neutralized, and who had done it.

"We are aware of your houseguest," Howard said. "Lance Corporal Wendel has enough clearance that you may take him into your confidence. But only when you have to."

"Understood," Dixie answered. "We have verified that the building is secure. I think this may be an initial attempt to probe our defenses. We are keeping a low profile and trying not to draw attention."

"Very good." Howard ended the call, and Dixie locked his systems before going in search of Robert, who was already putting the ladder and equipment away.

"What did you find?" Dixie asked quietly as soon as they were back in the house and up in the office.

"Three cleats. From the look of them, they've been there a little while, but not too long. The thing is… they weren't placed last night. But it's possible that someone tried to use them last night and didn't get what they expected. I found a fourth that had already failed, and I

made sure it would never be used. I was able to render the others unusable without too much trouble."

"Okay. So what do I do now? I already have alarm systems set up." This sort of thing was not his area of expertise. "I can't have Henri in danger."

"You're thinking systems. I'm thinking more physically. Have you ever thought of adding security bars to the windows?" Robert asked.

Dixie shook his head. "I've gone out of the way to make sure that all security efforts are out of sight. I didn't want to draw attention to the house in any way. Adding that sort of thing would only send a signal that I have something to hide." He blew out his breath.

"Then let's make it so that they can't get in Henri's window. There's a lock on it from the inside, and I'll make double sure all the windows on the street side are secured. While I was on the ladder, I placed blades along the glazing and sills to make sure that anyone who tries to get in that way will pay one hell of a price."

"The glass is the same laminate that they use on windshields, so it's pretty durable. The window broke shortly after we moved in and needed to be replaced." The fact that he had broken it and then seen to its replacement was another issue completely.

"So that pretty much cuts off that means of entry. I went up on the roof, and it seems clean. Maybe we need to keep an eye out and wait for them to make their next move," Robert suggested.

"Or maybe we've already deterred them. When they find their cleats gone, they're going to have to know that we're onto them. If they truly are trying to get to me and my work, they'll figure out that I have

resources and that I'm not going to just sit here and do nothing."

Robert agreed silently. "Still, I think we have to make sure that we all stay safe. No going out alone, and we make sure we're always aware of our surroundings. I know I promised to take Henri to the museum, but I think you should go along with us, even if it isn't really your thing. Let them see you and Henri aren't alone. If they want to get to any of us, they have to take on us all. We could hunker down in the house, but that would show fear. We need to project strength like the Marines we were."

"It's a good idea, and Henri will get a kick out of having both of us there. Though I have to warn you, he will go through the museum and point out each naked person he sees." Dixie patted Robert's shoulder. "The last time we went there, he finally turned to me and asked why no one in the paintings looked like him? Sometimes that kid really blows me away. All the figures in the museum are either perfect or painted for their ugliness. None of them are imperfect, yet shown as beautiful."

"Okay. Well…." Robert stammered slightly as he grinned. "There are worse things he could point out. Some of those guys have butts to crack walnuts." He bumped Dixie lightly. "He doesn't miss much, does he?"

"Nope." Dixie stood behind Robert and put his arms around him, letting his hands slide down his impressive chest. Damn, the power under his grasp was impressive. Part of him still wanted to pull away and not go down the same road they had before—it had hurt too much when it ended. He nearly drew his hands back, but Robert's pull was too powerful, the attraction

too great. He'd let him get away before, and who knew what would happen between them going forward. But right now, Robert was here and damn it, Dixie wanted him… just as much as he always had. Dixie remembered Robert as hard and strong, but he was probably even more fit now than he had been back then. "He doesn't miss a thing, and I'd like to think that I don't either." He sighed and leaned closer, inhaling Robert's deeply masculine scent.

"It's been a long time," Robert whispered, placing his hands over Dixie's. Dixie felt Robert's breath hitch and held his own. He drew closer, and Robert slowly turned. Dixie pulled back until Robert faced him, eyes dark and intense. "You and I keep getting interrupted, or other people come between us." Slowly Dixie stood, and Robert slipped an arm around his waist. "There's no one here now."

"I know. Henri is away at school; my work is done…." He stepped closer, their lips inches apart.

"What are you waiting for?" Robert asked.

"I don't know. Every time you and I get close, something happens. I keep expecting a knock at the door or the damn roof to fall in. I don't know. Given our past, it seemed as if the universe wanted to keep us apart. So I guess I was waiting for it to come calling."

Robert snickered and engulfed him in an embrace, taking his lips in a scalding kiss as he maneuvered him out of the office and toward the bed. "Is this okay?" Robert asked breathily, pulling away.

Dixie nodded, and then his chance to speak was gone. Robert took his lips in a bruising kiss that threatened to overwhelm him.

Damn, it had been a long time since someone had bested him in the strength department. Pierre had been

gentler in the bedroom and definitely more passive, as were the few other men he had been with. They all seemed to like *his* strength. But Robert was completely different. Hell, he lifted Dixie off his feet, propelled him toward the bed, and dropped him on the mattress. "Get out of those," Robert growled, kicking off his shoes before pulling his shirt over his head.

Robert was perfection—like a statue of one of the Greek gods in the Louvre, all muscle and sinew stretching under his smooth skin. There was no doubt about his power or the strength he held. Yet each movement seemed graceful and fluid. A lot of guys, if they were big, moved as though their own muscles got in the way. Robert wasn't like that.

"Dixie...." Robert's voice rumbled as he leaned over him. "You need to get these clothes off or else I'm going to do it, and I don't think I can be gentle." His brown eyes darkened even further, the color of a well that continued forever. Dixie snapped out of his reverie for a moment and got his socks off before tugging at his shirt. He managed to get it over his head as Robert dropped his jeans to the floor. Instantly Dixie's throat went dry.

Robert was naked, perfectly so.

"What the hell happened to you?" he asked, forgetting about his own pants as the long scar down Robert's leg drew his attention.

"A roadside bomb sent flying shrapnel my way. A piece of the vehicle sliced me up. One of the medics stitched me closed." He said it as though the whole thing was no big deal. Dixie took a moment to look Robert over more carefully. There were a number of scars that he didn't remember, and in his mind's eye, he

could easily recall the impressive man he had known so well all those years ago.

"You saw a lot of action after I was gone," Dixie said softly, and Robert nodded.

"It is what it is." He turned away slightly.

"Don't you dare hide them. Those are battle wounds, and you earned each of them." Dixie sat up, taking Robert's arm and slowly tracing the scar. Robert quivered but otherwise held still. "I know how tough it was, but what the hell did you do? Station yourself in front to make sure you took the damage?"

"I'm fine. A few of these are from after I got home. Police work isn't exactly a walk in the park either." Robert drew closer, pressing Dixie back onto the mattress. He pretty clearly didn't want to talk about that anymore, and when his hands began their own explorations, Dixie's mind centered on each and every touch.

"You're like a machine," Dixie said. "You take a beating and just keep going."

Robert shrugged. "There are times when I wonder how much longer I can be the punching bag. I don't recover like I used to."

"Right. You're an old man at thirty-one," Dixie teased, because Robert looked anything other than old.

"Sometimes I feel old, but not right at the moment." He smiled that bright smile that went almost all the way to his ears, and Dixie lightly cupped his cheeks in his hands, wondering just how many people actually got to see that smile. He knew when Robert was happy, and was very aware of when he had let his guard down, like when Robert was with Henri. But this smile was very different. This one was special and rare. Robert wasn't trying to hide anything or cover something up. He wasn't a carefree man. This was a smile of pure

joy, though, and Dixie was thrilled to see it, wishing it showed through a lot more often. Robert deserved more joy in his life.

"No. You don't look old either." Dixie guided him down into a kiss that seared through him. He ran his hands down Robert's wide back and held on as Robert proceeded to take him on a journey reminiscent of the one they had taken all those years ago. One thing that Dixie loved about Robert was his strength. Dixie was in control of so much in his life, and a great deal of responsibility rested on his shoulders. He had Henri and his career and their life here. Dixie had to keep both of them safe and secure. But lately his job had become more complicated, with a lot of added pressure. Doing his best to juggle the extra stress, while raising a son at the same time, added still more. With Robert, he didn't have to be the one in charge.

Hell, lying right here in Robert's arms, passion exploding inside him, and knowing that he was in safe, caring hands, actually meant that he could let go. Robert could be the one in control.

And damn, the intensity and energy that rolled off Robert made him feel like a surfer carried on a wave toward shore. Once caught, there was no way to stop it, other than falling off. And Dixie had no intention of doing that.

Robert had magic hands. That was the only way he could describe them. Wherever he touched, Dixie's skin flared into ecstasy. God, he was still partially clothed and his cock felt like it was trying to throb its way out of his briefs. He quivered with excitement. Robert hadn't even made a move toward his belly, let alone lower, and already Dixie found himself approaching the edge. He hadn't done that since he was

a teenager. But he was so far gone, he had already lost control of his own damned body.

DIXIE STARED up at the ceiling, breathing hard, with Robert next to him. He closed his eyes as Robert's hand slipped into his. Neither talked, which was a blessing. Instead, their breathing filled the room as they lay together.

"You know, that was…," Dixie finally said, breaking the silence.

"Yes." He rolled his head to the side, and Dixie met Robert's warm gaze. "Italy was so long ago, and yet…."

"I know. Some things about you are so familiar, and yet others aren't the same. We've both grown up, and…." Dixie sighed softly, not sure exactly what he was trying to say.

"It's different now." Robert gently stroked up his arm. "Do you remember that first night in our room? You practically had the covers pulled up to your chin." Robert bumped his shoulder. "You had never been with anyone before then."

"Yeah. Well, all that religion growing up had done a number on me. You sure as hell helped me get over my shyness. And after that…."

Robert snickered. "You turned into a horndog. Damn, you were pretty then. You still are. Though hotter now, and… more…."

"Old?" Dixie answered.

"No. I was going to say forceful, more sure of yourself. You know what you want and you aren't shy about asking for it." Robert kissed him hard. "I love that about you. I like that I don't have to guess. You're open and forthright, almost demanding. It's pretty hot."

Dixie liked that. "You think I'm hot?"

Robert leaned closer. "I always did," he whispered. "I've been with other guys, but none of them measured up. I realize now that I was comparing them to you. But they all came up short. I didn't realize why nothing had ever clicked. Well, now I do. None of them were you."

Dixie wasn't sure what to say. They had agreed to take things slow, only now it seemed like Robert was getting in over his head... and Dixie was going right along with him, full steam ahead, damn the torpedoes. The worst thing about it was that he *wanted* to go. This felt right, where no other relationship had since their time in Italy. Too bad Robert was only here for a few weeks. Dixie didn't know what he was going to do at the end of that time. He was pretty sure he was going to hurt like hell and that there wasn't a damned thing he could do about it. Disengaging wasn't going to work. And the thought of backing away now just to try to save himself and Robert from some potential pain seemed like the coward's way out.

"I know exactly what you mean," Dixie finally admitted.

"So where do we go from here?" Robert asked.

"How in the heck should I know? I don't have the relationship handbook any more than you do. But my guess is that we take things one step at a time and talk to one another. The first thing on the agenda is to get cleaned up and dressed. Then we should have lunch. From there, we'll figure shit out as we go." At least that was a plan.

Robert hummed his agreement, echoed by his belly.

Chapter 6

ROBERT WANDERED the city. For the past few days, to give Dixie a chance to work, Robert had taken the Metro to different locations and wandered through different sections of the sprawling city. He'd spent time in the Tuileries Gardens under the trees, taking shelter from a passing shower. He'd stood under the Arc de Triomphe, with its huge French flag flowing in the wind. He even did some shopping and sent tacky souvenirs back for the guys at the station. Let them eat their hearts out.

Robert checked his watch before turning back toward the Metro station. Henri was scheduled to be home from school in half an hour, and Robert had promised him a Mario battle. He'd even convinced Dixie to give him the code so he could disable the timer on the tablet. Just for today… and he'd been sworn to secrecy.

The subway ride was a little stuffy and definitely too warm. He took a deep breath when he stepped out of the station near Dixie's house and began ambling down the familiar-growing streets. He decided against stopping for a coffee but did make a detour into the patisserie for a snack for Henri.

"Mr. Robert," Henri called out as soon as he stepped inside. "I'm all ready." He had his tablet and everything.

"He was watching for you at the window," Dixie said with a smile.

"How about we eat these and then we can play?" Robert grinned as Henri bounced. They got plates and forks and sat at the table. "Did I get you the right one?" Robert asked Henri, who had already tucked into his cake with strawberries and pink cream.

Henri nodded and ate. "I'm gonna beat your butt," he said with a grin. "I'm really good at Mario."

"Henri," Dixie said with a touch of warning. "We don't talk that way."

He set down his fork, looking up at his dad. "But I am. I'm really good. It's not bragging if it's the truth."

Robert about lost it. "What if I'm better and beat your butt?" He cocked his eyebrows, and Henri gaped at him. "I've had lots of time to practice."

"Okay. Enough trash talk. You can play Mario after dinner and before bed. You have to get up early tomorrow because we're going to the museum, and I got tickets for first thing. That way the galleries won't be crowded and Henri can show you his favorites. Within an hour, though, the museum will fill and the Grand Gallery will be jammed with people."

"Sounds good. Is that okay with you? Will you be able to get up early, little sleepyhead?" Robert teased Henri.

"Yes. I'll get up, big sleepyhead," he countered and took another bite of cake. "I like Mr. Robert. He gets us cake."

"Is that the only reason?" Robert asked, mimicking Henri by pooching out his lower lip.

Henri shook his head. "I can kick his butt at Mario."

"We'll see about that."

AFTER DINNER, Henri did kick his butt—big-time, and more than once. Whenever he won, Henri jumped up off the seat and did this wiggle-butt dance in the middle of the room. Robert would have been tempted to lose just to watch the kid dance if his competitive spirit didn't run so deep. "Dude, you need to learn to be a good winner."

Henri wasn't buying that. He did that dance of his again after Robert's Princess Peach disappeared into the ooze at the bottom of the screen for the umpteenth time. Robert sat back and handed the tablet to Henri, who easily made it past the obstacle and on to the next level, his face a study in concentration. Robert was coming to see that Henri threw himself into everything he did with focus and intensity, like it all mattered so much.

"You know, this *is* just a game," Robert said gently as Henri reached the end of yet another level and paused the action. "You don't need to be so serious."

Henri blinked at him. "But I want to win."

"I know. But sometimes there are more important things than winning." He patted the seat next to him. "I like to win too. I always had to be first, the fastest, the strongest, the best. That was what I thought I had to be after my mom and dad died."

Henri put the tablet aside. "You were an orphan like me? Did you have a papa like mine who saved you?"

Robert put an arm around him. "No. I was older than you, and I had people who helped me until I was old enough, and then I went into the Marines, where I

first met your papa. But after my mom and dad died, I thought I had to be the best at everything to get people to like me. I tried to win everything just to show that I could do it."

Henri nodded. "Me too."

"Why do you think that?" Robert asked. "Your papa will love you no matter what. And he'll never, ever stop." Robert hugged him.

"Even when I'm bad?" Henri asked, and Robert shared a glance with Dixie, who was now standing in the doorway. "The kids at school, they say that Papa should give me back because of my hand." Robert could almost feel Dixie tense.

"Well, those kids are mean, and they don't know anything. Your papa will always love you, and he'll never let you go. You can do anything you want, I promise you that." Robert had to work to keep his voice level. He wanted to go down to that school, talk to the teacher and the principal, and rip their heads off. What kind of place were they running anyway? It took all his will not to look at Dixie. "And I'll tell you a secret. No one is good all the time—not your papa, and not me. We all do bad things sometimes. It's part of being a person and growing up. Do you want me to tell you a story about your papa?"

"When he was naughty?" Henri asked.

"Okay." This was going to be fun. "I can tell you about how naughty your papa can be. Let me think." He made a show of it, knowing Dixie had to be wondering what he was going to come up with. "Well, your papa and I were on vacation in Italy for a few days. It was just the two of us, and we were away from the Marines."

"Was Papa naughty?" Henri asked in a half whisper. "Did he get in trouble?"

"Your papa got both of us in trouble. We had a room with a view of the sea. All day long the sun made the water sparkle, and it looked so pretty and warm. We talked about going swimming and having a lot of fun. But things happened." Robert caught Dixie's gaze. "He and I ended up spending a lot of time in our room. But the last night, your papa decided that we needed to go out. That's when your papa was naughty. Did you know that your papa likes beer?" Henri shook his head. "And do you know what happens when people have too much to drink?"

Henri glanced at Dixie. "They pee a lot?"

Robert chuckled. Out of the mouths of babes…. "Yes, they do. But when people have a lot of beer, they get drunk and act stupid. Your papa was acting stupid and decided that we should go swimming. So he took me down to the water, and I took off my shoes to wade into the waves. Your papa took off everything and went in the water buck naked." He smiled as Dixie rolled his eyes, groaning softly.

"He was naked?" Henri asked, his little mouth hanging open. Robert wondered what Henri was think-ing. He found out quickly. "With fish? Did they bite his Mr. Shrimpy?"

Dixie doubled over with laughter, and Robert just about lost it right there.

"No. But he was in the water naked, swimming, and the police were not too happy about it. Thank good-ness I was still dressed and managed to get your papa's clothes on before they arrested him—*and* before he shocked the sisters of Santa Maria, who happened to be out taking a walk that night."

"Nuns? Papa flashed nuns?" Henri asked. Robert had no idea where Henri had learned that term, and it

seemed neither did Dixie, but Henri understood the situation in an instant.

"Yup, your papa flashed a group of nuns." He laughed right along with Henri. "But I got him dressed, and the police made sure we got back to our hotel. Then your papa and I slept that night, and we left the next day to go back to being soldiers again." After that, the corps had had very different ideas about their futures, and they'd made their decision, one he'd come to regard as his biggest mistake. "No more skinny-dipping."

Robert smiled, and Henri grinned. "I wanna go skinny-dipping, but no fish!"

Dixie hurried over and scooped Henri up. "How about we get you upstairs and you can skinny-dip in the bathtub? Guaranteed no fish." He carried a laughing Henri out of the room and toward the stairs. "Say good night to Robert. He already told you your story, so you get to go skinny-dipping and then right to bed. We're going to have a busy day tomorrow."

Henri waved and said good night before Dixie carried the giggling boy up the stairs, leaving Robert alone. The week he'd been here had been eye-opening in so many ways. The food was amazing…. And Dixie and Henri were a real family, while he was on the outside, looking in, wishing he could be part of it. Robert finished his water and set the glass on the table just as his phone vibrated.

"Hey, Captain," he said, recognizing the number. "What's up?"

"Robert…." He sounded so serious. "I have some news." Instantly Robert was on guard. "I've debated calling for the last couple of days, but I thought you would want to know. It's about little Grace, the girl who was hurt."

"What happened?" he barked without thinking.

"She's taken a turn for the worse. They got the bullet out and she was doing better, but an infection set in. They're treating it and she's a fighter. But right now, they don't know." He sounded heartbroken. "I promised to keep you informed, and I'm doing that. The doctors are doing all they can."

"I see." Instantly Robert was cold, and all the turmoil of that day, wrapped up with the loss of his sister, threatened to surface once more.

"This isn't your fault." He paused, and Robert wondered what he should say. Nothing came to mind.

"Thanks for telling me." What the hell else was he supposed to say? He couldn't do anything to help her. Just like the situation with Holly, things were out of his control.

"How is your vacation? Are you getting some rest?"

Robert hummed softly. "Paris is great, and I'm having a good time with my old friend and his son." He didn't want to say a lot about Dixie or Henri. They were here and part of what he'd found to make him happy. Telling the captain—or anyone—about them would be like sharing them, and he wasn't ready to do that. For now, they were all his. "If you hear anything more, please let me know."

"I will," the captain agreed, and they ended the call. Robert set his phone on the coffee table, sat back, and tried not to think too much about Grace… or Holly, for that matter. He needed to figure out a way past this.

DIXIE DIDN'T return for a while, and by then, fatigue was catching up with Robert. Even though he'd been here a week already, there were times when he grew

tired for no apparent reason. Robert was about to go out to his room and go to bed when Dixie came back down the stairs. "Do you have work to do?" Robert figured if Dixie did, then he'd go to bed and leave him alone.

"No, I'm good. How about you?" Dixie asked, and Robert stifled a yawn. "Sorry. If you're tired, you should probably get to bed. It's going to take a little while to get us ready to go to the museum on the Metro." Dixie stood still, and Robert could feel his gaze on him.

"I don't know what I feel right now." He explained about his captain's call. "I thought she was doing well. When I left the news was good, and now…."

"You understand that this isn't your fault," Dixie said softly. In his mind, Robert knew what Dixie said was true, but still, he'd spent the past hour running through every step of what had transpired, trying to determine any way he could have prevented that little girl from getting hurt. He went over it again and again but kept coming up empty. "Sometimes bad things happen."

"I know that. It's just that I thought she was going to be okay."

"And maybe she will be. Sometimes there are bumps in the road, that's all. You said she was shot in the back—that can cause a lot of problems."

"It was in the shoulder, and they thought she had been lucky." But maybe that wasn't the case. "I know there's not a damned thing I can do about it. Even if I was home, I couldn't help her."

"Maybe you need to deal with Holly first," Dixie offered. "You told Henri about how you lost your parents. And you know that losing Holly destroyed both your mom and dad. They were never the same

afterwards." Robert nodded slowly. "Maybe you need to stop blaming yourself."

"Me? How...?" Robert sputtered. That had to be one of the dumbest things he'd ever heard. "I didn't hurt Holly."

"No. But knowing you as I do, you blame yourself for your parents' reaction to her death. But you can't. Your dad would have done what he did no matter what. You were the best son you could possibly be. Being better or more perfect wouldn't have stopped your dad from taking his own life. That isn't your fault either." Dixie sat next to him, gathering Robert in his arms. "Your dad did what he did and made his own decisions. You aren't to blame for that any more than you were responsible for the asshole who hurt your sister. Shit happened, and then more got piled on again and again. But none of that is because of you."

"Then why do I feel like it was?" Robert asked.

"I don't know. But that doesn't make it so. You aren't responsible for the decisions that your parents made. But you were the one who paid the price for them." Dixie squeezed him harder. "I don't know what to say other than to try to let it go and to thank you for being honest with Henri. He asked me upstairs if I really would love him always, no matter what." Dixie sighed. "I want him to know that there is nothing that he could ever do to make me stop loving him."

"We all have baggage in our past." Robert just wished he could find a way to leave that behind some- how. He yawned again. This time he tried to cover it but failed. "Did you lock everything up and set the alarm?"

"Yeah. We're all in for the night."

"Then I think I'm going to go to bed." Robert stood, and Dixie came right along with him. He turned out the lights and then took Robert's hand and led him up the stairs. "Okay."

Dixie led him to his room and pushed the door closed. "Just relax and strip down. Tonight is about you." And to Robert's mind-blowing surprise, it was just that.

ROBERT WAS sore in the best way possible the following morning when a weight bounded on the bed. "Papa! Did you and Mr. Robert have a sleepover?"

Robert had been so comfortable and worn-out that he hadn't even thought about moving, and now a very active six-year-old was climbing into bed with them and they were both still naked. This was not a good thing.

"Henri, why don't you go get your bunny? He can join us."

"Okay." Henri climbed off the bed. As soon as he left the room, Dixie jumped out, pulled open a drawer, and tossed Robert a pair of shorts before pulling some on himself. They had just gotten back under the covers when Henri came back in, his stuffed rabbit under his arm, and crawled into bed next to Dixie.

"Are you excited about today?" Robert asked, wondering softly what time it was.

"God, it's only a little after seven," Dixie groaned. "The museum always takes an early start." Dixie settled back under the covers, and Robert hoped that if they were quiet, maybe Henri would rest for a little while more.

"Can we play Mario?" Henri asked. Apparently settling in for a little quiet time was completely out of the question. Henri might be lounging with them under the covers, but he was still about two seconds from full speed.

"Why don't you just relax?" Dixie asked.

"Because I'm hungry." He was already squirming. "I go make breakfast. We can have toast." That seemed to be it. Henri climbed over him and was on his way before either of them could get out of bed.

"You rest awhile longer. I'll go get Henri dressed and keep him from burning down the house." Dixie climbed out of bed, and Robert burrowed under the covers, trying to replace the missing warmth. But it didn't work. The warmth he really wanted was personal, not physical, and that had already left the bed.

After getting up, Robert gathered his clothes and tidied up Dixie's, which had ended up strewn across the back of the chair in the corner. Then he managed to leave the bedroom and make it out to his room without attracting Henri's attention, where he dressed and cleaned up in the tiny bathroom before heading to the kitchen. Henri was already making toast. But at least this time, Dixie had managed to convince him that not everyone wanted their toast nearly burned.

"Come on, eat your breakfast so we can go," Dixie encouraged Henri, who seemed to be having more fun making breakfast than eating it.

Henri sat down at his place, and Robert brought over a mug of coffee and sat across from him. Henri watched Robert as though he were trying to figure something out. "Did you get scared last night?"

"No." Robert glanced at Dixie, who shrugged. Great, he was no help at all, thank you very much.

"Then why were you sleeping with Papa? I sleep with him when I have a bad dream." He took a bite of his toast, still mulling things over.

"Robert and I are close friends, and...." Dixie sighed like he was out of his depth. "Okay. Henri, when two people, like Robert and I, really like each other, they sleep together. It's part of how those people show that they care for each other." Man, Robert never knew Dixie could tap-dance like a pro.

"Oh," Henri said. "So it's sex." He swallowed and took another bite, as though he hadn't dropped the equivalent of a nuclear bomb at the breakfast table.

"Henri," Dixie said cautiously once he could speak again. Robert used his mug to hide his smirk. This entire conversation was precociously precious as all hell. Like an innocent battle of wills, and Robert had no idea who would win. "Do you know what sex is?"

Henri nodded and then his eyes widened. "Do you?"

Dixie managed to hold it together. "Yes."

"Then why ask me?" Henri drank his juice, emptying the glass. "Can we go now?" He climbed down off his seat, looking at both of them.

"Henri," Dixie asked, patting his lap, and Henri climbed up. "I was asking because I wanted to know what you think sex is."

"Oh. I'm smart. I know what sex is. Marcus told me." He crossed his arms over his chest, and Robert pushed his chair away from the table, figuring now was a good time to give the two of them a chance to talk alone. "It's when a man and a woman love each other and decide to make a baby. They go in a room, take off their clothes. Boom, boom, boom... and nine months later, the baby comes out." He glared at Dixie as though daring him to contradict him.

Robert was actually impressed. Henri was largely right. "Oo-kay. Marcus told you all that."

"Yeah. He knows about things like that. His mommy had seven babies." As though that made the kid an expert.

"You do know that people can love each other and not be a man and a woman, right?" Dixie asked.

Henri nodded seriously. "Gay people, like you." He grinned. "So does that mean that gay people have gay sex?" He turned that intense gaze at Robert, and Robert knew he was in Henri's mental line of fire. Maybe this wasn't so much fun any longer. "Who has the baby?"

Robert groaned. Parenting was definitely not for the faint of heart.

"Yes. Gay people have gay sex, and that's part of how they express that they love each other. It takes an egg and sperm to make a baby, so gay people don't have babies without help. Instead, we can adopt special people like you." Dixie hugged Henri, probably to distract him. "Now go upstairs and get ready to go. You wanted to show Robert all of your favorite museum exhibits, remember?"

Henri slipped down and loped out of the room.

"Jesus."

"Yeah. Sorry. I should have gotten up and left your room, but I fell asleep and…." Honestly, he hadn't wanted to get out. Being with Dixie felt right.

"It's okay. Henri was going to start to ask questions eventually. It's best to be straightforward with him and get them over with instead of trying to put him off. He'll just watch and ask more questions later. By giving him an answer that satisfies him, he'll file it away and go on to something else." Dixie began cleaning up,

and Robert helped clear the table. Then he took over to allow Dixie to help Henri. Once everything was clean and put away, he got his things for a cloudy day and met the others at the door.

It was drizzly but warm enough when they left the house. Robert held Henri's hand while they waited for Dixie to secure their home. "I'm gonna show you the best stuff," Henri said as Dixie joined them.

"Do you wanna ride on my shoulders?" Robert asked, and when Henri nodded, Robert lifted him up. He was pretty light. Robert held his legs as they strode to the Metro.

Henri talked until they reached the station. Then Robert lifted him down, and Dixie took Henri's good hand and led him through the station while Robert followed close behind. There were a lot of people there, even on a Saturday morning. The three of them found seats on their train, with Henri sitting on Robert's lap, talking about all the special things they were going to see.

"What about the *Mona Lisa*?" Robert asked.

Henri shrugged. "It's small, and there are always lots of people around it." He made a face, and Robert chuckled. Okay, the *Mona Lisa* did not rank high on the Henri scale. "I like the ones with the babies." He turned to Dixie. "Can we get a baby someday?" he asked with the same enthusiasm as a kid would ask for a puppy.

"Maybe we'll adopt a baby brother or sister for you someday. But for right now, you're all the kidlets I can handle." Dixie tickled Henri as the train came to their station. They got off the train and headed up toward the exit.

The hair on the back of Robert's neck stood up, and he raked his gaze over the crowd of people. He felt

like he was on display, and that went right to his gut. Robert knew that sensation well—it had saved his life on more than one occasion. Staying close to Dixie and Henri, he kept his guard up as they exited the station. "Do you want a lift?" Robert asked Henri, who nodded. He had become aware that long distances became difficult for Henri, and if something happened, Robert wanted to be able to get them the hell out of there. This was not at all the kind of day he had expected.

He lifted Henri into his arms and held him so Henri could look forward, and they strode toward the glass pyramid in the center courtyard of what had once been the Louvre Palace. Robert couldn't help looking around, noticing a number of people who had come along with them from the station also get in line for the opening of the museum.

As he scanned the crowd, he caught a small movement, something most people would ignore. A man about his age, thin, with black hair, suddenly lowered his gaze when Robert looked his way. Robert turned away slowly, not wanting to give anything away. "I've always wanted to come here. My grandma had a book when I was growing up called *Treasures of the Louvre*, and I used to look through it all the time." He bounced Henri a little as the line began to move. Using Henri as a bit of a shield, he managed to glance back at the man he'd spotted earlier and found him watching them. This time his gaze didn't falter. Surrounded by all the splendor of the pyramid, the fountains, and the building itself, the most interesting thing to this man seemed to be their little group.

Robert made a mental note of the man as they continued forward. He didn't seem particularly physically threatening, and the metal detectors ahead would limit

the number of potential weapons that could be brought inside. So the most important thing he needed to do was keep Henri and Dixie in sight and safe. Dixie lived in his head; Robert lived by his guts. He'd make sure his guts protected both of them.

"Ready to go?" Dixie asked as they reached the security area. Richard set Henri down so he could go through with his father. Then he went through and they were inside, heading down into the subterranean lobby of the museum.

"Where do we go?" Robert asked Henri, keeping an eye out for the man who had been watching them. He didn't see him, and Robert thought maybe he'd been wrong as Dixie led them to the garderobe to put their things in a locker. Then they were on their way.

"This way," Henri said, taking him by the hand and leading him away before Robert could grab a museum map. Not that he needed one. Henri was like a full-fledged tour guide, taking them right to *Winged Victory*. "I love the angel," Henri said. "I like to think it's my mommy." Then he turned. "This way."

"No time to look?" Robert asked, because apparently Henri had his own timetable. They went up and took a corner.

"This is where the babies are," Henri explained, and Robert found himself walking down a mostly empty Grand Gallery.

"I know you're in a hurry, but can I look around for a minute?" He didn't want to rain on the kid's parade, but he was here among some of the greatest art in the world. Not that he was any kind of expert, but....

"Sure," Henri said.

Robert lifted him again. "How about you ride and direct," Robert said. Henri settled right in, holding on to his arm.

Slowly they walked down the gallery, taking in both sides as they went.

"See, that's the babies," Henri said, pointing, and Robert took him over to the *Madonna of the Rocks*. Robert couldn't help smiling at Henri's description of the Da Vinci. He stood still, taking in the painting, acutely aware of Dixie next to him, his scent occasionally tweaking Robert's nose. He sighed, and Dixie shifted closer, his shoulder brushing Robert's. They must have turned at the same instant, because their gazes met and Dixie smiled warmly, a gesture Robert returned. This moment was one of almost perfect contentment. He wished it could go on forever.

But just as suddenly, he sensed they weren't alone. Robert turned slightly, noticing their shadow out of the edge of their vision, about a quarter of the way back. Although the man turned to admire another nearby painting, Robert was pretty sure they were being followed.

They continued on, looking at the *Mona Lisa* and then the rest of the works in the long space before Henri guided them through gallery after mind-blowing gallery—Robert marveled at *The Raft of the Medusa* and *The Coronation of Napoleon*. It was becoming harder to concentrate on the art with Dixie next to him, pulling at his senses.

It was in one of those ornate rooms when Robert saw their shadow again, and any doubt he had about being tailed vanished.

"Do you want to see the booby lady?" Henri asked.

Dixie, who had been quiet, chuckled. "He means the *Venus de Milo*."

"Sure." And off Henri went, guiding him like a seasoned veteran right to her. "Do you have the entire museum memorized?" Robert asked Henri.

"No. Just the good stuff," he answered flatly, as though those art pieces were obvious. Before they could look through the ancient Roman and Greek art, Henri tugged at his shirt. "I have to go."

"Okay," Dixie said. Robert put Henri down, and they headed off in search of the facilities. Robert kept an eye out and waited outside the door while Henri took care of business.

"We're being followed," Robert told Dixie quietly as soon as they exited the bathroom. "I've seen the same man with us since we left the station."

Dixie nodded. "Yes. I'm followed quite often. The people I work for often keep me and Henri under surveillance for our protection. The man you saw is probably one of the same people who pass by the house regularly, like the one you saw the other day. I try to give Henri as normal a life as possible, and they help me by providing additional security when I need it." He seemed so damned calm about it. "There's nothing to worry about. The man over by the statue behind me isn't a threat."

Henri came out with a grin, but Robert felt a chill run up his back. He couldn't help thinking Dixie was taking things too lightly. Could there be another threat that was being overlooked? He couldn't shake the feeling that there was more to this than met the eye. "Where are we going next?"

"To the naked people," Henri announced with less energy than he'd had previously. The kid was finally

starting to run down. Dixie explained he meant the Greek and Roman statuary. Apparently they had only seen a small part of the collection. Dixie lifted Henri into his arms, and Henri put his arms around Dixie's neck and let his head rest on his shoulder. Robert doubted the boy would fall asleep, but a rest was probably a good thing.

They wandered through the statuary gallery and then on through the various other rooms. There was so much to take in, but after a while, all the art seemed to blur together. "Dixie, maybe we should get something to eat."

Henri liked that idea—they had been walking for quite a while. "Then we can figure out what to see next."

Dixie nodded. "This way." They made their way through one of the mezzanines to a small café and ordered quiches, a few pastries, and drinks. Dixie had Robert take Henri to the table and then followed with their tray of food. "Are you having a good time? I know it's a lot to take in." He placed Henri's plate in front of him, and the boy dug right in.

"It's wonderful," Robert said with a smile, grateful to sit down for a few minutes. "And I'm glad I got to come with you and Henri." He placed his hand on Dixie's. "It makes this extra special." He held Dixie's gaze until the man following them paused on the floor below them. Robert refused to actually look toward him, but he knew he was there, watching them. Still, he kept his hand in Dixie's. He'd be damned if he'd let some nameless security guy put him off.

"Everything is fine, and there's nothing to worry about," Dixie said. Robert followed his gaze to a man

sitting at another table. He was seated at an angle that allowed him to watch them.

Robert leaned closer. "Is that the guy you were talking about?" he whispered, making sure Henri wasn't paying them any attention for a moment. Dixie nodded. "He's not the man who was following us. I didn't make him." Dixie stiffened for a second and pulled out his phone. "The man I've seen is about five ten, black hair, a little longish, in jeans and a lime-green polo shirt." He kept his voice level.

"Who is?" Henri asked.

"It's not important. Just eat your lunch." Dixie's voice held a world of tension, and Henri seemed to sense it. He didn't argue but set down his fork to glare at his papa, even as Dixie texted frantically.

"Where is he now?" Dixie asked as the man at the other table got up and strode out of the café.

"Going back the way we came in," Robert explained, and Dixie texted before putting his phone down.

"Let me know if you see him again."

"I will." The man from the table strode through the lower area out the way the man in the lime-green shirt had gone. "It's going to be nearly impossible for him to locate the guy in this crowd." Dixie nodded. "Why would someone follow you here?"

Dixie shook his head. "Not now." He ate his lunch, and Robert did the same. His quiche lorraine was wonderful, but he barely tasted it. His mouth went dry and stayed that way. He wanted answers, and he wanted Dixie and Henri safe. Robert also wondered exactly what the hell Dixie was up to. Was he on the up-and-up, or were the people following him from law enforcement? No… he refused to think that Dixie might be up

to something illegal. He was his friend, his lover—at least for now, though his heart was quickly staking a claim. It sent a stab of pain through his gut to even think about the end of his trip.

Robert finished eating, his mind a whirl of possibilities that kept running through his head—until Dixie took his hand. Almost instantly, the adrenaline coursing through him lessened. "Just relax. Remember our training. Thinking clearly will take us a lot further than worry."

"How can you be so calm?" Robert mouthed.

Dixie leaned over the table. "Because this has been my life for a lot of years. I understand the game and how it's played. If nothing else, our tail has been frightened away, and if he hasn't left, he'll be caught, which is the best of all cases. Then we might find out something from him."

"Can we go now?" Henri asked.

"Finish your quiche and then we'll go look at more stuff if you want," Dixie offered.

Robert leaned over to Henri. "The rain has stopped, and the sun is coming out now. Is there more you want to show me, or do you want to go out into the gardens? You're the tour guide, so you get to choose."

"The gardens," Henri said. "And you get to carry me."

"Oh, I can?" he asked with a grin. Robert was glad that Henri seemed to like him. He tickled Henri and reminded him that people didn't get carried if they had empty bellies. Henri finished eating, then pooched out his belly to show how full it was. Robert put the dishes on the cart, and then they headed out.

"Do you see our friends? Either of them?" Dixie asked as they left the museum after gathering their

things. Robert shook his head. They headed through the courtyard and out past the fountains and across the road. Robert was glad he was carrying Henri, because a lot of cars passed, and it took a while to get across and into the former royal gardens.

"I like the animals," Henri said, pointing to the various statuary-topped columns.

"It's pretty here," Robert observed as they walked along the paths through the large park. "I never really gave a place like this much thought when I first thought of coming to Paris. It wasn't on my list of must-see things."

"Paris has a number of parks and open spaces, but this one is pretty special. People come here to see and be seen. They take walks in fine clothes on Sunday mornings when the weather is nice. It's sort of a holdover from the past. I like it because there's a lot of shade, and with the way the city is, it's nice to be in green space. Of course, there's the open parkland near the Eiffel Tower and other areas of the city, but this is special for me."

"Why?" Robert asked.

"Before he adopted me, Papa used to bring me here so I could play," Henri interrupted.

"Do you remember a lot from before your papa brought you home?" Robert asked Henri, who shrugged.

"Sometimes. Mostly just how lonely I was. The people there told me that I was different, and I had my funny hand and short leg. The other kids teased me, but I was smart, so I read a lot, even when I was little. Then Papa came in and said he would adopt me." Henri smiled. "He said that I was special." He sighed as though he had seen things beyond his years.

"Your papa is a very special man," Robert said, looking right at Dixie. Henri nodded and squirmed, so Robert put him down. Dixie took his hand, and they walked slowly down the path. "When I decided to come visit, I didn't realize how things would be." He knew he had to be careful because of Henri, but he was talking to Dixie.

"I didn't either."

"Why?" Henri asked.

Robert hesitated. "Your papa and I were good friends a long time ago, and sometimes old friends don't like each other the same way they did before." Man, that was a long-winded explanation. "But then sometimes, it's like the time apart didn't happen."

Henri looked at both of them like they were weird and continued walking.

The central fountain came into view, and Henri grew excited, tugging Dixie in that direction. Kids ran around the paved area, playing together and splashing the water with their hands. "You can go if you want," Dixie said, and Henri ran off.

"Are you sure that's a good idea, considering that we were followed at the museum?" Robert asked.

"Henri loves the fountain, and we're both here to watch him, as is our good shadow. He didn't catch up with the guy in the museum, but he thinks we scared him off. At least for now." Dixie was tense. "Besides, he loves this place. What am I supposed to do? Explain to him that my work is dangerous and that means he can't go out to the museum or play at the fountain?" Even as he explained, Dixie drew closer to where Henri was playing with a small group of boys. Robert didn't understand anything they were saying,

but knowing the language wasn't necessary for Robert to know the happy laughter and the joy in Henri's smile.

Robert could understand Dixie's decision, even as he watched Henri and the surrounding area like a hawk, looking for anyone out of place. "What I keep wondering is what they want from you."

Dixie sighed. "I've been approached by… shall we say less-than-reputable people to sell out the work I've been doing. Hackers and governments are always trying to break the encryption that we use to secure their data. What I developed will add security around the data that will make it almost impossible to access unless they have the system themselves. It was top secret, but word seems to have gotten out about it. And there are people and governments who will do or pay just about anything to get their hands on it. But I have no intention of handing over anything."

Robert nodded, watching Henri play, and then turned to Dixie. Seeing his huge, beautiful eyes filled with fear, Robert understood. His outward façade of calm covered up a core of worry. "I'll help keep him safe."

Dixie slipped his hand into Robert's. "My work doesn't usually attract attention, but what I stumbled on has changed everything. And it's put Henri in danger, something I never wanted to do."

That made sense. He wanted to ask Dixie more about it, but he instantly tensed, and Robert shifted his gaze to the fountain. He had looked away for just a minute… and Henri was gone.

"Where did he go?" Robert said, his heart rate increasing as panic rose in Dixie's eyes. For a split second, Robert couldn't breathe, and he was back at the

scene in Michigan, Grace being shot and…. Robert pulled himself out of his head. This was more important than his mental hedge mazes. With a proverbial slap on the face, he slipped into police officer mode. "He can't be very far. You go left, I'll go right."

Dixie nodded and took off. Robert ran around the fountain and then hurried off toward the trees. A group of boys ran around, calling out French as he hurried along the path, checking out the open grassy areas.

Happy laughter and yells made him turn, and Robert sighed as Henri stepped out from behind one of the trees, laughing as the other boys joined in. It was a game—Henri had been hiding. Robert texted Dixie immediately, knowing he would be frantic until he saw Henri again. "It was a game," Robert said as soon as Dixie was close enough to hear.

Dixie took steps toward Henri, but Robert held his arm. "Don't," he whispered. "Henri was only playing, and he has no idea how worried we were. Let him be happy." The terror in Dixie's eyes quickly turned to relief.

"We should have just gone home. I try to give him as normal a life as I can, and I don't want what I do for a living to interfere with his life, but I need to get it through my head that I can't just will everything to be okay." He began to shake, and Robert put an arm around his waist, holding him closer.

"I know, and it's okay. It was just a scare. Henri is fine." God, he never wanted something like that to happen again. "He's happy playing with the other kids." Dixie nodded but was still pale, which Robert could understand. "It's okay. It was nothing at all."

Dixie shook his head. "No, it's…. We were lucky. What if someone had tried to take him to get me to hand over work? What if—?"

"They didn't, and he's fine. He's just being a little boy." Robert squeezed lightly. "I was as scared as you were." He didn't go into his mini flashback.

Laughter filled the air around them as Henri and the boys raced back to the fountain. Henri got there last because of his leg, but it didn't seem to stop him, and the other kids continued playing as though nothing was amiss. Robert swallowed hard. "Your son is pretty amazing."

Dixie humphed. "Yes, he is. But what do you mean specifically?"

"Nothing stops him. He could whine because he can't run as fast as the others, but he just keeps going. And the other kids don't seem to mind that he's different."

"Because to them, he's just another little boy." Dixie met Robert's gaze, his eyes filled with tears. "If I lost him, I…." He inhaled deeply and then released his breath with a sigh. "He's the light I never thought I'd have in my life."

Robert didn't miss a beat, dropping his hands, and placing them on his hips. "And here I thought *I* was the light of your life and that you couldn't live without *me*. Now I find out there's another man." Dixie sniffed and then smiled… just as Robert had hoped.

"You're so full of shit," Dixie groused, turning away, probably to wipe his eyes. "Thanks."

Robert was quickly coming to realize that he'd do just about anything for Dixie. And the idea scared the hell out of him. He knew their time together had an expiration date, yet Robert couldn't help getting drawn

into Dixie and Henri's family. For the first time, he wondered how he'd ever go back to his life—and exactly what there was for him to go back to. The notion of leaving Dixie and Henri sent a chill up his spine, almost as cold as the one he'd felt when he thought Henri was missing.

Chapter 7

DIXIE DIDN'T let his guard down for a second the rest of the time they were out. It probably sucked for Henri, but the boy's game of hide-and-seek had shaken Dixie to the core. He'd always thought he'd struck a decent balance between Henri's safety and letting him have a life, but now he was reevaluating everything.

"Stop it," Robert said gently once Henri was in bed and Dixie had returned to the living room. "I know how you feel, and it wasn't your fault."

"You know, I could say the exact same thing to you," Dixie challenged.

"I know. I got a message a few minutes ago from my captain. Grace's infection is going away, she's apparently up and moving around, and her mother says that she can see the light at the end of the tunnel. So things worked out for her."

Dixie nodded. "True, but I bet Grace's mother wishes she had taken more steps to watch her daughter and prevent what happened in the first place. I have that chance with Henri, and I'm not going to allow him to be harmed." He sat down, eyes a little glazed over. Robert took his hand and held it, tracing the backs of

his fingers. Dixie closed his eyes and just enjoyed the simple touch, the comfort, while it was offered.

"You can't wrap him in bubble wrap." He smiled. "Well, you could, but the school and the neighbors are going to look at you funny, and he'd pop every time he moved. No kid wants that." Dixie scowled at him without even a twitch of a smile. "Come on, I was kidding. The least you can do is smile." Robert scowled back, and finally Dixie huffed a little but let his lips tick upward. He appreciated that Robert was trying to lighten the mood, but he wasn't sure he could do that right now.

"I have to keep Henri safe," Dixie whispered. That was all that really mattered. His son was his family—he was the center of his life, and the thought of losing him nearly made him sick. But he knew if anyone could help, it was Robert.

"I know you do." Robert turned on the sofa so he was facing Dixie. "And I'll help you. You know that." He leaned closer, sliding his hand around the back of Dixie's neck. It was an intimate gesture, and Dixie thought of resisting but didn't have the energy. It felt good to have someone who seemed to know what he needed. "You're a father, his papa, and I know you worry. You can't help it. I can't either." Dixie knew Robert understood—Holly's death and the fallout it had created for his entire family life pretty well guaranteed that. Robert was probably the only person he knew who fully got his mind-numbing fear.

"This is such a mess." It would be easy on his ego to say that this was his problem, one of his own making due to his work, and he needed to be the one to handle it. But the truth was that Robert, with his police skills, was more capable of handling this. Dixie was a

systems guy at heart, and this situation required Robert's strengths.

"I had your back when you and I were in the corps, and you had mine. We were brothers… more than brothers. We knew what the other would do before we did it. I trusted that you would look after me just like I did you. That's how it was," Robert said.

"And that was then…." Seven years was a long time—a lifetime ago.

"No. Those things don't go away just because of time or distance. We held each other's lives in our hands. You saved mine, and I saved yours. So don't try to be noble and push me away because you think you can do this all by yourself. You can't. You need someone to watch your backside, because there's a hell of a lot more to it now than there was back then."

Dixie huffed. "My backside is as high and tight as my hair, thank you very much." And he exercised to make damned sure it stayed that way. No gay man, no matter who he was, wanted a saggy ass.

Robert rolled his eyes dramatically. "I meant that your backside now includes Henri, you goof. And for the record, your ass…." He leaned closer. "Is as tight and hard as it was back then, and once this house is locked up tight and the alarm is on, I intend to take you up to that room of yours, close the door, and use that tight butt of yours to drive you out of your mind." Dixie quivered, and he might have actually moaned out loud. He wasn't sure. "I know you're on edge, but tonight, once the house is secure, you can let that go for a few hours and just be."

Dixie nodded. That sounded like absolute heaven. There had been so many times when he'd wondered if he had been doing the right thing bringing Henri into

his life. The work he did left him, and by extension, Henri, open to be hurt. But the thought of not having that little boy in his life…. He could still see those huge eyes and that adorable face asking him if Dixie was going to adopt him. He hadn't meant to adopt any child, and yet that single question had changed his life. "What if something happens to him? What am I going to do to keep him safe? He deserves a lot better."

Robert shook his head slowly. "What Henri deserves is a papa who spends time with him, takes him to his favorite places, loves him more than life itself, and will always be there for him. He needs everything that you already give him." Robert drew him closer. "No kid has the perfect life. I didn't, and neither did you, but you are doing everything in your power to see to it that Henri has the best one you can give. That's all any parent can do."

"But…." He knew he shouldn't be having all these doubts. "I keep wondering if I should just get out and do something else."

Robert clicked his tongue. "Come on, Dix. You know that there's no getting out of things like this. Once you're in, you're in until they freeze you out. You know too much—you can't just walk away. The people who want the information you have aren't going to stop stalking you just because you say you quit. In fact, they'll try even harder if they think you're a free agent. And then the government agency you work for will have no choice but to pull you back in."

He knew Robert was right. The men he'd directed and overseen had developed products and protocols worth many millions on the open market. The agency he worked for was not going to just write that off, no matter how many documents he signed about secrets,

and his security clearance. These were people whose job it was not to trust anyone. "So what do I do?"

"Well, first thing, we find out who these people are. And that means you need to get some additional help to catch these guys. If people are following you and trying to make contact...." He paused, thinking. "Maybe you should let them. Then you can send a clear message that you aren't for sale, especially if a couple of them end up limping home for their trouble. If you hurt them enough, they'll see that you'll be too expensive for any possible gain."

"Either that, or they'll come after me more." He wasn't sure that what Robert was proposing was going to help. But like Robert said, he had someone in his corner who was loyal to him and not the agency or anyone else. "I need to make some calls and get some more support."

Robert kissed him. It seemed like a weird time for that, and yet the familiar warm taste of Robert's lips soothed the hamster wheel of worry that had set up shop in his gut. "Go make your calls. I have a few things that I'm going to do while you're up there." He flashed a smile, and Dixie kissed him again before hurrying out of the room. He needed to make his calls before he got sidetracked.

WHAT HE'D hoped would be just a brief set of calls turned into two hours of debriefing and discussions about who was following him, who might have tried to penetrate the house, and about Robert. Thankfully, his employers didn't seem to have any problems with Robert or his presence in Dixie's life.

"Look, I've told you before that you need to use your best judgment on what you share with him. He has clearance, so if you need him to stay safe, then use him. But don't take any chances or try to be a fucking hero." Howard sometimes acted just like his former major in the corps—usually suave and careful, but easily rattled. And this situation seemed to have him on edge.

"We won't. But we aren't going to stand aside if someone threatens Henri."

Howard sighed. "I wouldn't think anything else. We'll have an additional security detail dispatched. They will make their presence known to you, but other than that, hopefully you aren't going to see them. They will do their job in the background. You know how things are done."

"Yes, I do." Everything was carried out as quietly as possible, without drawing any attention unless absolutely necessary. "I'm assuming that we will be followed and watched as before."

"They will coordinate more closely with you than our more routine security does. Now relax. We know what we're doing and we will keep you safe." When Howard ended the call, Dixie sat back in his seat. He trusted Howard. His boss was a company man through and through. Now all he needed to do was lie low until he was contacted. They'd put together a plan and execute it.

Dixie sighed and left his office and went back downstairs. Most of the lights were off and the room was dim. Robert lay on his back on the sofa, using one of the pillows for his head. His eyes were closed and his breathing level and steady, as if he were asleep.

Dixie checked the alarms and opened the refrigerator. He needed a beer, so he grabbed one and popped

it open, then grabbed a second and took it in to Robert. He set the bottle on the table and sat down, taking Robert's hand. "I'm sorry it took so long."

"It's okay. I was just resting." Robert's eyes slid open and he squeezed Dixie's fingers.

"I brought you a beer." Dixie sucked down a good share of his, letting Robert sit up before handing him the bottle. "We're getting some more security. They'll make contact. My superiors know you're here, and they are probably aware of everything about you, including your underwear size. You have clearance—"

"Don't tell me anything I don't need to know," Robert said. Dixie nodded; they both knew the drill. "I'll help all I can."

Dixie sighed. "I'm sorry about all this. You are supposed to be on vacation and enjoying yourself, not sitting here waiting on additional security."

"Don't worry about it. I'm in Paris, and there is plenty for us to see. Once the security arrives, we'll work up a schedule with them so they know where we'll be and what we're doing. From there, we can co-ordinate so Henri can show me all the things he keeps talking about."

"Sometimes I think he's going to grow up to be either a tour guide… or a world ruler." Dixie chuckled lightly. "He has…."

"Some of the weirdest interests of any kid I've ever met. He wants to go to museums and has his favorites. He'll sit and read a book, completely engrossed, and then put it down and be as active as any other kid. He's so smart it's frightening, and he sees everything. Looking in those big eyes, you know he's soaking in every word and expression like a sponge." Robert finished his beer. "Sometimes I swear he's going on twenty."

"And then he'll do something every six-year-old does." The way Henri's behavior shifted was both fascinating and a challenge.

"Exactly. Like the focus he puts into working out the code to the parental control."

"Yup, and he's doing it again. He knows it's been reset, and I'm also aware that he's trying to figure it out." He was so proud of his son.

"Will he be able to?" Robert asked.

Dixie shrugged. "Eventually. But he'll have to work for it."

Robert leaned back in the seat. "I think that's enough about Henri. Tell me about his papa." His eyes seemed to glow in the low light. "What makes you happy? When you go to bed at night, what is it you dream of?"

Dixie let himself relax. "I don't know." His mind was a blank. "I used to dream of a family, but I have that now. I have Henri, and we're a family, just the two of us." He closed his eyes, then chuckled. "If anything, I dream of nothing…." He knew Robert had no idea what he meant. "Here in the city, there is always activity. It's not like New York or the other big cities in the US. It's different here… but still, there's always this underlying sound." Dixie slipped his eyes open to look at Robert. "Last year I took a holiday, and we went to the Loire Valley. Henri and I stayed in a chateau with towers and huge, beautiful rooms. I wanted him to see a different part of France, and we had a lot of fun. Henri mentioned how quiet it was, and one night I took him outside after dark and we lay in the grass, looking up at the stars. It was almost silent, and the stars grew so close. I told him about the constellations and what they were. It was a time when it was just me and my son."

Robert leaned a little closer to him. "Sounds perfect."

He didn't nod or react, just held Robert's gaze in his. "Maybe it does. Lying on the soft grass under the stars, looking up, holding my son's hand as we talked. That night, the dew settled around us a little. I could feel the moisture on my cheeks, but neither of us moved. 'Papa, why don't we have stars like this in Paris?' Henri asked me, and I explained about the city and the lights." It had been magical. "But it wasn't perfect. The moment was special, and the quiet rested around us like a soft warm blanket, but I realized something. I had Henri, and he's the best. I love him with all my heart, and I know that Henri loves me. It's something that when I was in the corps...." He paused because his throat ached, and Robert, bless his heart, said nothing, but took his hand. "Do you remember the guys getting letters and videos from home? I used to be so damned jealous of them. They had wives, kids, whole families waiting for them, sending messages and video cards. I got next to nothing." Dixie hadn't meant to bare his soul, but Robert had asked the question, and once Dixie had started, he hadn't been able to stop. The box in his mind had been opened and the contents just came pouring out.

"I think I understand," Robert said. "You were on that grass looking up at the stars with your son, but it was incomplete."

Dixie nodded. "Yeah. I remember thinking that it would be perfect if I had someone to be with, to spend time with, someone who cared for me. Henri is wonderful, but he isn't...." The words failed him completely.

"Henri is your son—he isn't your lover, your other half... your...." Robert trailed off like he didn't

have the words either. "That someone who's always there for you."

Dixie found his voice again. "Yeah. Someone for me." The visual intensity between them was just too great, the energy nearly overwhelming, and Robert's gaze so laser-like that he needed to break it or he was going to crack open down the middle. "After we got home from that trip, I was determined to try to find someone, and that was when I met Pierre. God, what a mistake that was." He shook his head and closed his eyes, cutting this off before he lost control of himself. "I think I need to go up and check to see if anything else has come in." When he'd come down from upstairs, he'd needed a beer and conversation because his work was just too much. He hadn't expected their talk to veer into such dangerous territory that work would seem like an escape.

"Don't do that," Robert said. "Shit, don't run away because things get tough. We're Marines—we run toward the fire, not away from it."

Dixie paused. "Bullets I can take, but this…."

"Tell me about it." Robert once again took his hand and guided him over to sit next to him. "I don't do all this emotional stuff well. You know that. But I asked you to share your dream, so I guess it's fair for me to share mine." He sighed dramatically. "When I was a kid, I used to dream that Holly was back. That she wasn't gone and that Mom and Dad could be happy again. Then they were gone, and I used to dream that I had them back so I could try to make them happy somehow. It was exhausting because all I ever did was look back. I wanted what I'd had before, and that couldn't happen. None of us can go backwards, no matter how much we might wish it. Life has to move forward."

That was something Dixie knew well. "What did your dreams turn to then?"

"Well, in the corps, for a while, I had this dream about a certain member of my company. He and I spent a week together in Italy.... Then things changed and we were separated. So for a while, I dreamed that things were different once again. I went back to the corps and finished my tour, came home, and went to the police academy before joining the force."

"So where do you see yourself going?" Dixie wondered what Robert was getting at.

"That's just it. I worked a lot, pushing myself to get ahead. I thought my dream was to be the best officer I could be, maybe make lieutenant or captain someday. Be a good cop and really make a difference, just like we were trying to do in the corps." Robert licked his lips, but thankfully he didn't turn away. "I honestly think that over time, my dreams grew smaller and smaller. None of the big ones came true."

"Because they couldn't," Dixie supplied. "You can't bring back people who are gone. All you can do is move forward." God, he wished he had better advice to give than just ridiculous platitudes.

"And that's what I thought I was doing. Now I don't know." He sat back, resting his head on the top of the sofa cushion, looking up at the ceiling. "I kept myself busy all the time so I never had to think about things like this. And now...." He chuckled and straightened up. "Here I'm the one who asked the question that started this, and I don't have an answer to give you."

"You know, it's not that hard. Sometimes it's difficult to put into words, but when you close your eyes and think about what you really want and what would make you happy, you usually come up with something.

You don't have to tell me what you see, but you should be honest with yourself."

Robert scoffed. "You don't ask for very much, do you?" There was that smartass coming forward again.

"And you can smartass your way out of just about anything." Dixie knew it was a bad idea to push, and he was tired of talking anyway. It had been a tiring, exhausting day already. He set all the alarm systems, locking the house down tight, and then turned out the lights. He wasn't sure what Robert still wanted to do. He found himself standing at the base of the stairs until Robert hoisted himself up and slowly walked over. Without a word, he took Dixie's hand and led him up the stairs to his bedroom, then closed the door behind them with a snick.

"COME WITH me," Robert whispered in the dark room. Dixie reached for the light, but Robert stilled his hand. The single window that faced the courtyard allowed in a small amount of light, just enough for them to see the outline of the furniture and each other.

"Where are we going?" Dixie asked as a single flame flared to life. It caught a candlewick, and then Robert carried the point of light toward the bathroom. The small space seemed warmer bathed in the glow, and Robert set the candle on the counter before tugging off his clothes. In seconds he was bare and turned to start the water. Dixie got the idea quickly and did the same, letting Robert guide him under the spray. God, he was thrilled that one of the things he had done was to install a full shower when he'd redone this room. Dixie slid the door closed, and Robert held him tightly, the hot water cascading over them, wetting the skin even

where they pressed together. Robert's lips found his, and Dixie sighed softly, even that small sound echoing in the confined space.

Their kiss ended with Dixie breathless and Robert reaching around him. Dixie didn't move, letting Robert take charge of this particular dance.

The tile was cool under his back as Robert pressed him to it. He gasped slightly at the change in temperature until Robert's soap-slicked hands worked their magic. For a few minutes Dixie let go of his worry and tension under Robert's expert touch. Slick, strong hands worked his muscles, and the hot water soothed down to his bones. But it was Robert and the way he held him, combining his touch with the water and his embrace, that soothed down deep, reaching those places that no one had ever managed to before—not even Robert himself, all those years ago. Dixie was putty in Robert's hands, and he was more than content with that.

Under the water once again, Robert pressed against his back, hard muscle and firm arms embracing him, stiff cock pressed to his butt. Dixie's own stood at attention, and as Robert slid his hand lower, Dixie hitched his breath before moaning shamelessly as Robert's fingers surrounded it, gripping, stroking. Dixie closed his eyes and let the sensation of near bliss wash over him. His legs shook and he tried to steady himself, giving over to Robert's ministrations. "Don't fight it. Just let go," Robert whispered before sucking lightly on his ear. "You don't have to go it alone now. Just let someone else see to you."

Dixie whimpered and shifted his weight, desperate to stay upright even as his knees threatened to buckle.

His own body seemed to betray him, giving in easily, letting Robert propel him toward the edge. "I...."

Robert stopped and let his hand slip away. Dixie growled his frustration to Robert's soft hum. "We have plenty of time." Robert stepped back and turned off the water, then slid the door open. The cool air kissed his skin, bringing Dixie down to earth. Robert handed him a towel, and Dixie took it, stepped out, and began drying himself. Robert dabbed his back and then held him once again, his warmth replacing the chill. He kissed the base of his neck and then down his shoulder blade.

"What are you doing?"

Robert chuckled. "I'm sucking up a mark." He did it again, right at the base of his neck.

"Aren't we too old for hickeys?" Dixie asked. "Really?"

"Nope. Never too old, and tomorrow, there will be this little purple mark that will be mine. Come on." He took the candle and Dixie's hand and led him out of the bathroom. As soon as Robert had set the candle down on the dresser, he pressed Dixie back onto the bed. "Damn, you're gorgeous like that." Robert stood over him, his gaze as intense as any laser. Dixie could feel it, and heat rushed to his skin.

Robert climbed onto the bed, a hand sliding up Dixie's leg, while Robert's lips met his. Dixie thrust his hips upward as Robert cupped his balls, kissing him hard. Dixie whimpered and pressed to him, wanting as much heat and contact with Robert as possible. His engine was primed and revved, and Robert was the accelerator. He quivered with anticipation, and Robert didn't hold back. His hand slipped away, and Robert pulled back.

Then he was engulfed in Robert's hot, talented mouth. Dixie gripped the bedding, clamped his eyes closed, and let Robert take him on a passionate, wild ride. "God…." Robert took him deeper, and Dixie's head grew lighter. Every touch seemed important and only drove him higher. No one had ever made him feel this way. The world narrowed to just the two of them, all their cares and worries falling like raindrops and flowing away. "I'm…." Dixie gasped in warning, and Robert stopped once again. "What are you doing to me?"

Robert didn't answer. Dixie slid his eyes open as Robert stretched to the nightstand and pulled out supplies. A rip, a snick, hot fingers in preparation, and then Robert pressed to him. Dixie held his breath as Robert entered him, joining them physically as he kissed him hard, sliding deeper, the burn exquisite, the intensity mind-blowing, the intimacy perfection. "That's just what I want. You like this, eyes glistening, mouth open… for me."

Dixie groaned and pulled Robert into a kiss, devouring his lips while Robert took possession of his body. He had no idea how long he was going to hold his passion in check with Robert's power and intensity driving him crazy. Robert had already had him on edge enough that his mind and body were primed and ready to go. Dixie groaned each time Robert slid into him and gasped at the emptiness when he pulled away. "Where in the fuck did you learn all this patience?" It was driving him out of his mind.

Robert slowed his pace even more. "You really like this," he whispered. "I can tell. You gasp and your breath hitches. Each time that happens, I know I'm making you wild."

Dixie raked his hands down Robert's back. "You need to stop this."

Robert stilled in an instant. "You want me to stop? I can do that, if that's what you really want. I'll pull away and go to my own room."

"Don't you fucking dare," Dixie growled. "I mean you need to stop all this slow shit. I'm not made of glass."

"I know that." Robert held still, his cock pulsing. Dixie felt every movement, and it took his breath away. Fuck! Robert wasn't even moving, he hadn't touched him, and Dixie was on the edge. "I can tell exactly what you want and how close you are. I want you to stay there." Robert drew closer, and Dixie wrapped his legs around Robert's waist, holding him tight in case he got any more stupid ideas. "I want you right there for as long as I can keep you. No rushing, no hurry—just you and me in a bubble of passion that both of us will remember for the rest of our lives." Robert pulled away and slammed back inside him. "This is about you and me. It's time for just the two of us." Robert repeated his action, making Dixie shake.

"I know, but my head hurts, and I can't even see straight anymore."

"Oh, that's so good. I want you to take those pretty hands of yours and put them over your head. Your pleasure is mine. I'm claiming it for tonight. It's up to me to take care of you and hold you. It's also up to me to make sure that when we're done, you can't even remember your name." Dixie did as Robert asked, trusting him the way he always had. Pierre had been someone he'd thought would be good for him, but he'd been an ass. And Dixie had never shared anything like this with him. He hadn't held Dixie in his arms like this,

cradling him in his heat. But Robert was different. Dixie knew that Robert would never drop him—he would hold him up for as long as Dixie needed him. "That's it." Robert smiled in that dimness and then he moved, driving into him.

Dixie clutched the bedding as the entire frame moved along with them. All Robert's power and strength met his own. The air around them crackled with desire that Dixie only hoped didn't wake Henri, because there was no way in hell he could possibly stop this now. Robert's gaze bored into him, and Dixie couldn't look away even if he had wanted to. The connection between them was so deep, Dixie wouldn't have been surprised if Robert could read his mind or see into his soul. "Robert...."

"I know...." He reared back, stroking Dixie's cock. "Now, baby. I want you now."

Dixie wasn't sure if it was the endearment or just the words, but Dixie closed his eyes and let go. A wave built at the base of his spine, picking up speed until he could no longer control it. His entire body stiffened and his eyes clamped closed as a tidal wave of desire flowed through him, culminating in his release, which seemed to go on forever.

The room was very dark, and for a second Dixie wondered if he had gone blind. Nothing seemed to work, and he floated on clouds for a few seconds before falling back to earth. When his vision focused again, the candle flickered on the table and Robert lay next to him. "Are you okay?" Robert whispered. "You scared me a little. I thought I might have broken you." He smiled, and Dixie groaned.

"You didn't break me, though I think my head short-circuited." He lay still, not wanting to move,

just enjoying the afterglow. "What the hell did you do to me?"

"I hope I made you happy," Robert whispered, and Dixie hummed his agreement. Right now it took too much effort to talk, so he nestled closer, relishing Robert's warmth and care.

Robert was the first to get up. He went into the bathroom and emerged a few minutes later with some bath tissue. He wiped Dixie up and then left again, blowing out the candle on his return. Then Robert got back in the bed, and though Dixie wished he could stay still, he knew it was his turn to get up. He put on his robe and walked across the hall. Henri was sound asleep in his bed with his nightlight burning in the room. As usual, he was curled up, his covers at the foot of the bed. Dixie gently put them back into place so Henri would be warm and quietly left the room and returned to where Robert waited.

Each step reminded him of what the two of them had done, and as he climbed into bed, Robert put his arms around him, tugging him close. "Is Henri okay?"

"Yes. He's fine." Now Dixie could let himself go. Henri was good, the house was secure, and Robert was in bed with him. His world was in order, and he knew where everyone was. It wouldn't always stay that way, and Dixie hated the thought that the contentment that settled over him right now was only temporary. Eventually this rightness would end and Robert would go home, though he wondered what Robert really had to go home to. Still, Dixie would need to be able to go back to the way things were… somehow.

Chapter 8

THIS TIME Robert knew the men behind them. He'd been introduced in a roundabout way earlier in the week. The men had made their presence known as Dixie had said they would. He wasn't happy about the entire situation and continued to be on watch for anything out of the ordinary. It was weird being constantly followed, but at least now he had a way to signal them if he saw something unusual, like the woman in the courtyard outside the Palace of Versailles—the next destination on Henri's list—pushing an empty carriage. That was an old gambit, and he got a message through to security about her, but it seemed she was just a street person who wandered the courtyard, looking for handouts for her imaginary baby.

"Are you ready to go inside?" Dixie asked Henri. Thankfully Dixie had gotten them going early and had apparently booked one of the first tours of the day. It was already busy, but Dixie seemed to have expected that. It was Saturday, after all.

"Can we go to the mirror room?" Henri asked with a smile.

"Of course." The Hall of Mirrors was a place Robert was looking forward to seeing too. "We can see

all of it, and then we'll go out to the playhouse and through the gardens to check out the fountains. Okay?" Apparently Henri didn't play tour guide at Versailles. Instead, they met up with Louisette, their docent, at the appropriate place, and after being joined by two other couples, they entered the palace and began their tour.

It was a grand space, with glitter on top of opulence. Louisette took them through the various gilded staterooms, their lavishness meant to impress all who entered. The Hall of Mirrors was as stunning as he had hoped it would be, but in places the palace was starting to show some wear and tear. Robert saw cracks in the walls, and some of the floors were worn so badly that the wood rolled a little under their feet, and the fasteners to hold the boards rose slightly because the wood had deteriorated around them. Most of Robert's attention, however, remained on the people around them, though watching to see if they were followed was problematic because of the general flow of traffic. They had lunch after the tour and then passed under a large portico and out into some of the most amazing gardens in the world.

The vista of green with jets of water seemed to flow forever from the back of the palace. It was hard to judge how large the space was. It just seemed to go on and on. Robert put Henri on his shoulders so he could see better and to rest his legs as they wandered through the outdoor magnificence. "The resources it must have taken to build something like this…." It boggled the mind.

"Can we go to the playhouses?" Henri asked, and they wandered over to the Hamlet, a small village that had been built for Marie Antoinette and her children. Henri seemed captivated by the almost fairytale

buildings. At least none of the people tailing them seemed to have made it into the palace complex with them, and Robert felt himself relax. This part of the grounds was quiet, and Robert took Dixie's hand as they wandered.

"Are you and Papa boyfriends?" Henri asked. Robert felt Dixie tense for a moment. Robert kept quiet and let Dixie answer that question, though he was waiting to hear the answer himself. The two of them had slept together every night, though now, in the mornings, Robert left the bed before Henri woke up. He didn't want to upset their household, and he figured it was up to Dixie to explain things to his son when the time came.

"Is that okay?" Dixie asked rather than giving an answer.

Robert couldn't see Henri's reaction, but he couldn't miss Dixie's smile. "Okay, then." Dixie continued holding his hand, so both he and Dixie must have gotten the answer they needed.

After wandering awhile with Henri on his shoulders, Robert was beginning to come to the end of his energy. He had seen everything, including the fountain show. "Can I get down?" Henri asked, and Robert lowered him to the ground. Henri hurried over to the grand fountain pool to dip his fingers into the water. "I'm glad I got to come here with you," Robert said.

"What did you expect would happen during your visit?" Dixie asked.

Robert shrugged. "I figured you would have your own life. I was grateful that you said I could stay, but I figured I'd come and go and you would go about your life. I hadn't expected… any of this." He squeezed Dixie's fingers and then released them so they didn't

draw attention. "I never forgot you after Italy, but I didn't think things could be.... It was a long time ago, and our lives have changed—*we've* changed. I didn't think that there would be anything left but some sweet memories." Robert didn't look away from Henri. He'd learned his lesson in the park.

The boy turned back to them and asked a question in French. Dixie sighed and smiled. "He wants to watch the fountains again." Dixie answered him in French, and Henri nodded. "I told him that it was too long to wait," he said to Robert. When Henri returned, Robert took his hand. "How about we find a patisserie and have an afternoon snack?"

Always in the mood for cake, Henri agreed. Robert lifted him back on his shoulders, and they headed for the exit.

WHY WAS it that when he traveled on the Metro, he always felt as if he was being watched? Robert kept glancing at the other passengers, and even Dixie seemed jumpy. He kept Henri close to him, and they sat together in one seating area, each looking different directions. "I don't see our friends," Robert said softly.

"They're here, but...."

Robert nodded that he understood. He'd be more than happy to be back at the house and behind locked doors again.

"Why are you both grumpy?" Henri asked, looking at each of them.

Dixie forced a smile and then visibly relaxed, looking over his shoulder. Robert didn't turn, but he must have seen one of their good shadows. Dixie pulled out his phone, sent a few messages, then slipped it back

into his pocket. "Everything is fine. Robert and I are just tired. I'm surprised you aren't, after everything we've done today."

"Nope. It's because I'm not *old*." Henri grinned.

Dixie tickled him. "We aren't that old." Henri squirmed and giggled as the train pulled into their intermediate station. They exited and changed lines, heading to the one that would take them home.

By the time they were back in Dixie's neighborhood, Robert was exhausted. A stop at the patisserie helped, along with a coffee. When they entered the house, Henri climbed on the sofa with his tablet and fell asleep in about ten minutes.

A powerful knock on the door made Robert go still. He immediately went into cop mode, signaling Dixie to stay with Henri, knowing if this was a threat that he'd get him out. "Yes?" Robert said without opening the door.

"Koala," a deep voice said from the other side of the door, and Robert opened it slowly. It was one of the security men he'd been introduced to, and he relaxed, though just a little. "We caught one of the people following you." Robert stepped back to let him inside. "Do you recognize him?" he asked, showing Robert a picture.

"He was at the museum last week. Did he tell you anything?" Robert asked.

He shook his head. "We're going to take him into custody. Has he ever approached either of you?"

"No," Dixie said from behind him. "We saw him at the museum, but he hasn't actually tried to contact me directly." Dixie stood next to him. "Do you think he knows anything?"

"We don't know. He says he was hired to follow you and report back. So that's what he's done. We'll continue questioning him. I wanted confirmation that we had the right man."

"He's one of them," Robert explained. "I haven't seen anyone else, but that doesn't mean there isn't someone working with him." He turned to Dixie. "Have you identified anyone else specifically?"

"No. See what you can get from him. We need to know who's behind this and what they want." Dixie stepped closer. "I'm getting so tired of all this."

"We realize that, and we'll do our best." The man turned to leave, and Robert closed the door behind him.

"That guy reminds me of our first sergeant, remember? He was the biggest man I had ever seen up to that point, and he had those same 'look right through you' eyes." The two men were also equally intense and all business. "Where's Henri?"

"He's up in my room, playing on his tablet." Dixie went back to the living room. "I'm sorry about all this. This isn't exactly the vacation you expected. I can secure the house, but it's really getting bad when we can't even leave the damned building without a tail."

"What about Henri and school? He's been going every day. Maybe you should keep him home for a while until your people get this straightened out."

"I'll think about it. But I know Henri is safe when he's there."

"Maybe we should take him ourselves, then."

Dixie continued into the living room and sat down. "That isn't an issue." He grinned, and Robert pulled him into a hug and then kissed him lightly.

Little feet came down the stairs and they pulled away, but Henri must have seen them. Henri sat next to Robert on the sofa, the tablet on his lap.

"Is the scary man gone?"

"Yes. Everything's okay," Dixie said. Then he walked over and lifted Henri into a hug. "I won't let anything happen to you. Not ever. I promise you." He swung Henri in his arms until he giggled.

ROBERT GOT up and left the two of them alone. He found pasta in the kitchen and began making some dinner. It gave him something to do while they talked. Robert had spent a lot of his life on the outside looking in, so he was used to it. Mostly it didn't bother him—that was the way things were. In the corps, he'd been part of the team, so he'd never really felt like an outsider. He did in the department sometimes, though. Still, right now, he realized acutely that he wasn't a part of Dixie's little family unit.

"What has you woolgathering?" Dixie asked as he joined him. Robert hadn't even realized he had been staring at the wall.

"Just thinking…." He didn't want to say the words, but he'd been considering that maybe it would be best if he went to a hotel for the last week of his stay. The idea made his throat ache. But thinking about leaving was enough to make him shake, and the loss was only going to grow worse as time went by. How he had gotten so involved and emotionally entangled with Dixie and Henri, he didn't even know. He hadn't meant for it to happen. He finally found the words, but Dixie interrupted his thought.

"Henri asked me if his hand was gross," Dixie said.

"What?" Robert asked. "Where is he getting things like that?"

"Henri is smart, you know that. Sometimes too smart. He puts things together from what he's heard. I have no idea where the ideas come from, and as smart as he is, he doesn't necessarily have the words to express what he's thinking. I was afraid that the kids at the fountain might have said something to him. But I'm not so sure."

"So do you know where he got it?" Robert asked.

Dixie swallowed and paused. "He said just now that no one wants to hold that hand."

Robert's mouth hung open. "I… I pick him up so that he doesn't get tired. I don't have a problem holding his hand. I never thought…." He closed his eyes. He hadn't meant to hurt Henri in any way. Hell, he'd throw himself in front of a bullet before he'd allow someone to hurt him.

"I know, and I don't think it was anything you did that made him think of it." Robert felt a little relieved, but not completely. "I don't know where it came from. Like I said, sometimes he puts things together and gets these notions." Dixie sighed. "Anyway, that's what got him upset and wondering. It's happened before, and I reassure him each and every time."

"Considering his past, it makes sense that it will take some time for those feelings to dissipate. Does it happen often?"

"Less so over the past few months, but lately he seems to need more reassurance," Dixie said.

Robert nodded, his police psychological training kicking in. "You know, it could be something as simple as me staying here," Robert explained. "The last time you had someone close to you, Pierre, he scared

the hell out of Henri. So maybe because I'm here and we're getting close, he's worried about how things will be. I doubt that he thinks of me like Pierre—at least, I hope he doesn't." Just the idea of that guy being anywhere near Henri gave Robert the creeps. And between the police force and the corps, he'd seen just about everything.

"You know, you could be right. After that time when he joined us in bed, Henri hasn't come into my room, even though you're not there. That was something he often did, but he hasn't the last few mornings."

"Shit," Robert said under his breath. "I thought we were being careful. I didn't want to hurt him or…." He turned back to the dinner he'd been preparing and wondered again if he should stay somewhere else. Maybe then Henri's life could get back to normal. Robert already loved the little guy, and hell, he'd always loved Dixie, though he had never told Dixie how he felt. What was the point? He was only here for another week. Dixie's life was here, and his was in Michigan. As wonderful as Paris was, there was nothing for him to do here.

God, he was getting way ahead of himself now.

Robert put the pasta in to cook and opened a jar of sauce he'd found in one of the cupboards and put it on to heat. Yeah, it wasn't gourmet, but they'd had it before. Henri liked it, and the sauce had some flavor. "Would you like me to talk with him?" Robert offered.

Dixie patted his shoulder. "That's not a bad idea. It's on his mind now, so maybe if you sit with him, he'll open up to you."

"Okay. I'll let him set the pace." Robert shooed Dixie out of the kitchen because the space was just too small

for two people. He stirred both pots and poked his head into the other room. "Henri, can you set the table?" Robert asked, and Henri put his tablet aside and came over. "Do you need me to get things out for you?"

"No," he said and got the silverware before heading to the table. Robert continued his work but noticed that Henri kept looking at him.

"Did you have fun today?" Robert asked without turning around. He got out the plates and handed them to Henri, who carried them to the table without answering. Robert kept his attention on the food, but knew where Henri was and that he kept turning to glance at him. "If there's something you want to ask, fire away." That was as much of a prompt as he was going to make. The rest was up to Henri.

The boy set the plates on the table and returned to where Robert had set the glasses. Robert wasn't sure if Henri was going to open up, and that was okay, he supposed. This had to be about Henri.

"Why do you like Papa more than me?" Henri asked, and Robert stopped stirring the pot in surprise. He turned down the sauce and checked the pasta. It still had a few minutes.

"I don't like Dixie more than you. I like you both, but in different ways." He held out his hand, and Henri took it. Then Robert led him to the table and pulled out a chair. Robert patted the seat and took one right in front of Henri. Now that he was there, a sort of chasm seemed to open between them—he didn't have a clue how to explain things to this little boy. "Do you like your papa?" Robert asked, and Henri nodded. "Do you like me?" He nodded again. "Okay, do you like us the same?" When the boy said nothing, Robert continued.

"Of course you don't. Dixie is your papa, and you love him best in the whole world, right?"

"Yes," Henri answered, looking to where Dixie sat in the other room.

"And that's the way it's supposed to be. He's your papa, and you should love him the most. I like you a lot. And I like your papa too. But your papa and I have known each other for a long time, and we've done a lot of things. Do you understand?"

"But what if papa likes you more than me?" Henri asked.

Robert smiled. "Your papa loves you more than anything in the entire world, and he always will. No one will ever take your place. Not ever. I...." He had painted himself into a corner. "See, I'll tell you a secret. I love your papa, and I have for a long time. But I won't ever stop liking you, and your papa will never stop loving you. I promise you that. Okay?"

Henri nodded, and Robert hoped they were done talking about feelings. It was a minefield, and he'd nearly gotten caught in it. "Okay." Henri got down. "But why do you sleep in Papa's bed and make noises at night?"

Robert swallowed hard and had no idea what to say to that. "Maybe you should ask your papa about that," he suggested. Damn, he could feel the blush rising in his cheeks. How had a six-year-old so quickly managed to make him feel like an embarrassed teenager? "Why don't you do that now? But you have to promise me something."

Henri nodded seriously.

"You have to never doubt that your papa loves you. And your Uncle Robert loves you too. Once I leave, we may not see each other for a while because I will

have to go back to Michigan. But that doesn't mean that I don't still love you. Okay?" He hugged Henri, who then hurried out of the room, and Robert returned to the kitchen while Henri asked his father why Robert was sleeping in his bed.

Robert chuckled to himself. Dixie wasn't going to thank him for that. But those types of questions were best answered by Henri's papa. Robert had no idea how Dixie wanted to handle it, and he didn't want to give an answer that wasn't what Dixie wanted Henri to know. He returned to making dinner and got the food on the table before calling in the others. Henri seemed happy, Dixie a little wild-eyed, and as Robert sat down to eat, he realized that the number of meals he was going to have with them was beginning to really count down.

Chapter 9

Monday morning, Dixie woke next to Robert, and as much as he wanted to snuggle close, he kissed him gently and climbed out of bed. He was quiet, watching Robert for a few minutes as he lay still with the covers tangled around his thick legs. He could look at that form for hours. His gaze slid up his hips and along his side. Damn, he wanted to get right back in that bed. But they needed food in the house, and the best time to do the shopping was first thing in the morning, before Henri was up.

Dixie dressed quickly and left the room. He checked that Henri was still asleep before hurrying downstairs, grabbing his shopping bags, and leaving the house. He reactivated the alarm on his way out.

On the street, people were already bustling to get to work, and Dixie hurried down the walk to the corner, where he turned toward the grocery store. He walked quickly because he didn't want to be gone long. He knew Robert would care for Henri, but he liked to be there when he could be there for him.

After entering the store, he grabbed a basket and went from aisle to aisle, getting things for breakfast, lunch, and some ground meat for dinner because Henri

had asked Dixie and Robert to make burgers with onions again. It was a new favorite dish of his.

With his basket full, he stopped by the cookie aisle to grab some of the wafers with dark chocolate that both Dixie and Henri seemed to love.

"We need to talk," a man behind him said. "Don't turn around if you know what's good for you. Just listen." The voice was deep. "I'm aware of your tails and where they are. They'll never get here in time to help."

The threat made Dixie's blood run cold.

"I have buyers who will pay handsomely for your work. Enough that you and your cute little son will never have to worry about anything ever again." The way he said those words made Dixie want to bash the man's face in, but he didn't dare move in case he had a weapon. Instead, Dixie forced his mind to gather whatever information he could.

A woman turned down the aisle, and he felt the man shift behind him. "We'll be in touch."

Dixie turned to find no one behind him. He pivoted the other way as a tall man turned the corner. All he caught was a flash of black. He followed and glanced around, looking for someone who might be trying to get away, but when he reached the end of the aisle, all he saw was other shoppers going about their business. No one was wearing black. "Shit," he groaned under his breath, reaching to pull out his phone. Then he paused and headed for the checkout instead. He had no idea who was watching him, and the threat to Henri had been very real. They knew just how to get to him, damn it. Dixie steadied his breathing, dug into his Marine training, and went to the checkout, where he paid for his groceries as if nothing had happened.

He didn't know who was watching him, but he also didn't want to give anything away. So he played along as if he was considering the proposal. After all, they knew about his people and had managed to evade them. Once he'd paid the bill, Dixie strode back home without stopping, keeping his eyes on his surroundings. He didn't breathe normally again until he was back behind the doors to his place and had the alarm set once again.

"Papa," Henri called and wound his arms around his legs. "I saw Robert's butt."

For a second Dixie actually smiled. "You know you should knock before going into a room with the door closed."

Henri nodded, looking down. "I know, Papa, I didn't mean to. I was looking for you. I'm sorry." Henri held Dixie's leg, and Dixie placed his hand on his head.

"I'm not the one you need to say sorry to," Dixie said gently. Henri released him and stepped back, sighing and then nodding solemnly. "Where is Mr. Robert?"

"Shower," Henri answered and took one of the bags he was carrying, using both hands to carry it to the kitchen. Dixie let Henri help him put everything away and set out breakfast. Henri ate, and then Dixie sent him upstairs to finish getting ready for school. He hated the thought of letting him leave the house, but things had to appear normal. As Henri ate, Dixie made contact with his supervisor, Howard, to inform him of what had happened. He also requested a bug sweep of the house, just in case.

Robert joined him at the table as Henri returned. Dixie wanted to tell Robert what happened but was

reticent about talking about it in case someone was listening. Henri returned and went right up to Robert. "Papa says I need to say I'm sorry I saw your butt." He turned away and grabbed his school stuff just as Madame Brassard knocked on the door to pick him up. Henri hurried over with his things, said goodbye, and then left for school.

"What was that about?" Robert asked.

"Apparently after I left to go to the store, Henri came in the room to find me and… well… you weren't exactly presentable for company." He winked, and Robert groaned. Dixie figured what Robert's next question would be and put his finger to his lips, motioning to the courtyard. Robert followed him outside. A steady breeze had picked up, creating background noise, and Dixie stepped closer and explained to Robert what had happened and that he had requested a bug sweep.

"Why did you let Henri go to school, then? He could be in danger. They've already threatened him." Robert's urgency came through even though his voice was soft.

"Madame Brassard is more dangerous to anyone who might try to hurt Henri than you or me. She taught krav maga to various troops for years. If anyone tried anything, they'd find their arm ripped off and shoved down their throat. She's rather infamous in certain circles." He grinned.

"I see." Robert's eyes widened. "When will the equipment be here?"

"Pretty soon. It's being sent out today. Once it gets here, I can make sure no one is listening in the house." God, this entire situation was getting out of hand. "I need to write up a report on what happened and…."

Robert patted him on the shoulder. "We need to get someone in here to make sure there are no honey hooks into any of your data communications in case we missed something."

"Already done. I have special programs to check that my connections are secure." He patted Robert on the shoulder in turn. "I hate that you're spending your vacation in the middle of this mess."

"I'm not," Robert countered. "Now that I've gotten to know you again and Henri, I wouldn't back away from either of you for anything." Robert pulled him against his chest. "I have your back, now and always. Don't doubt it or worry. You don't even need to ask. I'm here for you both." Robert kissed him, and whether this was the right time or not, it didn't seem to matter. Damn, Robert knew how to kiss, and Dixie held on, giving as good as he got. When Robert broke away, he locked their gazes. "I mean it, Dix. Neither you or Henri needs to worry. I've got your backs."

Dixie smiled. "I know that. I only wish your trip to Paris could be more fun and…."

Robert growled. "Don't worry about my vacation. I'm here in Paris to be with you, someone I thought was a friend but who has turned out to be something much more. And more importantly, I'm here at a time when you and Henri need me. Keeping the two of you safe is what's really important. Not my vacation."

Dixie didn't know quite what to say. "What am I to you?" he asked, almost afraid to pose the question.

"Dix…." He swallowed, and Dixie looked deep into Robert's incredible eyes, wishing he had the right to ask him to give up what he had back home and stay. But no matter what he felt, that was something he couldn't do. Not because he didn't want to, but…

what if things didn't work out? What was he going to tell Henri if the boy got even more attached to Robert and then something happened like it had with… well, every guy he had ever dated? "You have to know how I feel."

"I… probably do." Dixie answered, able to see everything in Robert's eyes.

"What's going on? Is this one of those stoic Marine things? Because if you want to go down that route, then you know I can out-stoic you." He took a step back, crossing his arms over his chest.

Dixie rolled his eyes. "I know that's your Mr. Intimidation look, and it isn't going to work on me. You know that too. Remember, I've seen you covered in sand and doing just about anything to get the stuff out of your buttcrack."

"You had to bring that up, didn't you?" Robert glared at him for two seconds and then grinned.

"You know I did. And it seems to me that neither of us wants to be the one to break this particular piece of emotional ice."

Robert nodded. "Look. I have to go back to my life and see about that promotion to lieutenant I've got coming, and you need to stay here for your work and because this is your home, Henri's home. It's important; I know that. So there's no need for either of us to make any grand emotional pronouncements. We should just make the time we have together as happy as possible and take care of these assholes who are pressuring you, so I can go home and not worry about you guys day and night."

"You'd worry?" Dixie asked, realizing he'd been told something that maybe Robert hadn't meant to express.

"Of course I would," Robert whispered, and the two of them stood still, Dixie watching those intense eyes, hoping for something more. But it didn't seem to be forthcoming, and a sharp knock on the front door reached their ears through the open courtyard door, breaking the spell.

Remembering he had a job to do, he turned away from Robert and walked inside, to the hallway. Once he verified who was at the door, he took the package offered by the delivery woman. They said nothing other than sharing normal pleasantries before Dixie thanked her and closed the door once more.

In the small box was some bug detection equipment, and he slowly walked it through the house. In his mind, this was merely a precaution.

"What are your plans for today?" Dixie asked as he worked, trying to keep up a normal conversation as cover.

"I'm not sure. I was thinking that I'd take a walk, maybe down by the Champs Elysées. It's pretty famous, and I'd like to stand under the Arc de Triomphe. It's a wonderful day, and it would be a shame to spend all the time inside. What about you?"

"I have some work I need to do. But thankfully at the moment, nothing is really pressing." His boss had told him to take a few days off and to secure all his information. Dixie half expected that his accesses would be suspended for security reasons. He would also most likely be backstopped from taking any sort of actions. Which was fine—that was regular protocol and the safest thing, in this case.

The living room and kitchen were clear, as was the rest of the main floor. He went outside and checked the now largely unused guest room, which was also clear,

but when he stepped outside, the instrument pinged. He worked his way around the courtyard to a potted geranium in the corner. Sure enough, he found a small listening device in the surface dirt. Looking up, he realized it had most likely been dropped from the roof. Maybe that had been the reason for the clamps on the house. They hadn't been able to figure out a way inside, so they tried to bug the outside to gather information. Dixie checked the rest of the courtyard, finding another in a window box. It seemed strange to him for someone to bug outside, but he supposed they might be desperate enough to try anything. Either that, or Robert had interrupted their plans by discovering the cleats on the building.

Dixie didn't want to disable the bugs and tip off his listeners, so instead he carefully pushed dirt over both of them to dampen what they might pick up. Then he left the courtyard and headed upstairs. His own bedroom and office were clear, and so was the bathroom. He did find a listening device in Henri's room near the window. He shivered and clenched his fists that someone had gotten so close to his son.

Robert was standing in the doorway when he turned around, and Dixie pointed to the device. He clenched his fists, making a pounding motion. Robert shook his head and turned away, then returned with a glass of water. He gently lifted the bug and dropped it into the glass, then left the room. Dixie finished up with the rest of the house, pleased that no one had been able to penetrate deeply into his home. The listening device in Henri's room concerned him, and he vowed to better secure the boy's window.

"Anything else?" Robert asked when Dixie returned downstairs.

"No. Just the ones outside and the one in Henri's room."

Robert nodded slowly. "They didn't get far. That's good. The one from Henri's room has been disabled. It was weatherproof, but I let it sit in the water, and it fried out. Have your people look at it when you can. It might tell them something." He pointed to the glass on the counter in the kitchen.

"Thanks." At least that was done. "I need to let my boss know." Dixie excused himself and went up to his office. He sat at his desk, staring at the blank computer screen without moving. Dixie should be making his call and doing what he needed to, but his mind was elsewhere. Five more days and Robert was going home to a promotion he rightly deserved. This was his vacation, a break from real life. In a way, it was that for both of them.

Just like Italy seven years ago, life this time, rather than the corps, was pulling them in different directions.

Sometimes he wondered how in the hell he got himself into these messes. He'd known that Robert wasn't going to be able to stay, and yet he'd let himself fall for the guy all over again.

Henri adored Robert too, so now he was going to have to deal with not only his own loss, but Henri's as well.

Maybe he had been completely stupid to go down this road. He should have kept Robert at arm's length. He inhaled deeply. Yeah, he could say that all he wanted, but the truth was, he'd probably do the exact same thing all over again. Robert made him smile. Every time he looked into his eyes, Dixie saw home and family. Maybe that was what hurt the most. His life had

been so damned solitary, with the exception of Henri, and now he had found someone who fit—with him, his life, his heart, and his son.

Pulling his mind out of his circling thoughts, he turned on his computer and connected with Howard, relaying what he found. "Where do we go from here?"

Howard sighed. "I've put a hold on all your accesses as a precaution. We are also in the process of setting up a dummy project that you can pass on to them, if necessary, as a decoy. That will give them some information, but it will also lead them on a wild-goose chase. Hopefully that will give us a chance to track them down. It's going to take another day to finish putting it together. It will contain just enough information and functionality to keep them going. But after they use it for more than a few tests, the code will rewrite itself."

"Okay."

"We'll send it over tomorrow afternoon. Just stay inside. Our people are still keeping an eye on you. We had to switch them out because they had been spotted. But don't worry. Just lie low and keep that kid of yours safe." He ended the call, and Dixie sat back in his chair. Sitting still and doing nothing went against his instincts. *He* needed to do something to keep his son safe. Leaving it in the hands of someone else made him itch.

"WHAT'S UP?" Robert asked when Dixie strode into the living room ten minutes later. He'd been watching an action movie, and Vin Diesel was just about to launch the Mustang he'd been driving into one of those amazing car jumps.

"Well, it seems that they have plans, and we need to stay put." He flopped down on the sofa, and Robert

put his arm around his shoulders. "I'm officially off for the rest of the day." He sat back, and Robert tugged him closer. Dixie leaned his head against Robert's shoulders, inhaling deeply and closing his eyes at his rich musky scent, with just a hint of soap from his shower. He inhaled again, imprinting that scent on his mind. He didn't want to forget it any more than he wanted to forget the way Robert's hands felt on his skin or the rumble in his throat when the lights went off and Robert got all growly.

"I think I can find something to keep us busy," Robert whispered and lightly touched his chin. Dixie turned his head under the pressure, and Robert kissed him softly at first, then deeper, his tongue exploring. Dixie groaned and shifted, pressing against Robert, who enfolded him in his arms, pushing until Dixie ended up back against the cushions.

"You know, I like the way you think." Dixie shivered as Robert's hand slipped under his shirt and up his chest to his nipple, where he lightly plucked the sensitive bud until Dixie groaned and stretched his legs to give his dick some room in his pants. Damn, Robert knew how to touch him and just how much pressure to apply to give the maximum sensation.

"I know exactly what you like. I remember a lot about you. I always did." He tugged the fabric upward and only backed away long enough to pull Dixie's shirt off, and then his own, and drop them to the floor.

Skin to skin, enveloped in firm strength, Dixie held on as Robert ran his heated hands down his chest to tease the skin just above his belt. Dixie held his breath, drawing in his muscles, silently encouraging Robert to go lower. He wanted more of everything so badly, he could hardly stand it. Pushing his hips forward, he

silently begged for Robert to touch him, but Robert had his own timetable and slowed his caresses. Sometimes Robert's patience was such a pain in the ass.

"Do you want to move somewhere else?" Robert asked, disentangling them and standing. He offered Dixie a hand, and Dixie took it and let Robert tug him to his feet. He didn't release his hand but instead led Dixie up to his own room.

"Does it make me seem old that that I feel a little weird making love during the day?" Dixie felt a little naughty and kind of strange. "I know it's stupid and all."

Robert laughed as he pushed open the door and then maneuvered Dixie down onto the bed. "Maybe it's a little weird." He knelt over him. "You always were a little conventional, and yet, remember that day when we walked up the beach and found the deserted cove? You didn't seem to mind getting busy in the middle of the day then. So yeah, maybe you're just getting old."

"I am not. For the record, I'm a month younger than you are," Dixie protested.

"Age is a state of mind," Robert countered, chuckling softly, his eyes darkening as he did. "You just need to let things go for a while and relax. You and I were so carefree back then." Heat poured off him. "Sometimes I wish we could go back to that time."

Dixie wound his arms around Robert's neck, the mood growing more serious. "I don't. Yeah, we were hot for each other, but we were so young and stupid back then. We both had a lot more living to do before we could figure our shit out." He paused, still holding Robert. "If things had been different then, I wouldn't have Henri and my life here now. You wouldn't have had the experiences you've had either. Neither one of us would be the person we are right now. Our paths

would be different, and as much as I liked how things were back then, I wouldn't give up the person I am now. I like him, and I like the man you are now too. You're steadier and so much more interesting." He placed his hand in the center of Robert's chest.

"But you and I might not have lost the last seven years," Robert said.

"Maybe. Of course, we might have drifted apart because we were so damned young and stupid." He smiled. "Don't regret what happened, please. I don't. Not now. I did for a long time. But everything happens for a reason… just like you coming back into my life again. There's a purpose to it." He lifted his head and met Robert's lips.

"But it looks like history is going to repeat itself," Robert countered.

Dixie nodded. "And I suppose that may be inevitable. But remember all those amazing memories we made in Italy? They stayed with both of us. Maybe you and I can make some more this week so we'll have something to hold on to?" Dixie cocked his head to the side, and Robert closed the distance between them with a searing kiss.

Chapter 10

IT HAD been a long time since Robert had spent so much of the day in bed, and it felt wonderful. He sighed as he lay looking up at the ceiling with Dix asleep next to him, snoring softly. He didn't want to disturb Dix, but his mind refused to allow him to drift off. He slowly slipped out of bed and pulled on his boxers, left the room, and checked the time. Henri would be home in about an hour, so he went downstairs and made a call.

"Hey, Captain," Robert said. "I just thought I'd check in."

"Glad you did." He shuffled some papers. "Grace, the little girl you helped, has gone home, and she's doing very well." He cleared his throat. "How is Paris? Are you about ready to come back?"

Robert hesitated a second. "Yes," he lied, lifting his gaze as a nearly naked Dixie strode into the room. "I'll be in for my shift on Tuesday as planned." He was supposed to fly back on Sunday, leaving Monday free for him to get things together before he returned to work.

"You aren't bored on your own yet?" the captain asked. "My wife has been asking me to take her to Paris

for years, but what am I going to do over there? She'll want to see everything and...."

"It's beautiful, and you should experience it," Robert told him, feeling sorry for his captain's wife. Everyone should experience this city. It was truly magical—especially the mostly naked man who sat down next to him. "Is there anything I need to know?"

"No. Just come to my office on Tuesday so I can bring you up to date on the cases that await you. There are plenty of them. While you've been away, the criminals in town are definitely playing." He ended the call, and Robert shook his head, setting his phone on the table.

"It seems the outside world awaits."

"We always knew it did," Dixie said and checked the time. "I'm going to go upstairs to shower and dress." He kissed him before getting up to leave the room. "Henri will be home pretty soon, and I need to get some things done." The set of his shoulders—slightly rolled—showed Robert plenty. He looked the same as Robert felt. But there was nothing he could do about it, and moping wasn't going to help either of them. Still, he didn't know what to say. Leaving his phone where it was, he followed Dixie up the stairs. Sometimes words were inadequate... but when he followed Dix into the bathroom and closed the door, he let his hands and the hot water do his speaking for him.

THEY WERE showered and dressed by the time the knock on the door came. Dixie turned off the alarm and opened the door. Henri stomped inside, his expression pure storm. Dixie met Madame Brassard's gaze for a

clue to the problem, but she shrugged and told him in French that there was a note from the teacher.

"Okay. Thank you," he told her. "I'll get to the bottom of it." She smiled and turned with her daughter toward home. Dixie closed the door and reset the alarm. Henri was nowhere to be found, and Dixie went in search of his son.

"Henri," Dixie said when he found him in his room, sitting on the side of his bed, legs dangling.

"It wasn't my fault," he began in French and then began talking rapidly.

"Take your time and talk to me more slowly," Dixie said in English. Henri turned to him, tears running down his cheeks. Dixie picked up Henri's backpack, found the note, and read it. "You were arguing with the teacher?" That wasn't like Henri. "What happened?" It was best to let Henri tell his side of the story rather than jump to conclusions.

Henri huffed, crossing his arms over his chest. "She was wrong, and I raised my hand and everything. She didn't call on me, so I raised my hand again. When she picked me, I told her that Napoleon crowned himself Emperor and that there was a painting to prove it." He pooched out his lower lip as though that were the final word. "When she didn't correct herself, I told her she was wrong. Then she said that she was sending a note home. I was mad, and when she called on me later, I said I didn't want to talk to her." He lifted his gaze. "Can we get a better teacher? This one lies."

"But you like Madame Marie. She's a nice lady, and you know it." Dixie needed to smooth this over. He put an arm around his son. "Sometimes what's in a painting isn't real. That one you love so much was painted because Napoleon wanted to make himself

look important, like the center of everything. It isn't like taking a picture today."

Henri gaped at him. "So you're saying the painting is a lie?"

Dixie paused, trying to find the words to explain propaganda to his son. "It was painted so people would think what Napoleon wanted them to think. It was impressive and powerful, but it wasn't necessarily the truth. Do you really think the baby Jesus ran around naked with his mother as he played on rocks? He'd get his butt all scratched up. Art sometimes contains a message, because it was created when a lot of people couldn't read the way you can." He hugged Henri. "I think you need to say you're sorry to Madame Marie tomorrow."

Henri sighed like the weight of the entire world rested on his little shoulders. "But Papa, she…." He turned and hugged him. Dixie held him back. "She…."

"What is it?" Dixie said.

"I showed her the picture from my book." He pulled one of the Louvre guides out of his bag. "I showed her the book… and she was mean. The other kids laughed at me, and François told me that was what I got for being *un infirme*." He sniffled, and Dixie held him closer. "She heard and didn't say anything. But when I told him he had *un âme infirme*, she scolded me." Henri was crying fully now, and Dixie rocked slowly to comfort him.

Dixie knew he was going to have to go in and speak to her. "I'll talk to her, okay? But you can't call people names, even when they do it to you. Mean people use names, and you don't want to be like that." He didn't blame his son for defending himself, and he fully intended to get to the bottom of this. "I'll take you to

school tomorrow." He sighed as he let Henri cry out some of the world's unfairness.

"Is he okay?" Robert whispered from the doorway.

Dixie nodded. "Give us a minute."

"I will. But when he's ready, I have some cookies downstairs for him." Robert smiled, and Dixie nodded, then mouthed a thank-you.

"Are you angry at me?" Henri asked, his voice thin.

"I'm a little disappointed, but I'm not mad. You're my son, and I love you. And I'll be sure to find out what happened." He would get to the bottom of this, and if Madame Marie was out of line, he'd see to it that she understood where her boundaries were. He had met her on a number of occasions, and she had always seemed capable, if a little distant. Not that it would matter. Henri would be finishing the school year soon, and then he'd have a new instructor for the next year. "Do you want some cookies?"

Henri nodded and sat up, wiping his eyes. "I'm sorry I was bad."

What did he say to that? "You know how you feel when someone tells you you're wrong? Well, maybe Madame Marie felt like that. Next time you should ask her to talk, just the two of you. Maybe you are right, but maybe she is, and that way no one gets hurt." He got up, pulling Henri up with him. Then he hugged Henri again. "Come on."

He held Henri's hand and they went down to the table, where Robert was waiting for them. Henri sniffed as he sat at the table, then sighed and finally took a cookie. Dixie sank into a chair, wishing he could have a beer.

"Kids used to call me names," Robert said.

Henri lifted his gaze, mouth open. "Did you beat them up?"

Robert shook his head. "I just ignored them and walked away. They were really mean sometimes, but you know what I did? I grew up, got bigger and all growly. Arrrrr." He made a face. "Your daddy used to get picked on too, but he grew up smart, just like you will."

Henri actually smiled for a second. "I can do anything."

"Yes, you can. So I'm counting on you to be the smartest and best person you can be. You do what you do best. I found out that if I did that, what others said didn't matter. You need to work out your mind because you are really smart. And if you're nice, then some of the other kids will like you. And maybe some won't, but you be yourself anyway." He shrugged. "After all, you seem pretty amazing to me." Robert knelt down, and Henri slipped off the chair and went right into his arms. Dixie was relieved that this bit of drama seemed to be over, but he still had to have a talk with Henri's teacher. "Now, let's finish these cookies."

"Do you have homework?" Dixie asked. "You need to do that before you do anything on your tablet." Dixie thought he should take the tablet away for to-night as punishment, but Henri seemed to have gotten the message about talking back.

"Yes, Papa," Henri answered softly. He finished his cookie, then went back upstairs to get his backpack. A few minutes later, he came back down and sat at the table. After pulling out the sheets of paper, he handed them to Dixie to look over.

"Finish your math problems and then you can play *Minecraft*," Dixie said, and Henri settled into the chair

to finish. It didn't take him very long. In less than half an hour, Henri put his papers away, got his tablet, and sat in one of the chairs.

"I don't get how he can disappear into that game so easily," Dixie said. "I tried playing it with him, and it's mind-numbing for me."

"Yeah. Maybe. But you remember how the guys used to disappear into the video games on their downtime when we were deployed? They'd play for hours without moving. It's completely immersing and it's fun for him, I guess." Robert cleaned up the small mess from their cookie break. "What should we do this evening?"

"I was thinking dinner at the café. It's just up at the corner, and I'm going a little stir-crazy." Dixie was beginning to feel like the walls were closing in around him, and unless he wanted to give away his intentions to the people watching him, he needed to act normal.

"What about…?"

"We're going to give them a chance to make contact. And if they do, and you're there, maybe we can get a little more information from them. But we're going to have to keep an eye on Henri all the time. The café isn't far—just a block. The house will be alarmed up, and we're not going to be gone all that long."

"I don't know if it's a good idea," Robert said.

"They're going to have to make contact at some point. We can either make it easy for them or difficult. If we're lucky, they'll make a mistake." He was really hoping to put this whole thing behind them soon. Robert didn't seem convinced, though. "We're Marines, remember? We can sit here and wait for something to happen… or put ourselves out there and make it happen."

Robert rocked his head to either side. "Okay. Then let's have dinner out. But you should alert your people that we're doing it. That way they can help keep watch as well."

With that settled, Dixie made the appropriate calls and then wondered what he was going to do. Normally he would work to keep himself busy, but because of the threat, his accesses had been locked up. And going out for a walk or sightseeing with Robert was out of the question. He was really starting to hate these stalkers with a passion. Not only were they after him, but they were dictating what he could and couldn't do, and that bothered him as much as anything else.

"Hey," Robert said softly as he sat next to him, tugging him close.

"Papa, are you and Mr. Robert going to kiss? You can, you know. I promise I won't look when you get mushy." Henri continued watching them for a few seconds before returning his attention to the game. "I see you kiss sometimes. François says that boys should only lip-kiss girls, but I told him he was wrong because Papa kisses Robert all the time and that you said it was okay to kiss the people you care about."

"That's right," Robert said. "It's okay to kiss the people you care about… *really* care about."

A wave of heat rushed through Dixie, and he leaned closer. Robert's intense gaze drew him in, and it took all of Dixie's will not to kiss him right then. Not that a kiss would be a problem, but stopping it afterward might be. Robert's kisses were like potato chips— having just one was impossible. Still, Robert drew him closer, his kiss gentle but intense, and all too short.

"I wanna kiss too," Henri said, setting his tablet aside. Robert, bless his heart, lifted Henri off his feet

and gave him a big smacking kiss on the cheek. Dixie did the same to a chorus of giggles that shifted the mood, which was great. He needed something to break the rapidly heating atmosphere. Not that there was anything he and Robert could do to ease the tension building between them. Henri was here, and they needed to keep things as normal as possible in front of him.

Robert tickled Henri, earning peals of laughter, and Dixie sat back, wondering what the hell he was going to do when Robert was gone. The thought made his heart ache, and there wasn't a damned thing he could do about it. Henri was going to miss him too.

"Do you have to go on Sunday?" Henri asked.

Robert hesitated. "I have to go back to my job. There are people who need me to help them when I get back there. And you and your papa are going to need your house back."

Henri seemed to be thinking, and Dixie wondered what his son was going to come up with. "But you kissed Papa, and you said you kiss the people you care about. And mommies and daddies kiss. I know Papa is gay. I won't have a mama because he doesn't like women that way, but he likes you. So you should stay and be Papa's special person. And if you stay, then you can be my special person too. I'll even share my cookies with you." Sometimes the leaps Henri made were startling, and Dixie was more than a little curious at how Robert would counter his proposal. There were times when he had a great deal of difficulty refuting Henri's arguments, especially when his son used his own words against him.

"I'd love to stay, but…." Robert paused as though he was starting to wonder. "I have to go back to my job there. They're expecting me back. But I'll miss

you all the time. You know that, right? And I'll miss your papa." A cloud passed over Robert's expression and then continued on. If Dixie hadn't been watching him so closely, he might have missed it altogether. Henri was really taken with Robert, and things were going well between them, but it wasn't realistic to expect Robert to agree to leave his life behind after a few weeks—even if he did fit in seamlessly with their lives.

"But I saw you kissing Papa, so that means you like him." Henri was so earnest as he pleaded his case. Usually Henri used those sad eyes and pooched lips on him. This time, though, he and Henri were on the same side, hoping Robert would give in. But that wasn't likely. Who went somewhere on vacation and stayed?

"Henri," Dixie broke in, "you need to give Mr. Robert a break. I know you like him, and I do too, but when he came here, it wasn't forever. It was just for a few weeks to visit." He hated disappointing his son, but this was something unavoidable. "The best thing we can do is make sure we have a good time while he's here. And take lots of pictures so we can look at them later. If you want, you can get your tablet."

Henri hurried to get it and used it to take images, moving around Robert as if he was some kind of a fashion photographer. When he was done, he reviewed them and deleted some before presenting his final choices to them. "Is there no limit to what you can do?" Robert asked Henri as he hugged him. "Now I need some pictures of you and your papa."

Dixie lifted Henri on his lap, and Robert used his phone to take pictures of the two of them. Then Robert showed them to him and Henri.

"Is that someone's tummy I'm hearing?" Dixie asked Henri. "Maybe we should get ready to go to the café for dinner. Go get your shoes and we'll leave in a little while." Dixie sent messages in order to make sure everyone was in place, and by the time they left the house, Dixie couldn't help wondering how many sets of eyes were on them.

"PAPA, CAN I get the red meat with the toast?" Henri asked once they were seated. It was a warm evening, so the glass walls in the front of the café had been opened to the sidewalk.

"I don't think so, buddy. I know you had some when we went out with Pierre once, but I think it's best if you have something else." He still hated that Pierre had fed Henri tartare. It had surprised him that Henri really liked it and he sometimes asked for it, but he didn't want Henri eating raw meat. Yes, it was prepared carefully and raised with care, but he didn't want to take any chances with his son. "What else would you like?"

"Coq-au-vin?" he asked, and Dixie nodded as they approached the front door. They were seated immediately, and Dixie helped Henri get settled. Robert chose the duck, and since he was hungry for beef, Dixie got the steak.

"I like the food here," Robert said. "The atmosphere is simple, but yet you know you're in Paris. You don't need to hear French. It's in the air, the scent, the people, the energy…." He grinned.

"Papa, I gotta go," Henri whispered, and Dixie got up with Henri to take him to the bathroom. He got Henri inside and waited for him to use the toilet. Once he

was done, he washed his hands and waited while Henri did the same. As they left, a man came in, brushing past him. Dixie knew immediately that something had been pushed into his pocket, but he didn't stop, instead memorizing all the details he could as they went back to the table.

"Did you meet someone?" It took Dixie a second to realize Robert was speaking in code of sorts.

"I think so, yes." He continued to smile as he pulled out his phone and sent a quick text with the description of the man who had passed him. "Our friend is coming back from the restroom now." He sipped his water and didn't turn in that direction, even as his heart beat faster. He was curious what he had been passed, but he wasn't going to look at it now. Let them think they had gotten away with a clean note drop.

"I see him," Robert said softly as he drank the water. "Henri, take my picture, would you?" Robert asked. Henri slipped out of his seat and took a few pictures of Robert on the phone Robert handed him. When he handed it back, Robert looked through them and smiled, nodding. "You do great work." Robert ruffled Henri's hair, and Dixie knew Henri had gotten a picture of the man.

The server brought their dinners, and they settled in to eat while a steady stream of people passed ten feet from their table. "Is it good?" Robert asked Henri, who nodded and dug right in, and then coughed once and grabbed his throat. "What's wrong?" Henri's eyes grew wide as saucers and his mouth moved, but no sound came out. "Henri…."

"Get back," Robert said loudly, jumping to his feet and pulling Henri up. He went to his knees and bent Henri forward, firmly patting his back between

his shoulders. In those seconds, which seemed to go on for an eternity, Dixie's hands shook, and all he could see was his little son, scared and unable to breathe. His son's hands clutched at Robert, and his lips were turning blue as Robert got behind Henri and thrust his hands upward, jerking Henri.

Dixie had never been so happy in his life to hear his son cough and then inhale. "Papa," Henri said, crying as Dixie gathered him into his arms. Robert gathered what Henri had brought up in a napkin. Their server hurried over, as did the café manager.

"Is he okay?" the server asked in French, and Dixie assured him that Henri was, even as he clung to him.

"It was a piece of chicken bone," Robert said, showing the manager what he had found.

"Is terrible," he said to Robert and turned to the server, who took Henri's plate. "Does he want something different? Dinner is complimentary, of course."

"Henri, are you still hungry? Do you want some frites?" He nodded, and Dixie ordered him a side of frites and some vegetables. The manager hurried away, and Dixie rocked his son, the pounding in his ears finally subsiding. "You saved him." His own throat seemed to have stopped working for the moment. Dixie offered some of his food to Henri, who nibbled on a few of his frites and took a small bite of his beef. When Henri's replacement meal arrived, he sat down and ate slowly and deliberately.

"Buddy, you scared us," Robert said.

Henri put down his fork. "You saved me," he said softly and got out of his chair, went to Robert, and hugged him. "I love you." Dixie barely heard the words, but they were definitely said. Henri went back to

his seat, and Robert didn't move, presumably stunned into inaction.

Henri ate some more, and slowly the spell over the table fell away and they all returned to their meals. Though Dixie noticed that they both kept a close eye on Henri.

Dixie never, ever wanted to go through something like that again. He could still see Henri turning blue, slipping away from him. Dixie knew that he couldn't wrap Henri in bubble wrap and keep him safe from everything, but the thought that something could happen to his son was enough for his appetite to take wings and fly right out the door. Still, he forced himself to eat and for things to be normal. Now was not the time for him to fall to pieces; he could do that once he was alone and behind a closed door. Showing his fear was only going to upset Henri more, and his son was calm and seemed to be eating normally and doing okay, especially once the manager offered them dessert at the end of the meal.

"I DON'T want to eat chicken anymore," Henri pronounced on their way home. "I might choke again." He had been quiet for a while, and Dixie had wondered what was going through his mind. Henri pondered things and was smart, but there were times when his reactions were a little extreme.

Robert came to the rescue. "You never want to eat fried chicken?" He made yummy sounds. "It's the best. The skin is crispy and the chicken nice and juicy. So good. Have you ever had it?" Henri looked up at him like he was crazy and shook his head. "It's so good."

"Yeah. Your grandma used to make it every Sunday when I was a kid. It was so yummy." Dixie paused

their walk back toward home. "Besides, I know you got a chicken bone in your throat, but that was an accident. If you had choked on a piece of cake, would you never have cake again?" He tickled Henri, his little cake monster. "You're okay, and Robert helped you." Dixie couldn't help hugging Henri to himself as another wave of relief and concern washed over him. "Let's go home so you can get your bath and into your pajamas."

"Can Robert read me a story?" Henri asked.

Robert sighed and nodded. "I will. But you only want me to read one of the stories in French so you can laugh at how I say the words."

"You can read an English story," Henri conceded. Dixie released Henri, and he went to Robert, who lifted him up, and they continued their way to the house. "You should stay," Henri said, patting Robert on the shoulder. "I like it when you're here." Henri rested his head on Robert's shoulder, and Dixie had to agree with his son. He liked having Robert here too.

Chapter 11

ROBERT READ Henri his second story before slipping out of his room. He was finally asleep, and Robert was more fatigued than if he had run ten miles. He pulled the covers up over Henri before leaving the room and closing the door partway. "He's asleep," he told Dixie when he got to the living room.

"Did he say anything more about choking?" Dixie asked.

"He just asked about fried chicken. I really think he's fine. It was an accident, and the manager offering him dessert and being so nice to him really helped." Robert sat next to Dixie. "I think it's his papa who's worried and scared."

Dixie nodded. "I kept thinking…. What if I lose him?" Dixie shook, and Robert held him. There was nothing he could do other than be there and let Dixie process his fear. People often thought that Marines didn't feel fear. They were people—of course they did. But part of their training was to learn to process it and then move past it.

"But you didn't. And Henri is okay and is getting over what happened." Somehow Robert didn't expect

Dixie to move past it as quickly. They sat quietly, Robert's arm around Dixie, and he just let him think.

After a while, Dixie reached into his pocket and pulled out a small piece of paper, which he placed in Robert's hand. He unfolded it. Of course, the note was in French. "What does it say?"

"Basically, that if I don't want anything bad to happen, I should gather a copy of my encryption program and protocols and have them ready for delivery in the next few days. They say they will be in touch again."

"Okay." Robert pulled out his phone. "But we have a picture of the man who dropped that into your pocket. It's not the clearest image, but it isn't too bad. I bet your people can clear it up." Robert sent it to Dixie, who forwarded it on.

"They're on it," Dixie told him. "Maybe now we can identify who is behind this. Not that it really matters. I can't turn over the program, but I hope we will have something soon enough."

"Are they planning a dummy drop?" Robert asked. He figured Dixie and the people he worked with would create something that looked authentic but wouldn't have key components. That was what he'd do, which also meant that whatever they put together would need to be good enough to pass an initial inspection. Otherwise their friends would be back… and the second time with more force.

"That's what they tell me. They know they'll be on guard, so it's taking a little time." He sighed and leaned closer. "You know, I probably never would have gotten involved in any of this if I had known how much cloak-and-dagger was involved. You know me. I much prefer a fight out in the open to these games."

"Hey. It will come to an end soon, and then, hopefully, you can go back to your regular life. Once it gets out that you aren't an easy mark, they'll look somewhere else." These people were only after the information on Dixie's program. It was what they wanted. If they left behind a string of victims, then that would draw attention, and that was the last thing spies and espionage agents wanted. The shadows provided them cover, and they wished to stay there if at all possible.

"I sure hope so." He yawned, and even though it was early, Robert stood and began switching off the lights. Dixie set the alarm, and they went upstairs together. Dixie checked on Henri while Robert got cleaned up and climbed into bed. He lay on his back, hands behind his head while he waited for Dixie.

This vacation had been nothing at all like he had expected. Robert had figured he'd come to Paris to see some things and have some fun. He hadn't expected to encounter intrigue and a fascinating little boy, or to have his heart stolen by his old friend. Now he needed to figure out what he was going to do.

"OKAY. I'LL look for the files. From their note, I expect that they'll be in touch soon." Dixie's voice drifted in from his office. "I see. So you're setting me up as a sacrificial lamb." Robert hated the sound of that and got out of bed. "No, I get it. You have to make it look like you're suspicious so they'll believe that I might actually sell you out. It doesn't mean I like the idea, but I get it." Robert leaned against the doorframe. "I'll look for the information. Thanks." Dixie hung up and turned toward him.

"I take it they decided that just giving you the fake files wasn't enough."

"No. Apparently there are rumors, and a few suspicions that have been voiced. Granted, they aren't real, but I don't like that idea. What if someone believes them in the future?"

"It's a decoy," Robert explained. "It happens all the time. If you're being given fake data to feed to them, then the people after you have to believe it's real and that you're desperate and willing to sell it to them. They need to seem attractive to you, and a little suspicion would mean that maybe you aren't exactly squeaky clean." It made sense to him.

"Yeah. Apparently it's nothing specific, just a little talk that they've let get out, but it should be enough to keep the fish on the line." Dixie sighed. "I better get dressed, because Henri is going to be up soon and I need to take him to school so I can meet with his teacher." He sounded completely thrilled about the idea.

"Is there anything you need me to do while you're gone?" Robert asked.

"Not really. I'm a little at loose ends. Maybe once I get back, we can go do something. The idea of spending another day closed up in the house holds no interest for me. Besides, they can't make contact if I'm locked up here." Dixie used the bathroom and then dressed. Robert took his turn afterward and found Dixie and Henri at the table.

"Am I going to be in trouble?" Henri asked. "I'm sorry and I'll be good."

"No. I need to speak to Madame Marie this morning," Dixie said gently, but he had this determined papa bear look in his eye.

"Can Mr. Robert come with us too?" Henri asked as though Robert was going to be able to change whatever was going to happen.

"If he wants to. But that isn't going to stop me from talking to your teacher. Now eat the rest of your breakfast so we aren't late." Dixie finished his coffee and then prodded Henri to be ready to go. Robert walked along with them. Henri was unusually quiet. Usually he talked all the time, a running tally of his observations, but today he held Dixie's hand, remaining mostly quiet, which had Robert wondering what Dixie was going to find out.

ROBERT TRIED to remember the last time he was inside a school. This one looked pretty typical, except that all around him the children spoke French and the area was extremely compact. He supposed that some things were universal, including boards hung with children's drawings and lots of primary colors. He stood outside the office waiting for Dixie, who had been inside with the teacher for longer than he had expected. At one point another woman had joined them, but other than that, it was quiet.

On the way over, no one had accosted them or even seemed to be paying attention to their two-block trek to the school. But that didn't mean that he hadn't been watching like a hawk. He crossed his arms over his chest, continuing to wait, letting his thoughts run while he did. Honestly, Robert could hardly believe he was actually waiting outside a school office, and if he were honest, he wouldn't do this for anyone other than Dixie and Henri. Normally in this type of situation, he'd simply have stayed at home. But time was precious, and

that meant doing whatever Dixie needed to get done. After a lot of time spent alone, he had learned that even mundane things could be special if they were shared with someone else.

Robert didn't know how long they were going to be, so he slipped out a side door and checked out the area. He needed something to do, and if they were being followed, then he wanted to be able to double back on their tail. Robert made a quick turn just outside the door, headed away from the school for a block, and then circled around. He knew how to move stealthily and how to make himself seem smaller, staying with the flow of sidewalk traffic, using others as cover. At a corner past the school, he made another turn and doubled back using a narrow alley between buildings, looking out for people watching him. He saw no one suspicious and returned to the school by a few more byways, just to be sure. Robert needed to do something—the frustration with waiting for Dixie's people was working his nerves.

The door opened and Dixie stepped out as Robert returned. Dixie's shoulders were loose and his arms moving freely. "Merci," he said and then continued to where Robert waited. "We can go." He strode toward the exit and didn't say anything until they were outside and the door had closed behind them. "She heard those kids yesterday and did nothing about it," Dixie said. "Just like Henri told me. His teacher chose not to act, but I doubt she's going to do that again."

"I take it you had a productive talk," Robert observed, not indicating that the man from the café the night before was across the street, walking down the sidewalk the same way they were heading.

"Yes. I explained what Henri told me, and she explained how he had acted. I told her that I already spoke to Henri about his behavior and that I was here to talk about hers." He smiled. "I was actually proud of myself. I kept my cool and spoke calmly. The headmistress then came in, and we had a conversation about the kind of behavior that was acceptable for her teachers." Dixie kept speeding up the more he talked. Clearly he wasn't as calm as he said he was.

"I take it you got your point across without punching anyone out," Robert teased as he glanced across the road toward their observer. "That's a good thing."

"I did, and I'm also convinced that Madame Marie is a good person and a good teacher. She had a difficult day yesterday, and it happened to involve Henri. She promised that she would not overlook the other kids picking on Henri. She agrees that Henri is extra bright, and she is going to make recommendations about more advanced work for him next year."

"More advanced?" Robert asked. "Does she want him to skip forward?"

"Not yet. But she thinks that's what he needs in order to be challenged. Right now Henri is doing advanced work in his class, but she thinks he needs more of a challenge and that he's more than capable of doing third-year work rather than going into a second-year class." Dixie didn't seem happy.

"Is that bad?" Robert asked.

"Yes and no. He has friends, and he'll be leaving them behind," Dixie explained and stopped a second before continuing. "We're being watched."

"I know. Keep walking. I have them in my sights. As long as they stay over there, we're fine. Your people are there as well, just farther behind. I saw one circle

around, so they're going to try to cut them off, I think." It was what Robert would do in this situation, especially if he thought he had the upper hand. "You were saying?" he prompted.

"I don't want his life disrupted."

Robert took Dixie's hand. "Henri is going to have a life like neither of us could imagine. He needs to be challenged, and this new class can do that. He gets bored. Have you seen him do his homework? He whips through it as though he's barely thinking about it at all. As for disrupting him, I'd say that not challenging him would be doing the little guy a disservice. If he isn't challenged, *he's* going to become disruptive. Not on purpose, but he isn't going to have enough to do. After all, he's almost seven, knows more than kids two years older than him, but is still only seven years in maturity."

They reached the front door. "That's what I'm afraid of. What if he grows up too fast?" Dixie unlocked it and turned off the alarm as they stepped inside. He shut the door and reactivated the exterior alarms before proceeding inside.

Robert gathered him into his arms. "Not that I've ever had a kid, but I don't think that's something you can stop. Henri is going to grow up, and you'll always be his papa." Robert closed his eyes, inhaling Dixie's scent. "Do you know how jealous I am sometimes?"

"Of me?" Dixie asked.

"Who the fuck else? Of course of you. You're the one who had the guts to build your own family, and because you did that, you found the most amazing kid on the planet." He held Dixie tighter. "And you're the most amazing parent I've ever known." Robert whispered the final part.

"You know, most guys don't find a guy with a kid sexy. As I've found out already."

"Bullshit." Robert pulled away. "I happen to be a connoisseur of sexy men, and let me tell you that there's this one guy who has a son, and I think he is incredibly sexy." He smiled and met Dixie's gaze. "The problem I have is that he lives in Paris, and I am going to need to go home in a few days, and I don't know how I'm going to keep from leaving my heart in the City of Lights." He had to turn away because his emotions were way too close to the surface.

"Robert…," Dixie said softly. "Don't hide from me. That's what you and I did all those years ago. You and I could handle just about anything on the battle-field, but we didn't talk to one another and we didn't open up. So, yeah, it was hard when the corps separated us, but we could have fought it or requested different assignments. Hell, you and I could have fucking kept in touch with each other. But it was easier to just go our separate ways, blame the corps, and then just go on. So don't say stuff like that and just turn away." Dixie inhaled deeply, and Robert's throat tightened again.

"But I have to leave, and it isn't like I can just come back next weekend to visit."

"No. That's true. But it's up to us to make an effort if we want something more than another few weeks together followed by seven years before we see each other again. And I think that starts with the two of us admitting that we have feelings for each other and that we look at them square on rather than hiding. I have no idea what's going to happen or how the two of us are going to make things work with an ocean between us."

"I don't either," Robert admitted. "But you're right. If something is worth having, it's worth fighting for." He tugged Dixie back into a deep hug, and then he tilted Dixie's head upward. Robert kissed him hard. They didn't have immediate plans, and Robert guided Dixie toward the sofa and then down onto the cushions. Maybe the two of them could recreate some of the urgency that drove them all those years ago.

"You know," Dixie said as he cupped Robert's cheeks in his hands, "this sofa is way too small, and there's a perfectly good man-sized bed upstairs…." He smiled, his eyes darkening. Robert nodded just as Dixie's phone rang. Talk about a mood killer.

"I gotta check this." They both sat up, and Dixie pulled out his phone, furrowing his brow before answering the call. His expression darkened further and became downright cloudy as he listened. "Okay. I understand." He hung up, his hand shaking. "I guess notes aren't good enough any longer. They want the program, and they're willing to pay several million dollars to get it." He took a deep breath. "And they're willing to hurt Henri if they don't." Dixie's face began to redden, and his eyes grew hard as steel. "I want to get these guys, and I want it bad. This waiting around is driving me crazy."

Robert nodded. "Me too. My instinct is to go out there, kick some ass, and take names, but we can't do that right now. We have to play this game out." He grinned. "You know, usually I'm the one raring to go and you're the one trying to talk some sense into me." It was a frustratingly craptastic turn of events. He clenched and unclenched his fists, his pulse racing, but at the moment, he had nowhere to go. Robert was smart enough to realize that this was a game of wills

and counter moves, which was so not in his wheel-house, but that didn't make the waiting any fucking easier. Still, he knew that things were about to change and that these people were going to pay for what they were doing… one way or another. "Okay. When do you get your package to give them? We can hand it off and have this over with." He smiled. "You know, after all this drama, maybe you should think about getting out of Dodge yourself. Put some distance between you and them. Maybe visit Grand Rapids for part of the summer while Henri is out of school." He was determined to make an effort.

Dixie nodded. "I'll definitely keep that in mind." He held his head in his hands. "But there's too much for me to think about now." He was pale, and his hands shook. "I can take bullets and shell fire, but not some-one threatening Henri." His phone rang again, and Dix-ie snatched it up. "Yeah… they just made contact. The number was blocked of course…. Okay, I'll put him on." Dixie set the phone on the table and placed it on speaker.

"Mr. Wendel, I'm Howard Winters, your friend Dixie's supervisor. We are aware that you know what's going on. You're also in the home there, which is some-where we can't be without arousing suspicion. Dixie has been under surveillance for quite some time be-cause of the nature of his work. Not because we don't trust him but because we know there are organizations that would love nothing more than to get their hands on Dixie's work."

"Yes. And those people have been coming closer and closer." Robert crossed his arms over his chest, glaring at the phone as though Winters could see him. Not that it mattered. He was pissed that they were

putting Dixie and Henri in such danger. "My question for you is, what are you going to do about it?"

"You certainly don't pull any punches." He didn't sound intimidated, which ticked him up a notch in Robert's estimation. "We have a package that is being delivered to your phone, Mr. Wendel. Dixie will know how to download and decode it. He will then remove it from that device and place it on a drive for delivery. Have they said what to do?"

"Not yet," Dixie answered. "They said they would call with detailed instructions, but they also said they will know if the program is correct and that they are watching me and Henri. They know who is coming and going, and they are not squeamish when it comes to children." Dixie's voice broke, and Robert put an arm around him.

Robert's phone chimed with a message. He opened it to find the file that Howard had mentioned. He handed the phone to Dixie.

"I have the file and will get it all set for them. Are you sure this is going to work?" Dixie asked.

"Yes. We had to take a chance, so it will work perfectly the first three times, and then it won't after that. The core algorithm will be replaced and deleted. And the details of your work will be safe."

"What about Dixie and Henri? Will they be safe?" Robert understood that the people Dixie worked for were worried about their assets and property, but he was concerned about the family who lived in this particular house. If anything happened to them, he wasn't sure what he'd do. But he knew he'd feel their loss in a big way.

"Yes. We'll be able to track anyone who uses the program and take them into custody. From there, we'll

do our best to turn their assets to ones we can use, and if not, we'll put them away for a long time."

"Dix, you don't need to do this. I know Howard here wants you to, but you don't have to. You and your family are being threatened. You don't need to put yourself and Henri up as bait."

Dixie nodded slowly. "I do need to do this. I can't run away. What kind of Marine would I be then? What kind of parent? I have to do everything I can to remove this threat. I need to keep Henri safe and make sure that I keep my self-respect in one piece." Robert understood that and respected it. "I need you to have my back."

"Oh, I will. Just like in the corps, there is no way you are going out there alone. I will be there, like always." He had come to realize that the time for waiting was over, and there was no fucking way he was leaving this up to Dixie's boss or anyone else.

"You have the files. Do your preparations and take it from there. Giving them what they think they want should get them off your back. When they make contact again, make sure they understand that they are never to contact you again." He continued talking, but Robert pulled Dixie's attention.

"Make sure they know that you have information on them. That they haven't been as stealthy as they think they have. Just hint at it. Let them sweat it out a little. Tell them that the deal is a go, but that if anything goes wrong, you can hurt all of them as well. Even the playing field." Robert held Dixie's gaze. "If you don't have some strength here, then they'll figure they can come back to the well over and over again."

"Good idea," Dixie agreed and turned back to the phone. "I'll make all the preparations and let you know when they make contact again. By the way, you might

want to let it be known that my access has been suspended but that you're investigating whether I might have copied files. That should convince them that I'm desperate and have gone to the dark side."

"Will do." Howard ended the call, and Robert tugged Dixie close.

"Just sit here a second. I know you have things to do, but I'm serious. You don't need to do this."

"I know what you're saying, but I can't let years of work go for nothing. What kind of parent would I be to Henri if I ran scared all the time?" He pulled back.

"I didn't mean it that way, and you know it," Robert countered. "I'm worried for you. That's all." He drew closer, Dixie's scent filling his senses. "I don't think I could bear anything happening to you." He slipped his hand around the back of Dixie's neck. "Just be damned careful, and no matter what, I have your back. Once they make contact, we'll figure out how, but you aren't going out there alone." Fucking hell, he'd throw himself in front of a bullet if it meant that Dixie and Henri would stay safe.

"I know you do, and I hope you can understand that I have to do this. It's a matter of honor. I can't let people think they can pressure me like this and get away with it. Once this little game is over, I'll be reinstated, and then I'll be able to develop something brand-new."

Robert kept quiet, but he wasn't sure that was true. The fiction building around Dixie and this situation wasn't something that could be turned off like a switch. Yes, Howard could give Dixie back his access, but there were always going to be people out there who would think that with enough pressure, they could get what they wanted from him. Henri was the center of Dixie's world, and that meant Henri made Dixie vulnerable…

and that wasn't likely to change, no matter what. "I have to ask you something, and you may not like it. But have you thought of going into business for yourself? Maybe doing something completely different where you call the shots?"

"Maybe," Dixie answered. It wasn't the answer that Robert had expected. "I used to think of starting my own physical security company. There are a lot of people who need private security and advice on the development and installation of systems to keep them safe. But I don't know the people who can get something like that started. Yeah, I have the expertise, but not the connections or the money, and that's what starting a business takes. And I have Henri to provide for."

"Everything comes back to Henri," Robert said softly.

"Of course it does," Dixie snapped.

"I meant," Robert began, catching Dixie's change in tone, "that it has to. Henri is what's most important. He has to be safe, and he needs to grow up with every chance in the world." Robert closed the distance between them. "And Henri needs to have his papa there for him next week, next year, and for the next decade." Damn, Robert flashed on an image of him and Dixie with a much older Henri, who stood on stage with his violin, taking a bow. He could see Henri as a stunning, handsome young man, and more than anything he wanted to be part of that picture. That was a pipe dream, but that didn't stop him from wanting it.

"I'm well aware of that." Dixie stood up and headed for the stairs. "I need to get this file ready so that when they make contact, I can arrange the exchange and get this done." He climbed the stairs, and Robert couldn't take his eyes off him. He wasn't convinced

that this exchange alone was going to bring this to an end or leave Henri and Dixie safe. Somehow Robert felt that task was going to have to fall to him. Howard was concerned about his programs and the security of what Dixie had developed. But Dix and Henri deserved more than just what they could provide, and Robert intended to see that they got it, even if he had to pay a price to make it happen.

Chapter 12

DIXIE TAMPED down his nerves for the millionth time. He needed to keep control if he was going to have any chance at being effective. After his call yesterday, everything had been quiet, which only ramped up his wonder about what was going on. To top it off, Robert was as cool as a cucumber, and that got under his skin. Not that Robert had done anything wrong, but how could he be so relaxed when so much was on the line?

"Dix," Robert said as he came up behind him, settling his hands on Dixie's shoulders. Dixie jumped slightly even though he knew he was there, just because he was wound so damned tight. "They're going to contact you soon. Henri is at school, and they have that place locked down after the heads-up they were given. No one is going to get inside unless they have four forms of ID and are willing to give a DNA sample." Dixie knew he was kidding, and he was well aware that no matter how much planning was done, there were always holes that could be exploited.

"I should have kept Henri home," he sighed.

"And what were you going to do? Take Henri to the handoff?" Robert massaged his shoulders, and he

tensed more until his muscles finally released and he was able to lean back and let Robert work his magic. He had that ability to release the worry that Dixie usually kept buried inside.

Dixie started and grabbed his phone when it rang. "Oui," he snapped.

"Bring the program to the Arc de Triomphe today at noon, right under the flag. You'll be approached. Just hand it over."

"All right," Dixie agreed as they had planned. "But I want the money first. You'll get nothing until I get paid."

"We call the shots, not—" the gruff voice began.

Dixie didn't give them a chance to finish. "I have what you want, and if you intend to get it, then you'll have the money in my account today. Once I have it, then I'll meet you for a drop, and not before." He sat back. "And don't think for a second that I haven't seen you all around. You haven't been as smooth as you think you've been. I have descriptions and even pictures. So get this: once you have your programs, don't attempt to contact me again. If you do, then what I have gets turned over. Now get the money into my account and we'll talk." Dixie hung up, and Robert grinned, hugging him. "That ought to get their attention."

"Yup. They have to be second-guessing who they're dealing with. Keep them on their toes and wondering what's next. They've come this far and are close to getting what they want." Robert grinned. "They'll jump through hoops in order to bring this home."

Dixie sure as hell hoped so. He wasn't sure what he was going to do with the money that was supposed to be deposited. Part of him wondered if these people even had it to begin with. If they didn't, then maybe this

entire deal would collapse and he wouldn't have to go through any of this at all.

About fifteen minutes later, he received a notice of a deposit to his bank account. Dixie checked the balance and whistled, showing the balance to Robert. "What the hell do I do now?"

"Transfer that money to another account. Get it out of there. I'm going to leave the house and make my way to the Arc. Message me if anything changes. I'll be watching from somewhere. I'm assuming that the house is under surveillance."

"Then how are you going to get out without being seen?" Dixie asked.

"I'm going to go out through your neighbors'. I can get through their window onto the courtyard. They're at work, and I'm just going to pass through their place. They won't even know I've ever been there." Robert leaned down and kissed him hard. "Message me if anything changes. I half expect them to change the drop point when you're halfway there. Just message a location and I'll get there. But don't let them see you do it." He kissed him again. "I'll see you back here once this is over." Robert left, and Dixie watched him step out into the courtyard just as he received a message.

The money has been sent, and you know where to be and when. He didn't bother answering and received no further information. Dixie messaged his boss that the deal was happening and left the house, walking as normally as possible toward the Metro station. He wondered where the people who were watching him were. Clearly he wasn't as good at spotting a tail as Robert was, because he didn't see anyone the entire way to the station or on the train as he rode to the center of the city.

At the Charles de Gaulle–Etoile stop, Dixie got off the train and immediately left the station. He had ten minutes and wanted to get this over with as soon as possible. He checked his phone and there were no messages, so he went under the large traffic circle to the arch and approached the massive structure.

Dixie had been here many times, but after this, he would never look at the place the same way again. There were many places to take refuge in the shadows and many locations where people could linger. The meandering crowd alone made for plenty of cover, and Dixie felt like he stood out as he waited, his hands shoved in his pockets. He wished he knew where Robert was. That alone would tamp down some of his nerves. But he had to keep his head clear and know that Robert was man who did what he said he was going to do and that he could rely on him.

BACK AND forth under the Arc Dixie wandered, taking a look upward at the huge flag that flew over his head. Then he continued on, watching around him. A few times he thought he might have caught someone's eye, but they passed by, leaving him wondering what was going on and checking the time over and over. He was about to give up when he turned around and nearly ran into the man from the café.

"I believe you have something for me," he said.

"Yes. I do." He didn't move.

"Then hand it over without making a fuss," he added in a heavy accent. He must have gotten his dialogue from American television.

"And you tell your people to leave me alone from now on. I have pictures of everyone who's been close

to us over the past few weeks, including you. Good ones. That will be enough to lead me to whoever you're working for." He smiled slightly.

"Yes. Like they'll believe you. We already know you're under suspicion." He smiled, revealing a perfect set of caps.

"Am I?" He flashed an equally fake smile. "Then I have nothing to lose by killing you right here, do I?" He kept his hands in his pockets. "I've been trained to do just that, and you'd never see it coming. By the time anyone discovered you, even in this busy atmosphere, I'd be long gone, and you'd be a stiff who stopped breathing hours ago." He kept his voice light even as his heart pounded hard. "Now, I got what you sent, and I always keep my word. Make sure you do the same or I'll find you."

"And I always keep my word as well. You have a lot to lose," he hissed.

"And I can take care of what's mine. Can you do the same? Or should I prove my prowess, right here and now? I'm sure your employers can find some other lackey to act as their mule." Dixie didn't move an inch, holding the man's icy gaze until he turned away. That small gesture told Dixie all he needed to know. He had the upper hand, and he intended to keep it. "I never want to see you or any of your cohorts again. Is that understood?"

He nodded once, and Dixie pulled his left hand out of his pocket and gave him the drive, keeping his right in his pocket.

"This had better—"

"Just take this, quit your threats, and move on, or I'll shiv you right between your ribs and into your heart

before it can beat one more time." He was done with these people.

The man's hand closed around the drive, and he stepped back, then turned and melted into the crowd within a few seconds. Dixie turned as well, walked across the plaza and back to the underground crosswalk leading to the Metro station, and used his pass for the trip home.

Dixie watched everyone around him the entire trip. A few times he thought he might have seen someone paying attention to him, but then they got off, and Dixie rode the crowded train the final leg to the journey feeling a little less on edge. He hoped they were done with him and that he could return to normal once again.

Dixie unlocked the door and was immediately on guard when the alarm wasn't engaged. "You made it back in one piece?" Robert asked when he came around the corner. "I watched the handoff and got some good shots of him—much better ones than we had from the café. I also got a few pictures of the two men who came along with him. They fanned out around the circle as he approached. They left once the handoff was complete."

"I was afraid I was being followed the entire way home," Dixie explained. "It creeped me out a little."

"I didn't see anyone, and I was behind you a lot of the way. I didn't ride the same train as you, and my train was more direct, but the men left the Arc going in the opposite direction you did."

Dixie sighed. "So you think this could be over?" That was all he wanted.

"I don't know. But they think they got what they wanted. They may test it, find out that it works, and then go from there. Who knows—they will probably

sell what they have to someone else, and it could be two or three people away from you before anyone discovers that it's worthless. At least I hope so."

"Me too." At least no one seemed to have been following him, which meant they were happy enough with what they had. But they also knew where he lived, and unless he packed up and got out of Dodge, they knew where to find him. "I need to make a few calls." Dixie went up to his office and closed the door to report in on what happened. His boss was thrilled that the exchange went off. "What do we do now?" Dixie asked.

"No worries. In the next day or so, we'll report that we've suffered a major setback in our encryption efforts. Apparently the program that we thought was ready still has a number of issues and it's unreliable." He seemed almost giddy. "They'll think that the program is bad for everyone rather than that we messed with their copy." Damn, it was almost clever in its simplicity.

"Jesus, you played this whole thing." Dixie wasn't sure if he was impressed or worried as hell. Maybe Robert was right and it was time for him to begin some kind of disengagement from these people. His project was coming to an end and they would have something else for him, but maybe a new assignment wasn't in the cards and he should simply figure a way to get the hell out. He wasn't sure what the heck he was going to do.

"It's our job and part of what we do. You all develop programs that will help forward government interests. It's our job to protect them, and that means playing the game better than our opponents." He sounded as though Dixie were stupid and he was explaining something to a child. Dixie hated that tone and ground his back teeth.

"And you were willing to use me and put us out as bait?" He heard the snap in his own voice.

"No, we weren't. You had backup, and we've had people watching your home as well as your son's school." He sounded so reasonable that it made Dixie's hackles rise. Maybe he wanted a little more emotion to match some of his own.

"Yeah. But I was expendable. If things had gone wrong, you'd have closed ranks, written us off, and moved to protect your assets without worrying about us." It was a revelation. He had always thought he was important to the department, and yet he'd always known those were the rules of the game, but like a lot of people, he'd thought he'd been different. Yeah, it seemed he had pulled it off and should go up in the estimation of the department leadership, and things had seemingly worked out. But he was still angrier than he probably should have been. After all, they had kept his family safe—well, them and Robert.

"You are talented, and we protect our people. And for the record, you are not expendable." He kept his calm, which impressed Dixie. "Sometimes the games are required in order to protect our assets, and you are one of those. Never forget that. This was a situation where we had to play things carefully… and it worked, and we will continue going forward and do everything we can to protect you and your family."

"But when can I go back to a normal life with my son?" That was all he cared about. Henri was what mattered.

"Soon."

Dixie wanted to relax, but he knew he couldn't, not yet.

"We'll have your back; you've had ours for a number of years." He sounded so certain. Dixie would need to think things over. For now, he didn't argue and figured it was best to sleep on it and make up his own mind. Maybe it was just the entire situation getting to him. A little time and distance would probably be in order. "We aren't pulling the extra security for a while. So rest easier, and we'll keep our ears open for any chatter that might be directed your way." He ended the call, and Dixie sighed before returning downstairs.

While he was gone, Robert had pulled out some fresh bread, cheese, tapenade, and a bottle of wine. "Let's have something to eat."

Dixie sat down and broke off a piece of the bread while Robert poured the wine. "I guess it's as over as we can hope for." He wished that there had been a complete resolution, with the bad guys in jail and out of commission, so he would know that everything was going to be okay. That was probably too much to hope for.

"Probably. Sometimes I guess we have to be content with a 'happy for now' resolution and go on from there." He sipped from his glass. "There are so many times back home when I answer a call and I know that the right thing would be to take the perpetrator into custody, but then people don't press charges and they walk. I may have stopped what was happening at that moment, but not what would happen tomorrow when another call would come in. Sometimes we have to take what we can get and hope for the best."

"Well, hoping for the best isn't going to keep Henri safe."

"You may be right, but those guys raced off like rabbits once they had what they wanted, and they didn't

look back. Keep a low profile, and we'll watch over Henri." Robert sighed. "It's my hope that this is over." He took Dixie's hand. "Damn it all, I wish I had some answers, but we're guessing and shit, the same way we used to have to use our gut instincts and what little information we had when we were stuck on that sand pile."

"Yeah," Dixie sighed. People had been out to kill them back then, and hopefully that wasn't the case now. But he had no idea what these people were up to and what they might do if they found out that what they had been given was in essence worthless. Maybe what the boss had planned would work. It was what he had to hope for.

He ate some more bread and cheese and drank a little more wine than he probably should have. It tasted good, and Dixie needed something to calm his nerves. "What the hell has happened to me?" he asked once lunch was over and he plopped himself on the sofa. "I had nerves of steel, just like you. I could hear gunfire whizzing over my head and keep firing, just like you. Now I worry all the fucking time and can't even hold my lunch wine." His head was a little swimmy, and he rested it back, closing his eyes, hoping the feeling would pass.

"You became a parent. In the corps, we looked after ourselves and our brothers and they looked after us. We were strong because we were a team. No questions asked. Life was that simple sometimes. It isn't now. There are no rules out here, and you have Henri to look after. It's not complex—he needs you... all of you." Robert sat next to him, a warm hand gliding over his cheek. "He's your world, period." The loneliness in Robert's voice touched Dixie deeply. Without opening

his eyes, he touched Robert's cheek, knowing right where it was.

"Yes. And maybe I was hoping that when I found the right person, my world might just get a little bit bigger." Dixie drew Robert closer.

"So were you sucking down that wine because of what happened today, or because I have to leave?"

"Both," Dixie answered honestly, drawing Robert nearer. "I know the simple answer is to ask you to stay and keep asking until you say yes. Henri would ask you over and over too. But that isn't fair to you or to us." He didn't dare look into Robert's eyes or he would ask those questions and keep right on asking, no matter the consequences. Why couldn't life be fair, if just for once?

The sofa cushions dipped and then Robert was right there, tasting his lips. The wine from earlier colored their kiss, and Dixie gave himself over to it in an instant. Robert was going to leave in a few days, and Dixie was determined to make the most of the time they had. This wasn't a time for games or coyness. Dixie wrapped his arms around Robert's neck. This was a time for taking what he wanted, because it wasn't going to be on offer for much longer.

"Let's go upstairs," Robert breathed, and Dixie hummed his agreement. It was time to make some noise—an impression—something for him to remember when Robert was no longer here and he was once again alone in his bed staring at the ceiling.

Chapter 13

THE NEXT couple of days flew by. It seemed to Robert that he closed his eyes at night and when he opened them, the time had simply vanished. Dixie had pulled Henri out of school for a few days, and they went to the Loire Valley to explore and get out of the city. The change was amazing. The chateau they stayed at was all white stone with deep blue trim, and they had dogs that seemed to sense when Henri was near. They ran over every time they saw him, and Henri more than once got covered in grass stains from where he ended up as part of a wonderful puppy pile.

"You really should get him a dog," Robert said as they packed up the car to head back to the city.

"Robert," Dixie warned, "I know you, and I know my son and the way he has you wrapped around his little finger. Don't you dare get him one." There was no heat in his voice.

"So you're saying that the Maltese puppy that looked so adorable in the pet shop window and that I arranged to have delivered tomorrow isn't going to have a happy home?" He took a page from Henri's playbook, pooching out his lower lip before smiling. "I'm kidding. I would never do that to you. But I'm

serious. You should get him a puppy. Henri is old enough, and having a puppy to care for would be good for him. Teach him responsibility, and a dog would give you some company when Henri is at school." He closed the trunk of the car and turned to look over their surroundings one last time.

All this was going to be so hard to leave. Somehow—he didn't know when—Henri and Dixie had filled that part of his heart he hadn't even known was empty, and now… well, he'd have to figure out how to exist without it.

"Papa," Henri called as he hurried up, the dogs right behind him. He hugged each of them, talking to the dogs to tell them that he was going to miss them and that they had to go inside so they didn't get hit by the car. Not that any of the dogs paid any attention, bounding around Henri in abject doggie excitement and adoration. The owners of the chateau joined them, holding the regal dogs' collars and saying goodbye as they got in the car.

"I really want a dog, Papa," Henri said as soon as the doors were closed. He sounded so grown-up. There was no whining, just a statement of fact. If it were up to him, Robert would get him one right away.

"I know you do, buddy," Dixie said. "But you go to school all day, and I have to work."

Henri settled in his seat, buckling himself in. "But Papa. You're lonely all day, and when Mr. Robert goes home, you'll be extra lonely. I'll even let my puppy sleep in your bed with you so you won't be lonely at night."

Robert glanced at Henri, tempted to give him a thumbs-up because dang, that was both observant and

a little manipulative. When he got older, this kid was going to be a handful, that was for certain.

Dixie paused, and Robert heard a soft groan. "I'll think about it."

Henri grinned. Clearly he knew that moving from *no* to *I'll think about it* was halfway to a *yes*. And that Dixie was a soft touch. "I really want a dog like those at the chateau. They were fun, and they really liked me."

"Those dogs are a little bigger than what we can have. They were full-sized poodles. Lovely dogs, though. Maybe we could get something smaller." Dixie gasped, Robert grinned, and Henri put his arms in the air like he'd just run for a touchdown. He hadn't meant to, but Dixie had just agreed to get a dog whether he wanted one or not.

"Okay. A smaller dog. Can we go to the dog store and look to see what they have?" They had barely pulled out of the chateau drive, and Henri was all smiles. Robert turned to Dixie, who he could tell was trying to figure a way out of this. He took Dixie's hand, squeezed it, and then kissed the back of it.

"How about we go home and let your papa think about it some more?" Robert said. "A dog is a big responsibility, and that means that both of you have to love it and take care of it. It isn't just an Henri thing. A dog is a Papa thing too."

Henri sighed dramatically. "I know. But I really want one, and I'm not a baby. I'd love a puppy, and I'd take care of him, take him for walks, and even clean up when he poops." He was so earnest. "I'd feed him and walk him and everything."

"Henri, give me a chance to think about it." Robert had to give Dixie credit. It was clear to him that

Dix was feeling a little pressured, but he kept it out of his voice.

THE RIDE to the city took quite a bit longer than it had on the way out. Robert sat back while Henri pointed out all the sights, talking a mile a minute about everything he saw. As they pulled up to the house, Dixie pulled into his parking spot. They all got out, and Henri stood near the front door while Dixie opened the trunk and Robert helped pull out the luggage.

"Papa!" Henri screamed.

Robert turned as a man hauled Henri down the walk, a hand over his mouth. Henri struggled and kicked at the man, but it didn't seem to be doing any good. Robert dropped the bag in his hand and took off, chasing Henri and the man down the walk to a small black van.

The back door slid open, and both Henri and the man disappeared inside. Robert had no intention of stopping, barreling full speed to the van. He knew full well that if they got away, there would be little chance of getting Henri back anytime soon, and the thought of another kidnapping, one more loss in his life at the hands of people like this, was too much to bear. He slammed into the side of the van and yanked on the passenger door. The stupid people inside hadn't hit the door locks, and it came open. Momentarily shocked, he hesitated a second before grabbing the driver with both hands and pulling him across the seats and out onto the sidewalk. Dixie was right there to take him, manhandling him to the ground while Robert stepped inside and headed toward the back.

"Mr. Robert!" Henri cried as Robert met the kidnapper's eyes.

"If you so much as hurt a hair on his head, I will yank you out of here and make you wish you were dead. I know how to hurt you for hours and not leave a damned mark. You got it?" Robert growled and bared his teeth. He was prepared to rip this guy to pieces.

"Henri!" Dixie called. Robert got the side door open, and Henri jumped out and into his papa's arms. Dixie had the first suspect on the ground, sitting on his back as he rocked Henri in his arms.

"Dude, you made the worst mistake of your life trying to take that little boy." Robert reached for him and pulled him out of the van by his jacket, not caring what he might bang him up against. Once on the sidewalk, he got both men against the buildings. "Talk."

"The guys are on their way," Dixie said.

"How long do I have?"

"Maybe five minutes," Dixie answered.

Robert turned to both men. "I can cause a hell of a lot of hurt in five minutes. Broken legs, arms, cracked ribs... and no one will see a fucking thing." He smiled predatorily. "So don't even try me. Understand? I'm going to turn you over to some men, and the two of you are going to disappear. You do know that." God, he loved the flashes of fear that shone in both men's eyes. "No police, no protection."

A black car pulled up, and two official-looking men got out. Robert figured that was an illusion for anyone who might be passing by. Both men were about his size, one maybe a little bigger.

"Hello, Maurice," one said with a grin as he grabbed the man on the left. "Let's go." He manhandled the man to his feet, bound his hands, and roughly

worked him into the back seat. A second car pulled up, identical to the other. The second man was secured and placed in the back. The cars then glided away without any additional fuss, with the black van driven behind. Two minutes tops and the sidewalk was empty except for where Dixie still held Henri to his chest.

"The bad men are gone," Dixie whispered. "Uncle Robert took care of them, and they aren't going to be back." He seemed on the verge of tears as Henri still shook in his papa's arms.

"It's okay now. They're gone, and your papa is here and nothing is going to happen to you," Robert said, gently rubbing Henri's back. "No one is gonna hurt you." His gaze met Dixie's. "Let's get him inside and off the sidewalk." He was pretty sure that Dixie's people were going to want a full picture of what happened.

Dixie lifted Henri and carried him inside the house, then closed the door. He set the alarm and then brought Henri into the living room. "Did he hurt you?"

Henri shook his head.

"You know it's okay to be scared. But you were really strong. I saw the way you fought him and kicked at him. That was really brave," Robert told Henri. "You did the right thing." Henri's fighting slowed down the kidnapper and gave Robert a chance to get to them. In a situation like that, seconds mattered, and Henri's fighting and wriggling bought him those precious moments he needed to get to them and stop the men from getting away with Henri.

"Really?" Henri asked, rubbing his eyes and wet cheeks.

"Yes. You helped me stop them. That was super strong of you," Robert answered. Those few seconds,

combined with the fact that there had been no way in hell that he was going to let anyone take Henri. Robert had lost his sister, and little Grace had been hurt on his watch. These guys were not getting away with Henri. He'd have ripped the fucking van apart with his bare hands before that happened. His heart still raced, but it finally began to slow to a normal beat. Henri was safe and largely unharmed. That was what mattered. Robert left the room and went to the courtyard, where he paced back and forth.

"Uncle Robert?" Henri asked. Robert had lost track of the amount of time he'd been out there, but his clothes were sticking to him, so it must have been a while.

"Henri." He grinned and knelt down, and the boy went right into his arms.

"You saved me," Henri whispered as he cried on Robert's shoulder.

Robert tightened his hold, shaking his head. "Of course I did. You and your papa are special, and you were really brave." He rocked slowly as Henri continued crying. "Your papa loves you so very much." And those bastards had tried to use that against both of them. Henri hugged him tighter, and his tears slowly stopped. "They were bad men," Robert reiterated. This was maddening.

"Are they gone forever?" Henri asked.

Robert backed away slightly and looked at where Dixie stood in the doorway. "Yes, I promise with everything I have. Now why don't you go to your papa, and maybe we can have some ice cream and cookies."

Dixie came forward and took Henri's hand. "Come on. Let's go get us all something to eat." He

met Robert's gaze, mouthing a thank-you before taking Henri inside.

Robert stayed where he was, crouched down near the ground, wiping his eyes but unable to stop the tears. That little family of two had captured his heart, and he had literally thrown himself at a vehicle to try to keep it intact. But now he was going to go home, and that family, the one he could almost see himself part of, was going to stay behind. Robert took a deep breath, harshly wiping his cheeks. All there was to do was to make the most of the little time they had.

"YOU LEAVE tomorrow," Dixie said once they were alone in bed. The house was quiet, and Henri was asleep. He had had nightmares every night since the attempted kidnapping, and Dix sat up with him each time it happened, doing his best to comfort him until he calmed down. Robert hoped he slept through the night tonight.

"I know." He rolled onto his side. "And you remember your promise." He smiled, sliding his hands over Dixie's chest.

"I do. I'll get Henri that puppy he wants." Dixie smiled slightly. "I can't fight both of you."

"He deserves a puppy after what he did, and you know it."

Dixie sighed. "Maybe I'll find a puppy that will guard him. One that will love Henri to death and rip apart anyone who tries to hurt him." The attempted kidnapping had left a dark cloud over Dixie. Robert hated to see it, but he knew that feeling and what that kind of situation did to people.

"Hey… it's going to be okay. We got them and turned them over to your people."

"Yeah, it seems they tried to take Henri as insurance to get me to keep feeding them information. They apparently turned traitor and gave up their contacts. We're going up the line now. But it seems they're running out of strings to pull. Still, this should put an end to whoever thought they were going to get information through me. We also got the drive back, so it's been destroyed." Dixie closed his eyes. "They're going to continue working to track down the people behind this, but I doubt they're going to get anywhere. They've gone to ground and are probably very good at covering their tracks. We'll need to be careful for a while, but hopefully they will have enough trouble of their own." He seemed resigned, which was a disappointment. Robert would have liked to know who was pulling these strings. But that was above his pay grade, as they used to say.

"Why are you so relaxed about it?" Robert asked.

"Because it's not the answers I got but the way they were given to me. I was being told a story, what they want me to know. I suspect that they've gotten a lot further along than they said, but this was what they decided to tell me." He smiled. "The people I work for don't like to be taken for a ride."

Robert sighed and nodded. "Okay. So what do we do from here?"

Dixie rolled over and drew closer. "Let it go, I guess. We aren't going to get the details of what's going on behind the scenes. Those are being covered up and buried in the murky world of counterespionage. What we do know is that they feel secure enough to

give me back my access, and they have some new projects for me."

Robert closed the gap between them. "Is that something you want to do?" he asked. "This could be a chance for you to get out. They know you're loyal, and you could use the attempted kidnapping of Henri as a reason. No one would blame you."

"Exactly. I'm winding down my last project, and I'll figure things out from there. I have plenty of thinking to do." He drew Robert closer. "But right now, I'd much rather talk about something far more pleasant." He turned to the clock by the side of the bed. "We have just a few more hours and then we take you to the airport." Dixie closed the distance between them. "I think we should make the most of them." His kiss was heated, and Robert found himself throwing everything into it. He held Dixie as though his life depended upon it, cradling the man he knew he loved in his arms. Just like those years ago, they had one more night together, and Robert was determined to memorize every inch of him… even if it took the rest of the night.

"DO YOU have to go?" Henri asked the following morning at the airport, his arms closed tightly around Robert's neck.

"I do. I have to go back to work just like your papa does." He hugged Henri in return and then released him. "Now, you be a good boy for your papa. And don't worry, I won't let him out of his promise to get you a puppy."

Henri sniffed and turned to Dixie. "If he can stay, I will be okay with not getting a puppy." He turned, and Dixie lifted Henri into his arms while Robert struggled

to his feet, unable to breathe as the pending loss settled on him.

"Uncle Robert has to go, but we can call him, and you can talk to him on your tablet. Okay?" Dixie hugged Henri and then set him down. "Let me say goodbye too." Henri nodded, and Dixie held him. "We're going to miss you, both of us."

Robert hugged Dixie tightly, closing his eyes as his throat constricted. "It's been an amazing trip, and…." He squeezed Dixie tighter. "Oh, to hell with it. I'm not going away again without saying it." He pulled away, meeting Dixie's intense gaze, knowing he'd remember this as long as he lived. "I love you, Dix. I know it's a shitty time to say it, but I can't leave without you knowing."

Dixie's eyes widened and he swallowed. Robert inhaled deeply, picked up his luggage, and headed deeper into the airport. This time he hadn't chickened out and kept his feelings to himself. At least he'd said the words, and even though his heart ached, Dixie knew how he felt. Not that it changed much, but just saying the words had made it real. Robert held tightly to those feelings as he checked in for his flight, made his way to the gate, and finally boarded the plane that would take him an ocean away.

Chapter 14

His shift was just about over, and thankfully his radio remained quiet, so he headed back toward the station, ready to call it a night. Robert pulled into the lot, checked over the car to make sure it was clean for the next guy, then headed inside.

"Robert," Hank called almost as soon as he got in the door. His fellow officer must have been waiting for him. "Man, do you think you could take my shift for Saturday? My wife wants to go see her family. Mom's pretty bad, and she needs to make the trip. I don't want her to go alone." He shifted his weight from foot to foot.

"I can, yeah," he agreed. Robert had been taking fewer extra shifts and trying to build some sort of life for himself outside work. Not that it was working particularly well, but he was trying. "You can take Saturday for me the following weekend." Maybe he could go out and meet some people.

"You got it," Hank said.

"I'll let scheduling know," Robert told him, and Hank thanked him as he hurried out the door. Robert grabbed his things and sent a note about the schedule change, intent on heading out himself.

"Wendel," the captain called from his open office door. When Robert turned, he tilted his head inside. He'd been hoping to get out of here. He got up from his desk and went inside. The captain closed the door behind him. "What's going on?"

"Excuse me?" Robert asked, confused.

"Since you got back, you've done your job. No one can deny that. But there's none of your energy and enthusiasm. You're a leader, and the other men look to you. But these past few weeks, you've sunk to the back. You do what you're supposed to and then go home. What changed? Are you still dealing with the aftereffects of that kidnapping? The girl is doing well, and her mother thinks you're a hero." He sat down behind his desk. "I would have thought that your vacation would have given you some distance and you could see that you weren't at fault."

"It isn't that, and I'm fine," Robert answered evenly. "I had a good vacation, and I'm back on the job. You said yourself that I'm doing my job and you have no complaints with that. So I don't know why I'm here." He didn't want to talk about the empty shell that was his life outside work.

"You're here because I can tell that part of you isn't," the captain said rather gruffly. "You came back from Paris, and yes, you do your job, but it's like part of you is gone." He stood and leaned over the desk. "You know damned well that this job is no walk in the park. It requires all of our people to be on their toes. And you seem distracted."

Robert stiffened. "If I've been negligent in my duty, then can you provide examples?" He glared at the captain. "But I haven't been. I've been here on time. I've completed my assignments and calls the way I should.

My paperwork has been on time and complete." There was no reason for this. He crossed his arms over his chest as he waited.

"As I've said, I don't have any complaints about your work, but you're different, and I was concerned." Robert let his arms fall. "Did something happen while you were gone?"

Robert hesitated. "I had a good time and caught up with an old friend from the corps. It was a special trip."

"I see. And just how special was this trip? I know you saw the sights and things like that. I heard you telling the guys." The captain didn't miss much. "That was the only time in two weeks that I've seen even a hint of the gung-ho officer you were before your trip. So what happened?"

Robert shrugged. "It doesn't matter. The trip is over, and I'm here on the job. The rest is in the past, and there's nothing to be done about it." He met the captain's gaze. "Is there anything else you need from me?" He just wanted to get home, make some dinner, and then he could watch television until it was time to go to bed. The captain nodded, and Robert left the office.

"Uncle Robert, today is my last day of school," Henri said when Robert woke up at two in the morning and thought to call. Henri grinned into the tablet. "And look." He turned the tablet to where a blond-colored terrier puppy scooted along the floor. "Papa got me the puppy he promised. His name is Bobby, and I love him. He's funny sometimes, and he sleeps with me."

The tablet wavered, and then Dixie's face showed on the screen. "Henri, take Bobby out so he can potty, and then you need to get ready for school."

"Okay, Papa."

Dixie turned the tablet so Robert could see Henri and Bobby bound outside. "They're the best of friends. Henri loves that pup, and surprisingly he feeds him and takes him outside, even at night before bed. He even cleaned up after him when he pooped in the house, and then took him outside. Of course I had to clean up his cleanup, but still, he takes a lot of responsibility for Bobby, which is more than I expected." He was clearly a very proud papa. Not that Robert could blame him— he was pretty proud of Henri too. That little boy was a lot more grown-up than his years.

"That's amazing. I knew he'd love a dog, but to take care of him like that. I sort of figured you'd end up doing some of the work."

"Nope. Henri looks after him, changes his water, mops up the floor when it gets wet, and loves that dog no end." Dixie looked over his shoulder. "And you know he named him after you. He wanted to name the dog Robert, and I told him that the kids used to call you Bobby when you were young, so that's what he named the dog." Dixie's smile grew forced. "Damn, I miss you. There are nights when I wake up and wonder why in the hell I'm alone, and then…." He sighed. "Anyway, it's okay. I'll get used to it again."

"I know how you feel." He woke up every morning and for a few seconds he was back in Paris with Dixie, and then he'd wake up fully and remember that he was in Grand Rapids and Dixie was thousands of miles away.

"You don't look so good. Are you eating? Maybe I can send you some of that cheese you loved so much."

Robert nodded. "That was the best, especially as a snack at night with a little wine and some of that bread." The simplest food had been so special. Though maybe it had been the company and not just the food.

"It was." Dixie turned to look over his shoulder. "I need to get Henri ready for school and out the door. I'll call you later in the week. Okay?"

"Sure. I'll talk to you then." Robert yawned and said goodbye before closing the application and sitting back from the computer. He blinked a few times before getting a drink of water and going back to bed.

"HELLO," DAVID said a week later over the table at a Red Robin. One of the guys at work had set him up on a blind date, and apparently the only requirement for selection had been the fact that his fellow officer's cousin David was a gay man. "Where are you, honey?" he asked, patting Robert's hand. He was a smaller guy with loads of personality, effervescent energy, and bright pink hair.

"Sorry." Robert had promised himself that he would try to go out and meet new people. Tonight was his first foray into that arena. "I guess my mind slipped away." He forced his attention to the here and now. "What were you saying?"

"I was asking you about your job. I know you work with my cousin Hank. How is that working out for you?" He cocked his head to the side and smiled.

"I like my job," Robert answered.

David rolled his eyes. "Look. This is an evening out, not a walk to the guillotine. You don't have to be afraid. I'm not going to come charging to your side of the table and lambaste you with a handful of

glitter or spray your hair yellow. Though I think you'd look amazing no matter what color your hair was." He grinned.

"I'm really sorry," Robert said, putting his fork in his barely touched bowl of salad.

"Dude, what's really bothering you? I have this sense, and I'm sure you're a nice guy and all, but are you even gay? Did Hank mess up his signals? He's been known to do that. He once tried to set me up with a girl." He giggled with a bright smile that Robert knew he should be attracted to, and he was, but not in that heart-racing kind of way.

"No way. You'd light up a pride parade from half a mile away," Robert replied.

"He was in denial." David leaned over the table. "So what's really bothering you? Guy troubles? Hank didn't say anything about a breakup or anything. Of course, maybe he doesn't know."

Robert sighed. "It's nothing like that. I was... or maybe it's exactly like that." His mind did a complete one-eighty. "Look, I spent a couple weeks in Paris with an old friend."

"Boyfriend?" David asked. "Was it one of those friends-to-lovers things? How sexy is that? My best friend is a real hunk, but he has a boyfriend... or had. They broke up a week ago. I've liked him for years, but he doesn't see me that way." He shrugged and then sighed.

"Okay. I guess you told me yours." Robert reached into his pocket and pulled out his phone, then brought up a picture of Dix and Henri in the Hall of Mirrors. "This is my best friend from the corps and his son, Henri. I visited them in Paris. Dix and I reconnected after

some time and, well…." Robert swallowed hard as David took the phone.

"And you're in love with him," David said as he lifted his gaze. "You love both of them." He handed back the phone, shaking his head. "What are you doing here on a date with me?"

"And you're in love with your best friend," Robert challenged. "Who just broke up with his boyfriend and is now available. I can ask you the exact same thing. Is your best friend here in town?"

David nodded. It was now his turn to be far away. "But he's never seen me that way, and…."

"Have you told him how you feel?" Robert leaned over the table. "I'll tell you one thing. There is nothing more attractive than someone who's in love with you. Tell him how you feel and see what happens. Maybe he cares for you too but never thought you liked him?" Robert couldn't believe he was on a date with a guy, giving him advice on another man. This was almost surreal.

"You think so?" David asked.

"You're not going to find out unless you tell him. It's either that or end up like one of those characters in the movie who's in love with the hero but gets pushed aside until it's too late. I don't picture you as the pining-in-the-shadows type. So go for it." David smiled, and Robert found himself doing the same.

"There's only one problem," David said. "We have a plan for me, but what about you?"

It was Robert's turn to shrug. "Dixie is in Paris. It isn't like he's here… or even in the country. I have a job here, and…."

"A love life that has your straight coworkers setting you up with their gay cousins." David giggled again,

his eyes dancing with mirth. "I saw your face when you found that picture. You're aching for this guy, for both of them. You've been back here how long?"

"About a month," Robert answered.

"And you miss them so much it hurts… right?" David asked, and Robert nodded. He couldn't actually speak at the moment. "Are you scared?" David then grinned. "You are. A huge, hunky guy like you is scared."

"I am not."

David snorted. "Yeah, you are. You're scared of making the leap. You were a Marine, right? Hank told me. And people shot at you?"

Robert nodded.

"Sometimes they still do?"

Robert repeated the motion.

"And you're afraid that man and his son are going to reject you?" David shook his head. "If you love them, then you go get them. Have you told them how you feel?"

"I told Dixie at the airport."

David's mouth hung open and he rolled his eyes again. "Let me guess. You told this guy that you loved him and then you turned around and got on a plane." David smacked him on the shoulder. "Are you crazy? How could you walk away from that hunk and the most adorable kid on the planet? I mean, you told the guy you loved him and then turned and *left*?"

"Well, I wanted him to know how I felt even though I had to leave," Robert explained.

"Yeah. Like 'I love you, now I'm leaving' is what every guy wants to hear. If you love the guy and have been moping around for a month over him, then maybe you need to take your own advice and do something about it. Hanging around here, being miserable and

down in the dumps, isn't going to help anyone, least of all you." David grinned. "Call the guy, talk to him." His grin turned wicked. "Do you think Dixie feels the same way about you?"

Robert thought for a second and then nodded. Yeah, he really did.

David clapped his hands together. "Then do you have more vacation coming?" He practically bounced in the chair.

"Yes."

"Then get it scheduled and get your butt on a plane. Go to Paris, tell him how you feel and what you want. The worst he could say is no. The best he could say is that he feels the same way. Then the two of you can figure out what you want. But you can't do that with him over there and you back here."

"I'm really supposed to just get on a plane?" he asked, even as his heart beat faster and the "square peg, round hole" feeling that never seemed to abate for the past few weeks finally slipped away.

"Sure. Why not? Go see him. Did you hate Paris or something?"

"No. It was great."

"And you love the guy, like, with everything?" David sighed softly.

"Yeah. I have for more than seven years." Robert could finally breathe, and his appetite returned. He jabbed at his food with extra energy. "He's special."

"And the kid?"

"Amazing, and I love him. Henri wasn't happy when I left, and…." Damn, he'd felt like part of him had stayed behind. Robert finally knew what he needed to do.

"Then what the hell are you waiting for?" David asked, and for once, Robert didn't have an answer.

Chapter 15

"PAPA," HENRI said as he patted his side, "I'm hungry and I need to take Bobby outside." He patted again, and Dixie rolled over.

"Okay. I'm getting up." He pushed back the covers and sat up on the side of the empty bed. He'd never had trouble waking up and getting going, but the past few weeks, mornings felt like a chore. Dixie sighed as he got out of bed. He went downstairs, disarmed the alarm, and opened the door to the courtyard. Bobby bounded out and lifted his leg before scenting all around. Then, tail wagging, he half leapt and half ran toward Henri, crouching down to get Henri to play, tail going a mile a minute. "Make sure he has food and water and stay out here to play with him for a while." He returned inside to make himself some coffee.

"Will Mr. Robert call today?" Henri asked. It was Sunday, and Robert usually called between eight and nine. It was something both he and Henri looked forward to. Over the past few weeks, whenever he called, Henri would sit in front of his tablet and tell Robert all about his week and what he'd taught Bobby. It warmed Dixie's heart to hear Henri talk to him like

that. And seeing Robert every week was good for his own morale.

He wished that things had been different. Dixie knew that Robert had a job to do. Like everyone else, he had to make a living, and it wasn't as though he could transfer to the Paris police department.

"I hope so." He already had the tablet on the counter. "We have to remember, though, that to call us in the morning, it means it's the middle of the night there."

Henri hurried inside with Bobby right behind him. "Can't Mr. Robert sleep? Maybe he needs someone to read to him." Before Dixie could answer, Henri had taken off and returned with a book that he placed beside the tablet. "I'll read to him so he can sleep." Then Henri was off again, puppy sliding behind in his eagerness.

That dog was probably the best thing he had ever gotten for his son, and Dixie wondered why he'd waited so long. The two were inseparable. Once, just after they'd brought the pup home, Henri had tried sneaking him out of the house in his school bag for show-and-tell, Bobby's head poking out of the top of the backpack.

Dixie made breakfast, and they both kept watch on the tablet, but no call came in. Dixie didn't want to call Robert in case he was asleep. "Papa?" Henri asked, pointing once he had finished eating.

"Maybe he'll call later. How about you and I go out to the play park? Both you and Bobby can run and play for a while." They needed to get out of the house and have some fun.

"Can we go to the river where we can buy the books?" Henri asked.

Dixie smiled. "Of course we can." He loved that his son wanted books more than anything else. No matter what, Dixie would get Henri any book he wanted.

"Take care of your dishes and then make sure Bobby has had enough water, and we'll get ready to go. I'll get Bobby's leash." Bobby loved riding in cars and on the Metro trains. He sat on Henri's lap, watching out the windows the entire time.

"Okay, Papa." Henri cleared the table, putting the dishes in the sink. He rinsed them and then put the leash on Bobby, standing near the door, all ready to go. Dixie shrugged on a small pack with some snacks, a collapsible bowl, and some water. Then he disarmed the alarm system and opened the door.

Robert stood on the sidewalk.

Henri ran forward and hugged him while Bobby bounded around his legs. Dixie was speechless and stood stock-still. "What are you doing here?" he asked, stepping back.

"He came to see us," Henri said as though Dixie were crazy. "And to see the puppy, right, Uncle Robert?"

"Yes. I came to see you." He swallowed, and Dixie watched his throat work.

"How long will you stay?" Henri asked, but Robert looked right at him, his gaze heating Dixie from the inside.

"That's up to your papa. I have a week of vacation, but after that, I wasn't sure." He stood still on the spot, looking like what Dixie had been longing to see for weeks. Dixie took a step forward as Robert set down his bags, and then he was hugged to within an inch of his life. The strong arms he'd come to rely on to soothe away the worry transported him to happiness.

"You can really stay?" Dixie whispered.

"Yes," Robert whispered in his ear. "Do you want me to stay?"

"But for how long?" Dixie wasn't sure he could take Robert leaving a third time.

Robert pulled back, their gazes locking. "For as long as you'll have me."

Dixie smiled, the world blurring, and then he drew closer, winding his arms around Robert's neck as he kissed him. He closed his eyes and let the wave of happiness unlike almost anything he had experienced before wash over him.

"I wanna kiss too," Henri said.

Robert backed away, his hands slipping from around Dixie, and then lifted Henri in his arms. They each took a cheek, kissing Henri while Bobby bounded around their feet. Henri giggled, and soon they were laughing right along with him.

Epilogue

THE HOUSE had been decorated in a combination of American and French holiday decorations. Henri was so looking forward to the visit from Père Noël. It had been difficult to get him to bed after Mass, but he and Bobby were tucked upstairs under warm blankets as a light snow fell outside. Robert pulled open the curtains, watching as the snow drifted past the window.

"It's been quite a year," Dixie said as he came up behind him, sliding his arms around his waist, and then Dixie's warmth pressed to his back.

"It has. Lots of changes," Robert said. There had been his new job working in the same organization as Dixie, just a different area. Instead of technology, Robert designed security protocols and systems. He loved the work. But the best part was that he got to stay in Paris. The city was Dixie and Henri's home, and in a matter of weeks, he felt as though he belonged here.

"Any regrets?" Dixie asked, and Robert shook his head without a moment's hesitation. This was where he wanted to be. "Not for a minute?"

Robert turned. "Not for a second, even with the intensive French lessons." That he thought would be the death of him.

"I just checked my messages before coming down. It took a while, but we got a Christmas present from Howard. They found the information broker behind the kidnapping and put him out of commission." They had been on their guard for months, but Henri and Dixie were now truly safe. It had taken longer than Robert would have liked, but thank God it was well and truly over.

Robert leaned in to give Dixie a kiss just as a creak sounded on the stairs.

Robert smiled at Henri in his snowman pajamas. "What are you doing up?"

Henri rubbed his eyes. "Has Père Noël been here?" Henri asked, with Bobby now wandering the room, probably looking for treats.

"Not yet," Robert said. "Come on. Let's get you two up to bed so Père Noël can get here and not find a little boy still awake. Then he'll continue on down the street." Robert took Henri's hand and led him back toward the stairs. "Do you want me to read you a story?"

"Yes, Daddy," Henri said, and Robert turned to Dixie, wondering for a second if he'd heard right. But he had, and as Robert took Henri back upstairs with Dixie following behind, he knew that no matter what Père Noël put under the tree for him, he'd already gotten what he really wanted.

ANDREW GREY is the author of more than one hundred works of Contemporary Gay Romantic fiction. After twenty-seven years in corporate America, he has now settled down in Central Pennsylvania with his husband of more than twenty-five years, Dominic, and his laptop. An interesting ménage. Andrew grew up in western Michigan with a father who loved to tell stories and a mother who loved to read them. Since then he has lived throughout the country and traveled throughout the world. He is a recipient of the RWA Centennial Award, has a master's degree from the University of Wisconsin–Milwaukee, and now writes full-time. Andrew's hobbies include collecting antiques, gardening, and leaving his dirty dishes anywhere but in the sink (particularly when writing). He considers himself blessed with an accepting family, fantastic friends, and the world's most supportive and loving partner. Andrew currently lives in beautiful, historic Carlisle, Pennsylvania.

Email: andrewgrey@comcast.net
Website: www.andrewgreybooks.com

BAD
TO BE GOOD

ANDREW GREY

Bad to Be Good: Book One

Longboat Key, Florida, is about as far from the streets of Detroit as a group of gay former mobsters can get, but threats from within their own organization forced them into witness protection—and a new life.

Richard Marsden is making the best of his second chance, tending bar and learning who he is outside of organized crime… and flirting with the cute single dad, Daniel, who comes in every Wednesday. But much like Richard, Daniel hides dark secrets that could get him killed. When Daniel's past as a hacker catches up to him, Richard has the skills to help Daniel out, but not without raising some serious questions and risking his own new identity and the friends who went into hiding with him.

Solving problems like Daniel's is what Richard does best—and what he's trying to escape. But finding a way to keep Daniel and his son safe without sacrificing the person he's becoming will take some imagination, and the stakes have never been higher. This time it's not just lives on the line—it's his heart.…

www.dreamspinnerpress.com

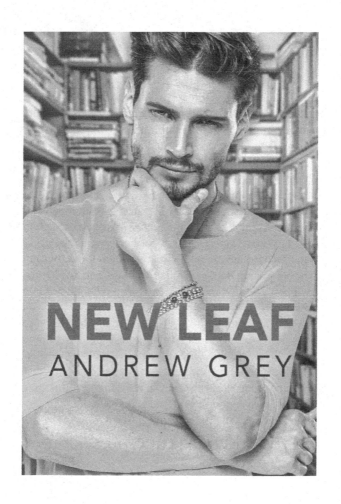

NEW LEAF

ANDREW GREY

When Dex Grippon's mother dies, he takes it as a sign—it's time to give up acting and return to his hometown. If he can find a way to save his mother's bookstore, he can preserve the one link he still has to his parents. But keeping an independent bookstore afloat turns out to be more difficult than he anticipated, and Dex isn't the only one who wonders what else his mom might have been selling.

Former cop Les Gable might be off the job, but he has to know what was going on at the bookstore, and he'll do anything to satisfy his curiosity—including befriend the new owner with an offer to help sort out his new business. Something about the bookstore doesn't smell right, and Les is going to find out what.

The problem is that his curiosity about Dex soon far outstrips his interest in what happened at the store. But as curiosity matures into love, the store's past threatens their future. Can Les and Dex untangle the mystery of the bookshop and escape with their relationship—and their lives—intact, or will the whole thing go up in smoke?

www.dreamspinnerpress.com

Everybody needs to be rescued sometime.

Veterinarian Mitchell Brannigan gets off to a rocky start with his new neighbor when someone calls the town to complain about the noise. Mitchell runs a shelter for rescue dogs, and dogs bark. But when he goes to make peace, he meets Beau Pfister and his fussy baby daughter, Jessica… and starts to fall in love.

Beau moved out to the country to get away from his abusive ex-husband, but raising an infant alone, with no support network, is lonely and exhausting. The last thing he expects is a helping hand from the neighbor whose dogs he complained about.

Mitchell understands what it's like to live in fear of your ex, and he's determined to help Beau move on. But when an unseen menace threatens the shelter and Beau, it becomes apparent that he hasn't dealt with his own demons.

With each other and a protective Chihuahua for support, Mitchell, Beau, and Jessica could make a perfect family. Mitchell won't let anything happen to them.

But who's going to rescue him?

www.dreamspinnerpress.com

Half a
Cowboy

Andrew Grey

Ever since his discharge from the military, injured veteran Ashton Covert has been running his family ranch—and running himself into the ground to prove he still can.

Ben Malton knows about running too. When he takes refuge in Ashton's barn after an accident in a Wyoming blizzard, he's thinking only of survival and escaping his abusive criminal ex, Dallas.

Ashton has never met a responsibility he wouldn't try to shoulder. When he finds Ben half-frozen, he takes it upon himself to help. But deadly trouble follows Ben wherever he goes. He needs to continue on, except it may already be too late.

Working together brings Ben and Ashton close, kindling fires not even the Wyoming winter can douse. Something about Ben makes Ashton feel whole again. But before they can ride into the sunset together, they need to put an end to Dallas's threats. Ben can make a stand, with Ashton's help—only it turns out the real danger could be much closer to home.

www.dreamspinnerpress.com

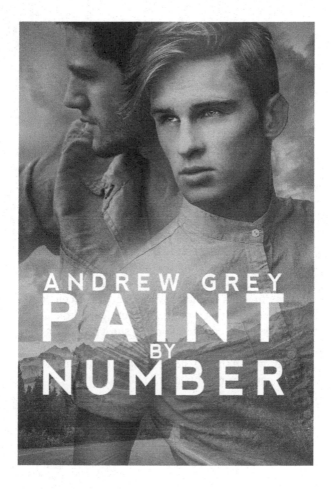

ANDREW GREY

PAINT
BY
NUMBER

Can the Northern Lights and a second-chance romance return inspiration to a struggling artist?

When New York painter Devon Starr gives up his vices, his muses depart along with them. Devon needs a change, but when his father's stroke brings him home to Alaska, the small town where he grew up isn't what he remembers.

Enrique Salazar remembers Devon well, and he makes it his personal mission to open Devon's eyes to the rugged beauty and possibilities all around them. The two men grow closer, and just as Devon begins to see what's always been there for him, they're called to stand against a mining company that threatens the very pristine nature that's helping them fall in love. The fight only strengthens their bond, but as the desire to pick up a paintbrush returns, Devon also feels the pull of the city.

A man trapped between two worlds, Devon can only follow where his heart leads him.

www.dreamspinnerpress.com

By ANDREW GREY

Published by DREAMSPINNER PRESS
www.dreamspinnerpress.com

Readers love ANDREW GREY

New Leaf

"For the majority, the story is like going for a walk in your favorite park… a pleasant excursion allowing for reflection and figuring out a way forward with life."

—Love Bytes

"If you like ex-police officers, ex-actors, hurt/comfort, with a touch of mystery and suspense and some mild man-sex you will love this one."

—TTC Books and More

Rescue Me

"Grey certainly captures the "spark when a dog and person click," as well as the attraction between Mitchell and Beau…"

—*Publishers Weekly*

"This was a beautiful story of overcoming abuse, of two men who each want to be in a loving relationship and have to put the past in the past."

—Paranormal Romance Guild